"Overcome."

On Blue Water ❧ By Edmondo De Amicis ❧ ❧ ❧

TRANSLATED BY
JACOB B. BROWN

Illustrated

Fredonia Books
Amsterdam, The Netherlands

On Blue Water

by
Edmondo de Amicis

Translated by Jacob B. Brown

ISBN: 1-4101-0455-9

Copyright © 2004 by Fredonia Books

Reprinted from the 1897 edition

Fredonia Books
Amsterdam, The Netherlands
http://www.fredoniabooks.com

CONTENTS.

TRANSLATOR'S PREFACE.

Edmondo de Amicis, in his book, *Sull' Oceano,*
"On Blue Water," has given an account of a voyage
from Genoa to Buenos Ayres in the *Galileo,* a
steamer carrying emigrants,—this and nothing more.
The narrative begins at the wharf at Genoa, and
ends when the tug leaves the ship's side in the harbor
of Montevideo. The ship does not even touch at
Gibraltar. The interest in the story, and it is not
small, lies entirely in the study of the types of humanity on board. The writer's observant eye has
singled out, his lively imagination has characterized,
and his ready pen has described at least twenty
different groups and characters taken from both ends
of the vessel, all dramatic, saying and doing in every
case just what such persons would say and do.
Nothing is exaggerated, nothing is improbable.
And these personalities are kept quite separate and
distinct without the mention of a single name.

De Amicis seem to have made the voyage on
purpose to write the book. The "commissary" on

board the ship, to whom the writer had due introduction, and who is himself a rare character, was
able to point out to his guest—so to speak—all the
life that was going on; and most inordinately must
he have enjoyed talking it over with so appreciative
a companion.

It has been well said that the beauty of De Amicis'
travels is that they are more than travels. They are
not merely the record of so many passages a day;
they are travellings plus seeings, listenings, feelings,
thinkings, talkings, love-makings;—all that a warm-
hearted, imaginative, educated young tourist would
engage in; yet they are told without displeasing
egotism or tedious detail.

His temperament is such that he is at home anywhere. He can go off like Mungo Park on an hour's
warning. He enjoys everything he sees, and sees
everything that is to be enjoyed.

ILLUSTRATIONS.

Illustrations.

On Blue Water

CHAPTER I

THE EMBARKATION OF THE EMIGRANTS

T was towards evening when I reached the wharf. The embarkation of the emigrants had been going on for an hour; and there lay the *Galileo* [1] filling up with misery as there passed over her gangplank an interminable procession of people, coming in groups out of the building opposite where the police official was examining passports. The greater part, having passed a night or two in the open air, lying about like dogs in the streets of Genoa, were tired and drowsy. Workmen, peasants, women with children at the breast, little fellows with the tin medal of the Infant Asylum still hang-

---

[1] Not the *Galileo* of the Società di Navigazione Generale.

ing around their necks, passed on their way, and
almost everyone was carrying something. They had
folding chairs, they had bags and trunks of every
shape in their hands or on their heads; their arms
were full of mattresses and bedclothes, and their
berth tickets were held fast in their mouths. Poor
mothers that had a child for each hand carried their
bundles with their teeth. Old peasant women in
wooden shoes, holding up their skirts so as not to
stumble over the cleats of the gangplank, showed
bare legs that were like sticks. Many were barefoot and had their shoes hung around their necks.
From time to time there passed through all this
wretchedness gentlemen in natty dusters, priests,
ladies in plumed hats, leading a lapdog, or carrying
a satchel, or perhaps a parcel of French novels of
the well-known Lévy edition. Then, suddenly, a
stoppage of the procession and, amid a shower of
blows and curses, a drove of cattle or a flock of sheep
came along; and when they were got on board, all
frightened and straggling here and there, they mingled their bellowing and their bleating with the
neighing of the horses in the forward part of the
ship, with the cries of sailors and porters, and with
the stunning clatter of the donkey engine that was
hoisting in whole piles of packing-cases. Then the
train of emigrants moved on once more; faces and
costumes from every part of Italy, strong, sad-eyed
working men, others old, ragged, dirty; women *en-*

ceinte, merry boys, half-tipsy youths, country fellows in their shirt-sleeves; and boys, and still more boys, who hardly had put foot on deck, amid that throng of passengers, stewards, officers, company's employés, and custom-house people, when they stood amazed or lost their way as if in a crowded square. For two hours these people had been going on board; and the great ship, moveless, like some grim sea monster that had fixed its fangs into the shore, still went on sucking Italian blood.

The emigrants, as fast as they got on board, filed in front of a table at which was seated the commissary, who told them off in messes of half a dozen persons each, writing the names upon a printed form which he handed to the eldest, that he might go at meal hours and get the ration. Families of less than six persons went in with their friends or with strangers, as the case might be. While this business was going on there was evident in everyone a lively fear of being cheated in the matter of half- and quarter-fares for children and infants; fruit of that invinci-

ble mistrust which the peasant feels for any man
with a pen in his hand and a registry in front of
him. Quarrels arose, there were protests and lament-
ations. Then the families separated; the men were
passed to one side, while the women and children
were shown to their cabins. And piteous it was to
see these women clumsily descend the steep ladders
and grope their way through the long, low between-
decks among innumerable berths, arranged in tiers
like the shelves in a silk-worm shed. Some, all perplexed, would inquire about a lost article of sailors
who did not understand one word they said; some
sat down wherever it might be, dazed and exhausted;
others wandered about vaguely, looking with uneasiness at all those unknown travelling companions who
were as uneasy as they; and, like them, confused
and frightened in this disorderly throng. Some who
had come down one ladder, and saw others leading
still on, down into the dark, refused to go any farther. Through the open hatchway I marked a woman
with her head in the berth and sobbing violently.
I soon learned that her young child had died almost
suddenly an hour or two before, and that her husband was forced to leave its little body with the
police to be taken to the hospital. Most of the
women remained below, while the men, having laid
by their things, went on deck again and leaned
against the bulwarks. It was odd enough. The
huge steamer, seen by most of them for the first

"Through the open hatchway I marked a woman with her head in the berth and sobbing violently."

time, must have been like a new world, full of
strangeness and of mystery; and yet not one looked
about him or aloft, or paused to examine any of those
many wonderful objects never seen before. Some
would fix an attentive eye upon a trunk, or a neighbor's chair, or the number on a box, or whatever it
might be; others munched an apple, or nibbled a
crust,—examining it at every bite as placidly as if
they had been in front of their own stable. Some
women had red eyes; some boys were giggling, but
their mirth was plainly forced. The greater part
showed nothing but apathy or fatigue. The sky
was clouded and the night was coming on.

Suddenly furious cries were heard from the pass-
port office, and people were seen running that way.
It proved to be a peasant with a wife and four children,—all found by the examining physician to have
the itch. The first few questions had shown the man
to be out of his mind; and, on being refused a passage, he had broken out into frenzy.

On the wharf there were perhaps a hundred persons. Very few relatives of our emigrants. The
greater part loungers or relatives of our ship's company, quite used to such separations.

When all were on board there ensued a kind of
quiet in the ship, and the dull rumble of the engine
could be heard. Almost all were on deck, crowded
together and quite silent. These last few moments
of waiting seemed an eternity.

"The huge steamer must have been like a new world to them."

At last the sailors were heard shouting fore and aft, "*Chi non è passeggiere, a terra,*"—All ashore that's going ashore.

These words sent a thrill from one end of the *Galileo* to the other. In a few moments all strangers were out of the ship, the bridge was hauled ashore, the fasts cast off, the

entering port closed, a whistle sounded, and the ship began to move. Then women burst out crying, youths who had been laughing grew serious, and bearded men hitherto stolid were seen to pass a hand across their eyes. This emotion contrasted strangely with the cool salutes that passed between the ship's company and their relatives on the wharf,—just as if it were a trip to Spezzia: "Don't forget me to the people at home.—You'll see about that parcel?—Tell Gigia (Louisa) I'll do as she says. —Post it at Montevideo, please.—It's all under-

stood about the wine, is it not?—Pleasant voyage to you.—Good-bye!" A few persons who had
just reached the wharf had only time to fling some
bundles of cigars or some oranges on board. These
were duly caught but some of the last ones fell into the
water. Lights began to twinkle in the city. The
ship slid softly along through the darkness of
the harbor almost furtively as it were, as if she were
carrying off a cargo of kidnapped humanflesh. I
made my way forward through the crowd of people
all turned towards the land and
looking at the amphitheatre of
Genoa, now being rapidly il-
luminated. A few were talking in low tones. Here and
there in the dusk women were
seen with infants on their laps
and their heads leaned hope-
lessly on their hands. From
the forecastle a voice called
out in sarcastic tone, " *Viva
l' Italia!* " and looking up I
saw a tall thin old man who
was shaking his fist at his native country. As we passed
out of the harbor it was night.
Saddened by this spectacle I

" Ⓥiva l'Ⓘtalia ! "

went aft again to the first-class cabin to find my
stateroom. And it must be confessed that the first

descent into these submarine lodging-places is de-
plorably like going for the first time into a prison
with its cells.   In those low, narrow corridors,
tainted with the reek of bilge-water, the smell of
oil lamps, the fragrance of sheep-skins, and with
wafts of perfume from the ladies, I found myself
in the midst of hurrying groups who all wanted
the steward, and were behaving with the low-
minded selfishness which characterizes almost all
travellers in the first bustle of getting settled.   A
half-light fell upon the confusion here and there, and
I caught glimpses of a beautiful blonde lady, three
or four black-bearded men, a very tall priest, and
the broad, bold face of an angry stewardess.   I heard
Genoese, French, Italian, Spanish.   At a turn of the
corridor I came upon a negress.   From a stateroom
came a solfeggio in a tenor voice.   And opposite to
that stateroom I found my own,—a cage of a place,
about a half a dozen cubic metres in size, with a
Procrustean bed on one side, a sofa on the other;
on the third a barber's mirror over a fixed wash-hand
stand, and beside the mirror a lamp on gimbals,
swinging to and fro as if to say, " What a fool you
were to set out for America." Above the sofa
gleamed a round window like a huge glass eye,
which seemed, as it caught mine, to wear a mocking
expression.   And, indeed, the idea of having to
sleep for twenty-four nights in that suffocating cubi-
culum, and the presentiment of the deadly dulness

the heat of the torrid zone, of the bumped heads I
should have in bad weather, for six thousand miles
— — But it was too late to repent. I looked at my
baggage, which said, O, so many things to me in that
moment; I handled it as if it were a faithful dog,
the last living relic of my house; I prayed God I
might not repent having spurned the proposals of an
insurance agent who came to tempt me the day before leaving; and then, blessing in my heart the good
faithful friends that had stood by me until the last
moment, I let myself be rocked to sleep upon the
cradle of my country's sea.

CHAPTER II

WHEN I awoke it was broad day, and the ship was rolling along in the Gulf of Lyons. Suddenly I heard the warblings of the tenor from the stateroom opposite; and from the one next to mine a sharp female voice, that cried: "Your brush! What do I know about your brush? Find it yourself." A voice that revealed not only momentary vexation, but a hard, bitter disposition; and which made one feel deeply for the owner of the missing article. Farther on another female voice was singing a child to sleep. It was a queer strain with a modulation which did not seem to belong to one of our race. I supposed it might be the negress I had seen the evening before. The song was marred by the low hissing voices of a couple of stewardesses disputing in the corridor about a *picaggietta* (a towel). I listened, and needed but few of their words to per-

12

suade me that if there be a woman in the world that can hold way with a Genoese stewardess, it is a Venetian one. A steward came in with the coffee. The first morning one notices everything. He was a handsome, disagreeable-looking youth, his hair dripping with oil, full of himself and smiling at his own beauty like a conceited actor. When asked what his name was he answered, "Antonio," with affected modesty as if that Antonio were the assumed name of a young duke disguised, with some amorous design, as a cabin steward. When he had retired I went out myself, staggering up against the bulkheads; and, turning into the main corridor, I marked the back of the gigantic priest of the evening before as he entered his stateroom. A step or two farther on I caught sight through the crack

"A steward came in with the coffee."

of the door, and just as the green curtain fell, of
a black-silk stocking being drawn by white hands
upon a shapely leg. The passengers were almost all
still in their staterooms, whence issued the sounds
of water being splashed, of brushes being whisked,
and of trunks being rummaged. On the poop-deck
were three persons only. The sea was ruffled, but
of a beautiful blue color, and the weather was fine.
No land was visible.

But the sight to see was the the third-class people.
The larger part of these emigrants, overcome with
sea-sickness, lay huddled together,—some thrown
across the benches like the dead or dying, with faces
all dirty and hair all rumpled, amid a tangle of
ragged wraps. There were families crowded in piteous groups with the dazed and dejected look of
houseless people ; the father sitting up asleep, the
mother with her head on his shoulder, the children slumbering on the deck with their heads on
their parents' knees,—mere heaps of rags with nothing sticking out but a child's arm or a woman's hair.
Women, pale and dishevelled, were moving towards
the companion-way, staggering and holding on. What
Father Bartoli nobly calls " the pain and anger of the
stomach " appeared to have made that clearance,
wished for by every good captain, of the bad fruit with
which emigrants always cram themselves at Genoa,
and of the feeds they are all sworn to take at the inn
whenever they have any money. Even those who

"Overcome."

had not been sick were haggard and cast down;
looking more like convicts than emigrants. It seemed
that the inactive and comfortless life on board ship
had already quelled in most of them the courage and
the hopes with which they had set out; and that in
the prostration of mind which follows the excitement
of parting a fresh sense had arisen of all the doubts,
the troubles, and the pangs of those last days at
home, when they were selling their cows and their
little bit of land, were having sharp discussions with
the landlord or the parish priest, or were saying their
last sad farewells. But the worst was below in the
great cabin, the hatchway of which was aft, near the
poop-deck. For looking down one saw, in the half-
light, bodies piled upon each other as in the ships
that carry home the corpses of Chinese emigrants;
and there came up, as from an underground hospital,
a concert of wailing and retching and coughing fit to
make one think of landing at Marseilles. The only
pleasant feature was the sight of a few bold spirits
who were crossing the deck from the galley with
their pannikins in their hands, to gain a place where
they might eat in peace. Some, by dint of miraculous balancing, succeeded; others, stumbling, fell
headlong and scattered their broth in every direction
amid an outburst of execrations.

I heard with pleasure the bell that summoned us
to breakfast, where I hoped to see a somewhat gayer
picture.

"Lay buddies together."

There were about fifty of us seated at a long table in the middle of a vast saloon, rich with mirrors and with gilding, and lighted by numerous air ports through which we could see the horizon swaying up and down. While taking their seats, and for some moments afterward, the guests did nothing but eye one another; concealing beneath a feigned indifference that prying curiosity which we always feel about unknown persons with whom we are to live for some time in unavoidable familiarity. The sea being a little rough, several ladies were missing. I soon remarked at the end of the table the gigantic priest, taller by the head than those around him; it was the head of a bird of prey, small and bald, with red eyelids, and a neck of interminable extent. I was struck with his hands as they spread the napkin, huge, bony, with fingers like the tentacles of a devilfish; in short, an unpoetical Don Quixote. On the same side, and nearer me, I recognized the blonde lady I had noticed the evening before. She was a handsome woman of, say, thirty years old, her eyes rather too blue, her nose without character; she was fresh and lively, and was dressed with an elegance perhaps a little too marked. She turned on her neighbors, as if she knew them all, the vague and smiling look of a dancer at the footlights, and I do not know what it was that made me quite sure she was the owner of those stockings that had caught my eye that morning. The legal proprietor of said silk was no doubt the gentlemanly quinquagenarian who was sitting next her. He had a kind and tranquil face, surrounded by a professional head of hair

"Her eyes rather too blue, her nose without character."

and pierced for two half-closed eyes, in which there gleamed the look of a cleverness more apparent, perhaps, than real, but which seemed habitual. Next him a couple of young ladies who appeared to be relatives or intimate friends. One was dressed in sea-green, and I was struck with her pale and hollow face, in strong contrast with her black, shining hair, which was like the tresses of a corpse. She had a large black cross about her neck. There was a droll little married couple, bride and bridegroom beyond a doubt; very young, both small, like two little Lucchese plaster figures. They ate with downcast eyes and talked without looking at each other, embarrassed, and shy of the others at table. I took him to be twenty and her not over eighteen, and would have wagered that not more than a fortnight had passed since their appearance before the city authorities; in short, a white nun and a theological student who had found out in time that they had mistaken their vocation. On one side of the bridegroom there sat in state a matron with imperfectly dyed hair, her bosom up to her chin, and a great face such as the caricaturists give a sulky moon. There were above the mouth unmistakable traces of an over-strong depilatory. She ate conscientiously, having down from those aërial sideboards that swayed above our heads like chandeliers, first the mustard then the pepper, and then the mustard again; as if she were trying to give a tone to a worn-out stomach, or to a hoarse voice which she tried from time to time with a bit of a cough. At the head of the table was the captain, a kind of Hercules, low of stature and frown-

ing of visage, red of hair and fiery of face. He talked
in good Genoese to his right-hand neighbor, and in
bad Spanish to the gentleman on his left. This was
a tall, old, dried-up person with long, very white hair,
bright deep-set
eyes, and an air
about him that
recalled the la-
test portraits of
the poet Ham-
erling. As the
greater part of
the passengers
were strangers
to one another,
there was but
little conversa-
tion, and that in
low tones, ac-
companied by
the jingle of the
swinging lamps,
and interrupted

"Next him a couple of young ladies who appeared
to be relatives or friends."

from time to time by the sharp slap on the table
with which some person seized an escaping apple
or orange. A phrase of Spanish, followed by a
burst of laughter, caused everyone to turn toward
the end of the cabin. "It is a party of Argentines,"
said the passenger on my left hand. As I turned

to look at them my attention was caught by the
handsome, manly face of my right-hand neighbor,
whose voice I had not yet heard.   A man of about
forty, looking like an old soldier, stout of body, but
evidently still active; hair already gray.   The bold
forehead and bloodshot eyes reminded me of Nino
Bixio, but the lower part of the face was milder
though sad, and contracted by a disdainful expression which did violence to the gentleness of the
mouth.   I do not know what association of ideas it
was that made me think of one of those noble Garibaldian figures of the year '60 which I knew from
the immortal pages of Cesare Abba, and I quite
made up my mind that he had gone through that
campaign and was a Lombard.

While I was looking at him my left-hand neighbor
dashed his fork upon the table, exclaiming, "It 's
no use ; if I eat I am ruined ! "

It was a withered little man with a face as of one
suffering from stomach-ache, and a great black beard,
too long for him, looking as if it were fastened on,
like a jack-in-the-box.   I asked him if he felt ill,
and he answered with the easy fluency of an invalid
when he is talking of his aches and his pains.

He did not feel ill, or rather he was not exactly
suffering from sea-sickness.   His was a special trouble,
rather moral than physical, an invincible aversion to
the sea, a sombre angry disquietude which seized
upon him the moment he stepped on board, and

which never left him until he landed, even though
the sea were like a lake and the sky like a mirror.
He had crossed several times, his family being settled at Mendoza in the Argentine; but he suffered
at the end as at the beginning. By day he felt a
languor and a morbid restlessness; by night he was
tortured with incurable insomnia and the darkest
imaginings that can pass through the mind of man.
His hatred of the sea rose to such a pitch that he
would, for a week running, never look at it. If he
came across a description of it in a book he would
skip the passage. In fact, he declared that if he
could reach America by land he would rather travel
in that way a year than make this trip of three
weeks by sea. So far down was he. A friend of
his, a doctor, had declared in jest, but he himself
firmly believed, that this violent aversion to the sea
arose from no other cause than a mysterious presentiment that he would be drowned in a shipwreck.

" *Scià se leve queste idee da a testa, avvocato!* "—O
avvocato, put that notion out of your head,—said his
neighbor on the other side. The advocate shook his
head and pointed with his finger to the bottom of
the sea.

Finding that this gentleman knew some of the
people on board, I asked him about matters and
things. How correctly I had judged! My right-
hand neighbor, he told me was, in fact, a Lombard;
he had heard him speak Lombard with a friend on

the wharf at Genoa; and a Garibaldian no doubt, the commissary had told him so that morning. "But how did you know?" he asked me; and I am afraid I felt rather proud of my power of guessing, and showed it. He went on with his details. The family at the end of the table, father, mother, and four children, was a Brazilian family going to Paraguay. The young fellow, with the blonde mus-taches, sitting next the youngest Brazilian was, he thought, an Italian tenor singer (he of the stateroom opposite mine) going to Montevideo to sing. The person speaking so loud at that moment on our side of the table was a kind of original, a Piedmontese mill-owner who, having grown rich in the Argentine, was returning thither for good, after a short stay in his own country, where, as it would appear, he had not had the triumphal reception that he expected. In fact, as early as last evening he had been heard to tell the story to a steward, and boast that Italy was not going to hold *his* bones. Here my informant stopped and said in a low voice, "Look at that arm."

It was the pale young lady with the cross around her neck whom I had already noticed. I looked and almost shuddered. It seemed not an arm but a poor white bone fresh from the sepulchre. Then I re-marked her eyes so dull and filmy, and with the ex-pression that seems to gaze at everything and see nothing. I remarked, too, that the Garibaldian regarded her with lids half-closed as if to veil the feeling of compassion which she inspired even in him.

The company, in short, presented to an observer a variety that was highly satisfactory. Amongst others I noted the strange bronzed face of a man of thirty-five; a grave and somewhat melancholy countenance. I could not take my eyes off him for a while after the advocate had told me he was a Peruvian, for the oblong head, the large mouth, and the thin beard answered well to the descriptions we read in history of those mysterious Incas that had always tormented my imagination. I seemed to behold him clothed in red woollen, with a fillet around his head, and golden earrings in his ears, marking his thoughts with the many-colored strands of a knotted cord; and I could almost see the gigantic golden statues of the imperial palace gleaming behind him, and gardens around him glittering with fruits and flowers of gold. But it was only the proprietor of a match factory at Lima, talking composedly of his business with his opposite neighbor.

When the fruit came on the conversation became somewhat more general and animated. I could hear the captain recounting an adventure which happened to him when he commanded a sailing ship, the upshot of which seemed, from his gestures, to have been a monumental serving out,—on his part, in some port or other, to some ragamuffin or other who had failed in due respect,—of kicks and cuffs. At the foot of the table the Argentines often provoked loud laughter by poking fun, as it appeared, at a French travelling salesman, the usual bagman to be found in all steamers, and who answered with the imperturbable coolness of an old hand, lavishing in reply witticisms out of the well-known repertory which all of his profession have at their tongues' end. While coffee was being served, the ship gave two or three rolls rather deeper than usual, and then, gazed at by all, there rose from the table a beautiful Argentine lady; but as she walked off staggering and supported by her husband, I could not verify—so to speak—that "wonderful grace of motion" which writers of books of travel ascribe to ladies of her country. But it was plain enough from the admiring curiosity of the company that she was already acknowledged as æsthetic lady-superior among the fair sex of the *Galileo*, and that it would be exceedingly difficult to dethrone her while the voyage lasted. Soon after this all arose from the table, looked one another over from head to foot as on sitting down, and then dispersed to the poop-deck, to the smoking-room, to their staterooms; already showing in their faces how bored they were at the prospect of the endless six hours which lay between them and dinner.

But I did not find it dull at all. One idea filled my mind, a reflection new and most delightful, unknown in any other condition than on board a ship

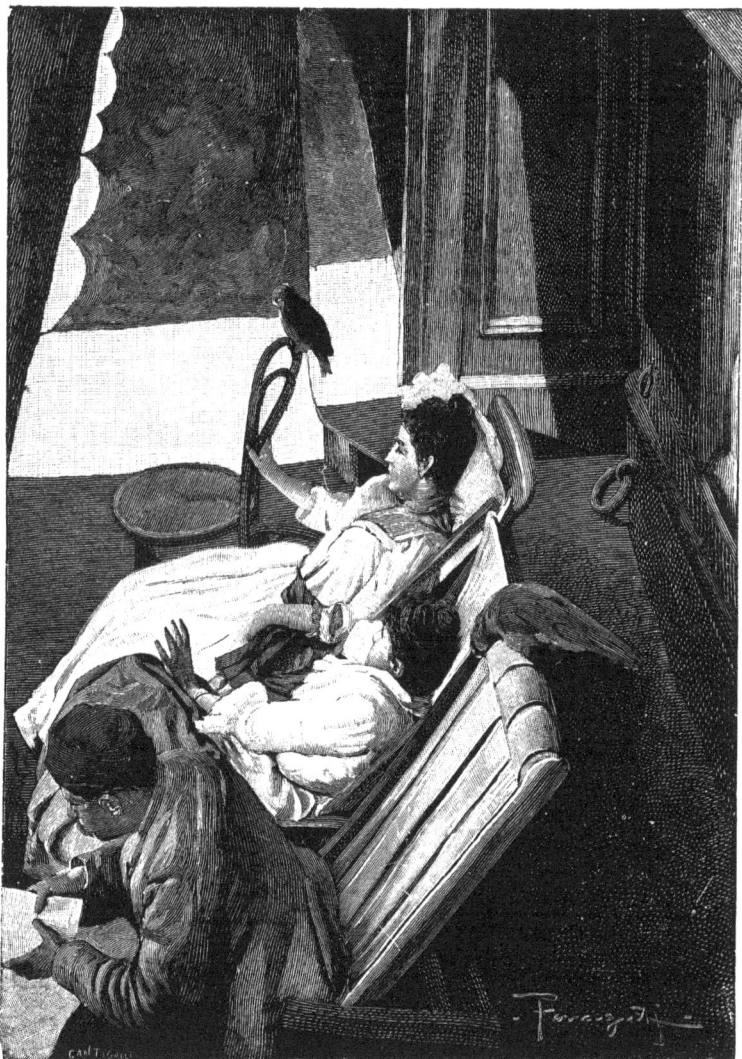

" Perfect freedom from care."

at sea,—the feeling of perfect freedom from care. I could say, in fact: Now for twenty days I am separated from the habitations of men, I can see none of my kind save those I have about me, these are for me the whole human race. For twenty days I am freed from every social tie, from every social duty; no trouble can assail me from the outer world, for no news can reach me from anywhere. A thousand misfortunes may threaten me, none can reach me. Europe may be convulsed, I shall not know it. Twenty days of limitless horizon, of undisturbed meditation, of peace without fear, of idleness without sting of conscience. A long stretch without fatigue across a boundless desert; a sublime prospect all around me, and an air most pure; strangers for my associates, and an unknown country for my goal. Prisoner in an island if you will, but an island that bears me where I wish to go, which glides along under my feet; and, like a palpitating slice of my native land, sends its own thrill into my sympathizing blood.

CHAPTER III

ITALY ON BOARD SHIP

I HAD, moreover, as a remedy for dulness, a letter of introduction to the commissary from a friend in Genoa, praying that official to put me in the way of making such observations on board the *Galileo* as should suit my purpose. Before we reached Gibraltar I waited on him. His quarters were on deck near the captain's office, in one of the long gangways running fore and aft, called by the officers of the ship Corso Roma because there was such a constant passing of people there. I found him in a nice white stateroom, adorned with photographs and full of handy little trifles which gave it a homelike air, altogether different from the boarding-house look of our sparsely furnished domiciles. He was a handsome young Genoese of fair complexion, who wore with ease the simple uniform of the vessel; and his grave regular features bespoke a power of acute observation and a fine

sense of humor.　He took me at once to his office
on the other side of the Corso.　Besides having
charge of the mails, he was a kind of justice of the
peace on board the ship; his duty being to keep
order and settle all disputes which might arise among
the third-class people.

There needed but few words to show me that I
was to have on the voyage a new and far more extended field of observation than I could have supposed possible.　It seems that, owing to the crowded
condition in which this multitude of emigrants is
forced to live, the diversity of their manners and cus-
toms and the agitation of mind so natural under the
circumstances, there arises in a day or two such a
complication of psychological facts and questions as
would not occur on land in a whole year among a
number four times as great.　I was not, however, to
hope in the first few days for any proper conception
of it all.　I must wait, he said, until things were a
little settled and arranged, until attachments and
sympathies had been formed, until jealousies and
quarrels had arisen.　I must allow time for original
minds to acquire their little celebrity, and the leading spirits to get their followers around them; the
"belles" must have the chance to become known,
the gossips of both sexes the opportunity to observe
and exchange ideas, and then I should see that life
on board would take the character and movement of
a huge village where all the inhabitants, idle from

necessity, were passing the day in the street and eating all together in the open square. "Imagine if you
please," he continued, "what sort of a daily chronicle
all this can yield." And as he said this the commissary shook his head with a slight smile which
gave token at once of the queer scenes at

which it was his duty to be present and the treas-
ures of patience he would be forced to draw upon.

On the table was a perfect mountain of passports,
an abstract of which he showed me. The *Galileo*
was carrying sixteen hundred third-class passengers,
four hundred of whom were women and children.
This, of course, did not include the ship's company,
which must have numbered nearly two hundred persons. Every place was occupied. The greater part
of the emigrants, as is generally the case, came from
northern Italy, and eight out of ten were from the
country. Many Valusines, Friulans, and farmers
from lower Lombardy and upper Valtellina ; peasants
from Alba and Alessandria who were going to the
Argentine for the harvest ; only expecting to put by
three hundred lire in three months, the journey being
forty days. Many came from Val di Sesia, many also from those lovely regions which crown our lakes,—
so lovely that it seems strange how anyone could
think of leaving them—weavers from Como, families from Intra, reapers from around Verona. From
Liguria the usual contingent, principally from the
districts of Albenga, of Sanova and of Chiarivari ;
divided into gangs by an agent who accompanied
them and to whom they were bound to hand over a
certain sum in America within a given time. Among
these were several of those sinewy women who work
in the Cogorno slate-quarries, and who can vie in
muscular force with the strongest man. Of Tuscans
but few. A handful of alabaster workers from
Volterra, plaster-figure makers from Lucca, and far-

mers from around Firenzuola, some of whom, as often
happens, may have laid aside the mattock to become
wandering musicians. There were harpers and fid-
dlers from the Basilicata and the Abruzzo, and some
of those famous braziers, the ringing of whose anvil
is going to be heard in every quarter of the globe.
Those from the southern provinces were principally
shepherds and goatherds from the Adriatic coast,
especially from the neighborhood of Barletta; and
many herdsmen (*cafoni*) from that of Catanzaro and
Cosenza. Then there were Neapolitan pedlers, specu-
lators in straw work who, to get rid of the import
duties, took their raw material to America and man-
ufactured it there; shoemakers and tailors from
Garfagnana, pick and shovel men (*sterratori*) from
the Biellese, field laborers from the island of Ustica.
In short, hunger and courage from every province and
of every profession; not to speak of many starving
creatures without profession, aiming at they knew not
what, going to seek their fortunes with blinded eyes
and folded hands, the feeblest and most unlucky of
all emigrants. Of the women, the greater number
had their families with them; but there were not a
few quite alone or accompanied by a friend of their
own sex. Among these several Ligurians who were
in search of places as cooks or waiting maids; some
were looking for husbands, allured by the hope that
they would not find so much competition in the new
world; and there were those who were going out with

3

views somewhat more extended and more easily realized. Amongst all those Italians there were some
Swiss, some Austrians, and a few French Provençales.
Almost all of them were bound for the Argentine, a
small number for Uraguay, a very few for the republics of the Pacific coast. Some did not even know
where they were going—to the American continent
generally—when they got there they would look
about them. There was a monk who was going to
Tierra del Fuego.

The company, in short, was of the most varied description, and promised well. Not only a large village, as the commissary remarked, but a little state.
In the third class was the people, in the second the
burghers, and in the first the aristocracy. Captain
and officers stood for the government, the commissary was the magistracy, and the press was represented by the register of complaints and remarks
which was kept open in the dining-saloon; besides
which the passengers themselves, to kill time, often
set up a daily journal. "You'll hear and see all
sorts of things," said my friend the commissary, "and
the comedy will grow more and more interesting
until the very last." He prepared me meanwhile
for the play by showing me some very curious docu-
ments, records of peasant ingenuity; letters of recom-
mendation handed by emigrants to the captain and
to himself, and written by persons wholly unknown
to those whom they addressed: "Signor Comandante

of the ship, I ask your good offices in favor of so and
so, a countryman of mine, admirable farmer, excellent
parent, and my very good friend, etc., etc." There
were those who had such letters as these signed by
Tom, and Dick, and Harry (*Tizi ignoti*), and addressed
to the authorities of Montevideo and Buenos Ayres.
Fine, handsome, smiling women, too, had presented
credentials, evidently apocryphal, from a father or
an uncle, as an indirect way of asking favor, and
making it quite clear that they would not be wanting
in gratitude. "I cordially desire," one would say,
"to introduce my sister, who being young and alone
among so many strangers, might be exposed to, etc.,
etc." And on the very first day he had found on
his table a note scrawled in pencil, without signa-
ture, a blind declaration of attachment, with a vague
hope that *he* would from sympathy recognize *her*
among all those people,—but he must not say a word
for pity's sake, must keep the secret and pardon the
indiscretion. "*Amore, alma del mondo,*—" "'T is love
that makes the world go round." And it was the
great business of these ocean voyages. Whether it
was, said the commissary, the result of idleness
which left too free thoughts already excited by the
emotions of the few days previous, or whether it was
a special psychological effect of the sea air joined to
an inclination to tenderness engendered of solitude,
it was, at all events, a fact that the "populace" of
the steamer gave him more trouble on that one ac-

count than on any other; and it would, beyond doubt stand as the dominant chord in the great symphony he was to be hearing for the next three weeks. "O, if I could only write a book!" he concluded, smiling.

And yet for the first few days the ark attracted me more than the animals. And I believe it is always so with those who travel for the first time in those colossal boats that carry blood to the New World and bring back treasure to the old. At first the brain is confused in that labyrinth of passages, of corners, and of nooks; by that jostle of sailors and of officers in coats of various pattern, going into and coming out of all kinds of furtive doors, like those of a prison or a public office. How can so much intricate structure be necessary to move and steer the huge vessel! But when one begins to understand a little, it is impossible not to admire the perfection which human wit has reached in planning, fitting, and settling into one another all those little holes of offices, of storerooms, of sleeping-places, of workshops of every kind, in each of which one sees as he passes by some person who is writing, or sewing, or kneading, or cooking, or washing, or hammering, crouched down, as it would seem, with hardly space to move, like a cricket in a hole, and yet appearing quite at ease, as if he had been born and had always lived inside there, floating between heaven and earth. The enormous machine that

moves all this is the nucleus; and the bow and stern are like the suburbs of a kind of stronghold called the midships, consisting of the second-class staterooms, the rooms of the officers, the engineers, the doctor, and the cooks; of the bakers' and pastry cooks' rooms, the kitchen and the baths, the galley, the pantry, the linen-room, the flag-room, and the post-office. And this central city, traversed by two long side gangways, all noise and bustle, and full of the smell of coal, of oil, of tar, and of frying, is covered by a huge terrace, like a hanging square, to which the enormous trunk of the mainmast and the two mighty smokestacks rising from among the boat davits and the ventilators, and at the far end the officers' bridge like an airy balcony, give a strange monumental aspect, which enchains the fancy as if it were some mysterious city. This deck, occupied principally by the third-class passengers, commands the whole fore part of the vessel, a bit of Noah's Ark, a huge place crowded with passengers, having along its sides the stalls for the horses and cattle, the coops for pigeons and fowls, and the pens for the sheep and the rabbits. At the far end the steam washroom and the slaughter-house; this way again the fresh-water tanks and the deck-pumps, the skylight of the canteen, and the hatchway of the women's cabin, covered by a strange-looking roof of thick glass, which serves the women for a seat. Above all the foremast, with its black shrouds and rigging

cut clear against the sky. Beyond all the forecastle, covering the sailors' quarters, the icehouse, and the sick bay, and forming another platform running to a point where plenty more people are crowded in among the huge blocks and the cap- stan and the anchor chains; and more hatchways, and more ventila- tors, until it is like an outwork of the main fort, from which the poop-deck at the other end of the ship, covered with its awning and peopled with ladies and gentlemen, looks small, confused, far off, and not at all as if it belonged to the same structure. Yet all this is only the outside of the mighty vessel. You are to imagine another world underneath, un- known to the passengers; endless bunkers full of

coal, enormous tanks of fresh water, provisions of
every kind, as if for a besieged city; enormous
stores of rope, of sails, of
blocks, of fire hose; an
interminable labyrinth
of half-lighted caves
crammed full of baggage;
passages where one must
stoop; ladders that go
down into the dark, black,
damp recesses which no sound
from the humming crowd above
can reach, where one would seem
buried in the granite vaults of a
fortress did not the trembling of
the walls inform him that all
around is thrilling with tremendous life, and that the frail structure is in motion.

And so examining the *Galileo*
piece by piece, and turning over
passports with the commissary,
I passed the first three days.
We had noble weather in the
Gulf of Lyons; but, reaching the
Straits of Gibraltar on the fourth
day, we found a thick fog that wholly concealed
the Rock, the coast of Africa, and the shores of
Spain, and made the passage very difficult. Not

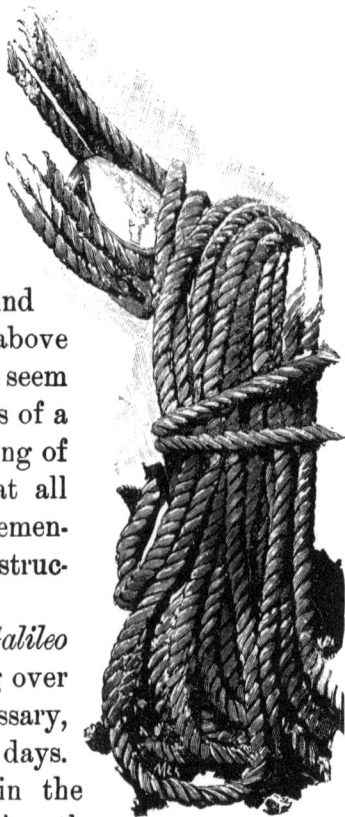

for the reason that disturbed the quiet of many
women in the third class who supposed, the commissary told me, that the ship had to thread her
way through a narrow passage between the rocks,
where she would scrape on both sides and run the
risk of being knocked to pieces like the boats that
go into the Blue Grotto of Capri, but that because
of the fog and the crowd of ships that meet there in
that ocean vestibule, where two continents almost
touch each other, there might easily occur a collision
that would send us all to the bottom and no time to
make our act of contrition.[1] We had, therefore, to
proceed with the greatest caution. And then a wonderful sight was seen, at once comical and solemn,
well worth being made a picture of, and called in
Genoese *A füffetta,*—"Fear and Trembling." The
Galileo was moving on very slowly indeed in the
midst of a dense fog which shut in the view a short
distance from the ship; the officers were all on the
alert; the captain on the bridge was sending down
order after order to steer to starboard or to port,
while the whistle sent out at every moment its note
of alarm,—a kind of hoarse wail like the presage of
woe. To the right, to the left, in front, behind,
were heard hoarse ill-boding answers from invisible
steamers, some far off, like roars from the lions of
Africa, some quite near, as of steamers on the point

---

[1] " Letter or line know I never a one
      Save my neckverse at Hairibee."—*Translator.*

of running us down; others weak and at intervals;
others again coming thick and fast as if to threaten
and entreat at once. At every sound those sixteen
hundred passengers, on their feet and crowded together on the deck, turned,
everyone, towards the quarter whence it came, with
wide eyes and suspended
breath ; and some would
hurry that way with frightened faces as if expecting to
see the huge bow of the ship
that was to run us down.
Not a voice was heard, not a
smile was seen in all that
multitude. As if by instinct,
families drew together, some
crowded around the boats,
others eyed askance the life-
preservers that were hanging here and there, and
all sent glances in turn from the captain, their
guardian angel, to the fog ahead, where death might
be lying in wait for them. One man only on the
poop-deck seemed to be indifferent. It was my neighbor at table, the advocate. Seated with his back to
the water, he appeared to be reading, and I was half-
inclined to admire his coolness ; but I was quickly
undeceived, for the book trembled in his grasp as did
never glass of liquor in the hand of a hopeless drunk-

ard. This lugubrious concert of signals lasted more
than an hour, amidst a deathlike silence on board the
ship, and the slow, slow progress of the steamer, as if
she were stealing through a hostile fleet,—an hour
that seemed to last forever. At last only far distant
sounds were heard from time to time, and the captain came down from the bridge, wiping his forehead
with his handkerchief, the signal of our deliverance.
We were passing Cape Spartel, and the *Galileo*
moved out upon the broad Atlantic accompanied by
a school of porpoises, which was greeted by the emigrants with a hurricane of yells and whistles.

The fog lifted almost at once. On the left appeared the coast of Africa, a chain of far-off mountains as clear as crystal, and the Atlantic rocked us
on its long, smooth billows, blue and fringed with
silver like carpets shaken by myriads of hands unseen, one after the other, far as the eye could reach;
and the *Galileo* seemed to draw over them, as she
foamed onward, a long, endless train of whitest lace.
The new sea was in no wise different from the one
we had left, and yet everyone seemed to toss his
head as if the spirit were more free and the eye had
greater range. We breathed the air with deeper in-
spiration, and with a new sense of pleasure, as if
it brought to us already the spicy breath of the
great South American forests to which our thoughts
were flying across those six thousand miles. The
sky was deepest blue, the dim and horned moon

hung low above the horizon, almost lost in the tender
azure of the sky. It seemed as if that ocean to which
we had all been looking forward with such anxiety
were saying to us, "Come on! I am mighty, but I
fight fair!"

"I am mighty, but I fight fair!"

CHAPTER IV

WO days later everything could be regarded as in order in the forward part of the ship, and I began my observations. When I went on the bridge, a little after eight in the morning, the hour for breakfast, the fore-deck looked like a country fair or a gypsy encampment with the tents down. Each party of emigrants had taken its place and passed the greater part of the day there. These places were, according to traditional custom, respected by everybody. Wherever one could sit without blocking the passage, in all the nooks and corners made by coils of rope or bales of hay or merchandise piled against the side of the ship, there nestled, like so many kittens, a little knot of kinsfolk or acquaintances with their stools and their cushions and their rugs. Some had crawled so completely out of sight that one might pass the place ten times and not know

they were there; for these poor creatures fit into
every hollow like water. Some of the emigrants
were still dipping their biscuit in their black coffee,
the tin pot on their knees; some were washing their
crockery at the deck tubs, or were serving out the
fresh water to their *ranchos* in so-called bidons, shaped
like truncated cones and painted red or green. Others,
again, were crouched up against the bulwarks in the

"Dressing the children."

posture of peasants well accustomed to lie upon the
ground; or were pacing up and down with their

hands in their pockets, as if on the open square of
their native villages. The women, meanwhile, with
their hair hanging about their shoulders, were making their toilettes before twenty-centime looking-
glasses, or dressing the children; passing soap, towels,
brushes, from one to the other, or mending clothes,
or washing handkerchiefs in a spoonful or two of
water; all busy, but plainly hampered by their narrow limits and the lack of a hundred things they
needed. Through the dense throng there moved the
long blue bonnets of the herdsmen (*cafoni*), the green
corsets of the Calabrese women, the wide felt hats of
the north Italian peasant. There were seen the caps
of peasant women from the mountains, red bonnets
from the Papal States (*italianelli*), coronets of pins
worn by the countrywomen of Brianza; white heads
of old men; wild black shocks of hair, and an amazing variety of faces, wearied and sad or laughing or
astonished; while many a dark and sinister look
gave reason to believe that this emigration carried
out of the country the fruitful germs of many a
crime.

But the sea being smooth, the air pure and fresh,
the greater part were in good spirits. And it was
to be remarked that the excitement of departure, in
which all thoughts had been absorbed, once over,
immortal womanhood had resumed its undying sway
even here. And that the more because, being scarce,
it commanded here, as in America, a higher price.

Very few of the men were looking out over the sea.
The greater number were scrutinizing the women
passengers. The young fellows astride of the bulwark, and one leg hanging outboard, their hats on
the backs of their heads, took on like bold mariners,
talking loud and laughing so as to attract attention ;
nearly all of them looking at the hatchway of the
women's cabin where were assembled, as on a kind of
stage, many young women with nicely dressed hair,
with ribbons and white dresses and bright-colored
kerchiefs neatly put on ; the enterprising portion, it
would seem, of the ladies of the third class. Among
these was conspicuous a rather pretty young woman,
a peasant of Capracotta, with sweet, regular features,
a countenance like a Madonna (ill-washed) charm-
ingly set off by a neck scarf which she wore crossed
on her bosom, all roses and pinks which looked
flamingly real to the eye. And I marked two girls,
one a brunette, the other with red hair, two bold
pretty faces, dressed with a certain town-bred co-
quetry. They talked with great animation, giving
from time to time a shrill laugh, and looking hard at
one or at another, evidently discussing their fellow-
passengers and reviewing the figures of fun among
the "emigration people." The commissary, who
came by as I was studying them, said they were
Lombards, travelling alone, and calling themselves
singers. They were two little devils, he said, and
were likely to give him a great deal of trouble on

the voyage. And as I did not know just what kind
of trouble was meant, he proceeded to set forth that
one of the greatest plagues of life on board ship
among all those emigrants was the jealousy of the
married women. A terrible business! The honest
women with infants in their arms were fit to kill
these impudent adventurers who, taking advantage
of all that confusion, were trying to *bewitch* their idle
husbands; and so furious quarrels arose in which he
had to do the moderator. "Ah! you 'll hear more
later on!" There were about a dozen of them this
time as if they had got together on purpose to plague
him. And then he showed me another girl, a
Bolognese, a heavy-artillery kind of woman (*donna
cannone*) sitting behind the other two with her head
high, dressed in black, a face like a lioness, dark, not
ugly, but,—Lord save us! She had a haughty co-
quetry of her own, the whim it would seem of standing pre-eminent, and of being longed for on account
of an ostentation of high-bred contempt for everybody be they who they might,—of an excessive
delicacy which would be soiled by a breath. And
she threatened everybody, boasting of a relative in
Montevideo who was in journalism, and who struck
terror into the government. On the first evening
she had come to the commissary to demand justice
because a peasant passing near had disturbed a
leathern pouch which she wore over her shoulder.
And on being asked once why she was going to

America, she had answered loftily, "To get a little air ! "

So here was one who was pretending to be out of her sphere ; but there were those who were really so, and the commissary looking about him for a moment pointed out to me some families and some individuals in corners as it were and keeping as far as might be apart from the crowd. These, to judge from their air and their clothes, ragged but of superior make and material, had evidently been forced to embark for America through some sudden reverse of fortune which had brought them down from competency to the streets, without even money enough to take a second-class ticket. There was, among others, a married couple with a little ten-year-old girl, who stood apart near the cattle-pen with the uneasy air of people who do not venture to sit down ; both about forty years old, feeble, and of most woe-begone aspect. They were shopkeepers. The woman, tall and thin, with red eyes, had seemingly just recovered from illness, and had passed the whole of the first day in the cabin, weeping over her little girl and not eating a morsel. "Yes," said the commissary, "there is wretchedness everywhere, but it seems worse at sea."

Meanwhile, looking down and right under the bridge, I discovered one of the most beautiful faces I had ever seen by land or sea, in the flesh, or in painting, or in sculpture, from the first day that I began to go about the world. The commissary told

4

me she was a Genoese. She was seated on a little
stool beside an elderly man who seemed to be her
father; and she was washing the face of a little fellow before her who was no doubt her brother. She
was a tall, blonde girl, with an oval face of the most
angelic regularity and purity of outline, eyes large
and clear, skin most fair and delicate; the body perfect, except that the hands were a little too long.
She was dressed in a fluttering white jacket and a
blue skirt which clung around limbs that seemed of
marble. Her dress, though perfectly clean showed
that she was poor; but her air was the air of a lady,
mingled, however, with a simple and ingenuous grace
of movement which accorded well enough with her
lowly station. She was like a ten-years child that
had grown to that stature in a day or two. Many of
the passengers were standing about looking at her,
and others turned to give a glance as they passed.
But for the whole time that we were regarding her
she never raised her eyes or gave the slightest sign
of consciousness that she was being admired; and her
face preserved a tranquillity, I might almost say a
transparency, which rendered any suspicion that all
this was put on a thing out of the question. So different was she from her surroundings that she appeared quite alone in the midst of a solitude, although
people were pressing upon her from every side.
How did this *dainty miracle* get there? And there
was evidently fame of her all over the ship, for the

next thing we saw was the cook of the third class
looking out of his own window and regarding her
with the air of an habitual admirer. This personage
with his imposing white cap, a bluff red face, and an
amazing stateliness, seemed to know that he was for
the emigrants the most important person in the ship,
—revered, dreaded, paid court to like an emperor.
"She too," said the commissary, shaking his head,
"she too will, without intending it, give me no
little annoyance." And he predicted a troublesome
voyage.

But though there was a good deal to make one
smile, the spectacle on the whole was one to wring
the heart. No doubt, in that large number, there
were many who could have got along honestly in
their own country, and who emigrated only to try
and rise out of a mediocrity with which they would
have done well to be content; and many others who,
leaving behind them fraudulent debt and ruined
reputation, were going to America, not to work, but
to see if there were not there a better chance than in
Italy for idleness and rascality. But the greater
part, it must be allowed, were forced by hunger to
emigrate, after having struggled vainly and for many
years in the clutch of want. There were those jour-
neymen laborers from around Vercelli, who, having
wife and children, and half-killing themselves with
work,—when they can get it to do,—hardly earn
five hundred lire per year; and there were peasants

from around Mantua, who, in the cold season, pass
over the Po to gather black bulbs and roots, which
they boil and eat, not so much to live as to keep
from dying before the winter is over; and there
were rice gatherers from lower Lombardy, who, in
the slimy water that is poisoning them, sweat for
hours under a scorching sun and, with fever in their
veins, earn a lira a day that they may have a little
polenta and mouldy bread and rancid pork to eat.
Then there were peasants from around Pavia, who
mortgage their labor to get clothes and implements,
and, not able to work enough to pay the debt, renew
the obligation, each year under harder conditions,
bringing themselves at last to starving and hopeless
slavery, from which there is no escape but death or
flight. And there were Calabrese, who live on a
kind of bread made of the wild vetch, something
like a paste of sawdust and mud; and in bad years
eat the grass and weeds of the field, and devour the
raw tops of the wild carrot, like cattle. And there
were those plowmen of the Basilicata, who walk five
or six miles to their work every day, carrying their
implements on their shoulders, who sleep with the
asses and the hogs on the bare ground, in hideous
hovels without any chimney, with no candle but a
bit of resinous wood; and who never taste meat
from one year's end to another unless one of their
animals happens to die. And there were many of
those unhappy eaters of *panrozzo* and *acqua-sale* from

Apulia, who, with the half of their daily bread and
one hundred and fifty lire per year, have to maintain
their families in the city far away from them, while
they in the country, where they are killing themselves with work, sleep on bags of straw in niches
dug in the walls of a cabin, where the rain drops
down and the wind draws through. And, finally,
there was a good number out of those many millions
of small proprietors who, brought down by a system
of taxation *wholly unexampled in the world* to a condition worse than that of their laborers, and living
in huts which many of these would shun with horror,
are so wretched that " they could not live in a healthy
way even if compelled to by the law." All these
were emigrating from no spirit of adventure. To be
sure of this one had but to mark how many there
were in the throng with stout, large-boned bodies
from which privation had worn the flesh ; how many
whose brave, haggard faces declared how long they
had fought and bled before quitting the field of battle. Useless to try and bid down the compassion
they awaken by raising the old cry of the outsider
that the tillers of the Italian soil are feeble and
slothful—an accusation long ago refuted by these
very foreigners, who proclaim the solemn truth that
in the south, as in the north, these laborers *pour
out their sweat upon the land to the extent of possibility ;* a truth proved, moreover, by the hundreds of
countries that call for their labor and prefer it.

They deserved profound and sincere compassion; and the more when one remembered how many of them, no doubt, had with them ruinous contracts drawn by forestallers of the market, who scent despair in their huts, and who buy it up; how many of them, too long ill-fed and broken with toil, bore in their bodies the seeds of disease which must be fatal to them in the New World. And it was useless to recur to the remote and complex causes of that misery, "before which," as one minister remarked, "we are as sorrowful as we are powerless," to the greater and greater impoverishment of the soil, to cultivation neglected on account of the revolution, to imposts increased by political necessity, to the heritage of the past, to foreign competition, to malaria. In spite of myself those words of Giordani would be in my memory like a refrain: "Our country will be blessed so soon as it shall remember that the peasants, too, are men." I could not but allow that human wickedness and selfishness was greatly to blame in this matter. So many indolent gentlemen for whom life in the country is but a careless sojourn of a few days, and the hard lot of the toiling classes nothing but the conventional complaint of humanitarian utopians; so many farmers without discretion or conscience; so many heartless, lawless usurers; so many middlemen and traders who must make money no matter how, foregoing nothing, trampling every consideration under foot;

ferocious despisers of the instruments they make use
of, whose fortunes rise from an unwearied course of
sordid oppression, petty larcenies, and small deceits,
from crumbs of bread, from centesimi wrung on
every side for thirty years out of poor creatures who
have not enough to eat. And then I thought of the
thousands of others who, stuffing their ears with
cotton, as it were, rub their hands and hum a tune.
And it seemed to me that there is something worse
than profiting by the misery we despise, and that is,
denying its existence while it is wailing and howling
at our doors.

I should have liked to go down among these people
and talk with some of them, but thought it better, on
the whole, to wait for a day when the crowd should
be less. To get rid of uncomfortable thoughts I
went to pass an hour on the so-called piazzetta or
little square, a part of the deck on the port side of
the ship between the midship-deck and the poop.
It had been given the name of the piazzetta because,
as the doors of the saloon, the smoking-room, and the
pantry opened upon it, there was there, of necessity, a
constant traffic of people ; and being, moreover, shel-
tered from the trade-winds which swept the poop-
deck above, the ladies congregated there to read and
do their embroidery work. The staterooms, too, on
one side, with their green window-blinds did give it
the look of a theatrical piazzetta, and the covered
passage that ended there was like a public street.

Here was where we read the daily bulletins of the
course and the distance made, with the latitude and
longitude, all posted up on a slate hanging at the
door of the saloon ; and here the officers usually came
to take the sun at noon, and here were retailed the
first bits of news in the daily chronicle of our voyage.
It was a nook where one smoked a cigar with calm
contentment, as if in front of the café; and there was
a kind of sense of being on shore and enjoying city
life. Now and then there came a little dash of spray
that sprinkled the books and embroidery of the
ladies, who would hastily make their escape, but
soon come back again. And it was here during the
first few days that the greater part of the passengers
had made acquaintance.

When I got there that morning, there introduced
himself with attractive ease a passenger whom I had
not before noticed, and who was to be my most
agreeable associate from that time until the end of the
voyage. It was a Turinese agent of a banking-house
in Genoa. He went to the Argentine nearly every
year, and was one of those men whom one gets to
know thoroughly in an hour's time. He had the
look of a comic actor, was well dressed, white hair
and black mustaches, a face so serious that it made
one laugh, eyes like a schoolboy's, a brain full of
notions, an inexhaustible good-humor, and a ready
flow of talk, slightly euphuistical but without affectation, tormented by a gossipy curiosity, thinking

of nothing but the people about him ; as indefatig-
able and sharp as an old detective, prying into and
finding out all about other persons' affairs, and excess-
ively skilful at making fun out of them for his own
benefit and that of the company, but without ever
being suspected by anybody. He knew the most
amazing things about several passengers with whom
he had made the voyage, and after ten minutes' talk
began familiarly to ask me if I knew this gentleman
or that lady. But I could not listen to him just
then, because my attention was attracted to another
personage,—the type of a curious set of people whom
I saw now for the first time.

It was the mill-owner, who was running down Italy
as he lounged in the middle of a group of passengers,
and gloried in his lately acquired corporosity as if it
were a mark of gentility. He was dressed like a
well-to-do farm steward ; had a huge gold ring on his
right hand, a snaky eye, a petulant nose, and a conceited mouth. From his face and his talk he seemed
to be one of those old emigrants who, having made
their fortune without getting any education, think,
on returning to their own country, that they will have
but to show their well-filled purses and hold forth
before the apothecary's shop in a mixture of lies and
bragging about all sorts of far-off things, to be elected
councillors and made syndics, and to mount on the
shoulders of their fellow-townsmen, who will of
course not dare to say a word because they have not

stirred from home. This one certainly must have had
a sharp awakening; and his scorched self-love must
have pained him cruelly under all his show of rude
joviality. Three months, he said, were enough to show
him that his native air would not do for him any more.
After twenty years he expected to find a transforma-
tion there,—some progress. He had instead found
the old ideas, the old prejudices, the same sordid life
and accursed greed. A hundred dogs around one
bone, when there was a bone; and no enterprise in
business; everything moving on leaden feet; a thousand perplexities; all misers, rotten, suspicious; an
entire want of *caballerosidad*. So saying, he sent
glances at the Italians who were near by, as if rather
enjoying the chance of wounding their national
pride. But the best was to listen to his vocabulary. It was the first sample I had come across of
the strange jargon spoken by our lower classes after
many years' sojourn in the Argentine, where, by min-
gling with the people of the country and with their
fellow-citizens from various parts of Italy, almost all
of them lose their own dialect and get a little Italian,
and then confound Italian with their own dialect,
putting vernacular terminations upon Spanish radi-
cals, and *vice versa*, translating literally from each
language phrases which in translation change their
meaning or lose it altogether, and occasionally jumping half a dozen times in the course of one sentence
from one language to the other like so many maniacs.

Amazed, I heard him say, *si precisa molta plata*, for " ci vuol molto danaro,"—much money is needed; *guastar capitali*, for " spender capitali,"—spend principal ; *son salito con un carigo di trigo*, for " son partito con un carico di grano,"—I set out with a cargo of grain. And in this horrible jargon he went on attacking the government, the behind-the-age (*atrasado*) government, the beggarly people (*mendigos*), the Chamber of Deputies, and even the works of art, remarking that as he passed through Milan he had found the cathedral much smaller than he remembered it. He glorified the beauty of the American plains, using a broad, clumsy gesture like a tipsy landscape painter. But he always came back to Italy with a sort of refrain, no doubt picked out of the leading article in some provincial newspaper. " Mediæval, you know, mediæval."

The bank agent, who was listening at the same time and laughing in his face, had had experience of that style of patriot, and told me that when such persons were in America they took the other side, or rather they abused everything, glorying in their own distant native land, compared to which they regarded as uncivilized, ignorant, and repulsive the land in which they had found refuge and in which they had grown rich. But he cut this talk short off to tell me that he had found a most delightful original among the crew, an old hunchbacked sailor who was set to keep order in the women's cabin. This

was an exceedingly delicate matter which required
in the employé not only the guaranty of very ma-
ture age indeed, but also the absence of every
æsthetic bodily quality which could possibly touch
the female heart. This hoary hunchbacked dwarf,
who had to separate the two sexes at nightfall and see
that no woman came out from the cabin during the
night, was a queer mixture of the buffoon and the
philosopher, who kept droning out all sorts of say-
ings against women, the torments of his life, with a
kind of pulpit solemnity, and sometimes with a turn
of expression so intricate that one could not understand at all what he wished to say. "You must
talk with him; you will be greatly amused. And
that other one," he went on, "have you marked
him?" And he pointed out the handsome, well-
pomaded steward of the first class, who went by,
tray in hand, casting languid looks upon the ladies.
This was a kind of marine Ruy Blas who looked
high, and tried in everyway to have it understood
that the lowliness of his social condition on board
was alleviated by mysterious and miraculous success
among the fair sex. Meanwhile he was sultan to
the two stewardesses, a mellow Genoese and a fresh
Venetian, each fit to tear the other's heart out for
jealousy, and who, with hands on hips and caps
awry, quarrelled noisily and coarsely in the corridors
of a morning while the ladies were ringing for them.
At that moment a passenger went by,—the Genoese

who sat on the captain's right at table,—a dumpy, good-natured little man, fifty years old or so, with but one eye, and a beard like a scrubbing-brush. In passing us, he made the agent a sign which I did not understand, and then went on deck. I asked what that sign should mean. "It means," said the agent, "that there is maccaroni with gravy to-day." So he sketched me the portrait of this gentleman. He was a well-to-do business man in Buenos Ayres, one of those many unhappy creatures who, though perfectly well on board ship, can neither talk, nor read, nor think, and are bored with a boredom that is un-imaginable, torturing, overwhelming, mortal. This gentleman, for a little relief, had gone into gastron-omy, for which he had a turn. He had established relations with the cook; he was the first to know in the morning what there was for dinner, and eagerly carried the news about. He was in and out of the kitchen twenty times a day, saw to the plucking of the fowls, chatted with the scullions, peeped into the baking-ovens, had talks with the pastry-cook and the canteen man forward, went down into the store-room and drank a dozen glasses of vermouth to hasten on the dinner hour. He conversed but little, and that always about gormandizing; and when not thus occupied, passed hours in his berth, his hands under his head, his eyes wide open, yawning grievous yawns as if hypnotized, or like a lion in a show; one yawn right after another, fit to make one

believe (if the idea of some people or other, I do not
know which, be true, that at every yawn there issues
from the man's mouth the soul of one of his ancestors) that he had long ago breathed out the soul
of father Adam.

"Do you know any more?" I asked. "Why not?"
(*Y como noo?* Pure Argentine, in sing-song tone.
All Italians take it up.) But this time, as the person
spoken of was near by, he lowered his voice and told
me in my ear to look to the left in a corner of the
piazzetta. Among the ladies there was one of forty
years or so, with large piercing eyes, rather sallow,
elegantly dressed ; a strange face, which at a little
distance, when it smiled and showed the beautiful
white teeth, seemed good and lovely, and most pleas-
ing ; but on drawing nearer there seemed to come out,
hard lines, evil little wrinkles. The mouth, too,
bitter with envy and disappointed ambition, revealed
a constant habit of unfeeling slander. Beside her
was a dried-up young girl who might have been
about fifteen years old ; a washed-out blonde, still in
short dresses, with a meaningless face bent over her
embroidery. The lady was skimming a book, but
would glance sharply up at every word or step that
she heard near her. Mother and daughter, the agent
said. He had made the voyage with them the year
before in the *Fulmine*. The mother had been taking
the daughter to Germany to master the pianoforte ;
both of Spanish descent, but born in Italy and

settled in the Argentine.   The mother had an arrowy
tongue fit to raise a tumult among the passengers,
and was so envious about dress that every new
toilette that appeared on board was like a knife thrust
into her body. "And what do you think of the
daughter ? "—"Nothing at all—an ill-developed
schoolgirl that might be playing with her dolls."—
"Never made a greater mistake in your life,—begging your pardon," cried the agent, and he took me
over to the other side of the piazzetta so as to speak
more freely.   That dried-up little thing that no one
noticed was a real psychiatric case worthy the attention of the alienist.   The year before in the *Fulmine*, one of the officers of the ship, a handsome
young fellow, a friend of his, used to chat now and
then with the mother, but probably never, during
the whole voyage, had exchanged twenty words with
"that ugly little (*acqua cheta*) still-waters," who regarded him with an eye of the most tranquil indifference.   And yet beneath all that there had been
burning a kind of love that never seems to break out
except on board ship in the silence of the cabin and
in the solitude of the ocean, where soul sometimes
seems to grapple to soul with the fury of the sinking
sailor as he grasps a floating plank.   As soon as they
landed at Genoa, the lady and the daughter set out
for Germany, and the young officer received next day
a letter of eight pages, "full of a passion so furious,
such phrases, such red-hot phrases you know—cries

of passion fit to make a man shudder,—a brutal *tu* at every line, cataracts of insensate adjectives, words that were sobs, kisses, bites—a language incredible, unspeakable—at thirteen years old! And in midst of this lava-flow, blunders in grammar and spelling; and between two leaves, some hair." Then, looking hard at me, "Only think—Some hair! The Lord knows where her wits were. And mark this! A letter giving no address and so without object— nothing but the ungovernable outbreak of soul and body tortured by twenty days of silence and enforced hypocrisy." I turned to look at the girl and could not help saying, "It is impossible." But the agent made a movement as if I had denied the light of the sun. It was quite true. "And so—?" "*A record of human nature.*—That's all."

As he said this the Garibaldian came by from forward. He passed near me and I asked him, almost involuntarily, from a kind of fellow-feel- ing, "Have you been among the emigrants?" He seemed surprised that I should address him, and nodded, yes—coming to a stand, but half-turned away like a man that means to talk but little. The agent, who no doubt perceived in this gentle- man an instinctive antipathy for men of his stamp, moved off.

I asked once more, " Have you seen those poor peasants?"

"The peasant," he said, looking at the sea, "is

an embryo burgher."[1] I did not at once catch his idea.

"The only merit they have," he went on, without looking at me, "is their not trying to put on that mask of patriotic and humanitarian rhetoric. Otherwise the usual egoism of domesticated animals. Their stomachs, their pockets. Not even the idea of elevating their own class. Each would like to see the others worse off so only he might get on better himself. If the Austrians came back and made them rich they would be for the Austrians." Then, after a pause, "I wish them joy."

"And yet," I observed, "when they are in America they remember and love their native country."

He leaned over the bulwark towards the sea ; then answered, "Their native land, yes ; not their country." (*La terra, non la patria.*)

"I do not agree with you," I said.

He shrugged his shoulders. Then without preface, and in the tone of one who means to be rid, once for all, of an importunate person, rather than to confide in him, he spoke his mind in a few quick, dry words. He did not even mourn for his country after all. She had fallen too far short of the ideal for which he had fought. An Italy of declaimers and plotters infested with old-time court-intrigue, dropsical with vanity, void of every great ideal, beloved by none, feared by none ; like an abandoned woman, now caressed, now

---

[1] *Borghese* is not accurately translatable into English.

5

buffetted, by one and by another; strong in nothing but the patience of a beast of burden. High and low, nothing to be seen but universal rottenness. A policy that licks the hand of the most powerful, who-ever he may be; a scepticism tormented by secret terror of the priest; a philanthropy inspired not by generous individual sentiment, but by timid class interest. And no honor, not even kingly honor. Millions of monarchists, incapable of defending their own banner in time of need, and ready to grovel on their faces before the Phrygian cap so soon as they see it reared aloft. A furious eagerness in all to reach, not glory but fortune; the education of youth directed to this end alone; every family a business firm, without any scruple, and ready to coin false money so only they can get their children on in the world; the sisters following the brothers, losing day by day from the education and life of woman all spirit of poetry and of breeding. And while popu-lar instruction, a mere pretence, was planting the seeds of nothing but pride and envy, misery was in-creasing and crime was flourishing. Could those men who gave their blood for the redemption of Italy come back to life, one half of them would blow their brains out.

So saying he turned away.

"I do not agree with you," I said. "We our-selves are the cause of the disillusioning that we have suffered; for we imagined that the liberation,

the unification, of Italy would bring about a complete moral regeneration, would do away, as by
miracle, with crime and suffering. We must not
judge the present state of things by an ideal standard
to which one nation is not much nearer than another.
We must judge it by the past, the horrible and dis-
graceful past. To have come out of that, no matter
how, is comfort enough."

He made no answer.

I asked if he were going to the Argentine, and
if he had any relatives there. He was going to the
Argentine, and he had no relatives there.

I then observed, for the first time, that he had behind his ear a deep scar as from the wound of a pistol-
ball.

I asked if he had made the campaign of sixty-six,
not supposing from his age that he could have been
in that of sixty.

But he had been through the last also, at sixteen
years of age.

I looked at him attentively and asked if he had
ever been hit.

Never,—he said, quite naturally.

But turning unexpectedly at that instant, and
taking me in the act of looking behind his ear, he
gave me a quick, searching glance, while a flush rose
to his cheek, and a flash of anger shot from his eye.
He frowned and turned once more to look at the
horizon with a sharp movement that said most

plainly, "Let me alone." But that look had revealed
to me a secret of his life, a terrible moment to which
he must have been brought by long and bitter suffering, and after a great change had been wrought in a
mind no doubt once firm and full of fertile force,
like his fine soldierly, athletic body.   And all enthusiasm, all affection, perhaps, was dead in him; but
the unbelief into which he had fallen, was not ignoble scepticism; for he suffered, and he still loved
the good in which, alas! he could no longer place
any hope.   I saw, moreover, that there could never
be anything in common between him and me,—or
anyone else for that matter; so I left him alone
there, looking at the sea.

And I went over to the other side of the deck to
look at it myself, for since the day we sailed it had
never been as now,—all bright, frolicking waves
which rose, lucent and tender, with a hundred softening shades of crystal blue and green, of velvet
and of satin, crowned by silvery tufts and plumes,
by crisp white crests and a thousand little rainbows
hung amid a mist of drops; and ever and anon a
high white spout of water through it all, like a cry
of joy from that crowd that was dancing in the sun
beneath the kiss of the trade-wind.   The swell would
roll up to the level of the deck and then sink out of
sight, like a threat that turns into a jest, and then rise
again, as if angry at not being able to say it, giving
place to other billows which kept running up and

looking at us, and then going out of sight with their secret, like the rest. And I could have remained there for hours to watch that ceaseless forming and dissolving of snowy mountain chains and hollow valleys, of solitary and fantastic tracts, thrown together, dispersed, collected, scattered again, like the surface of a world at the will of a god. But all this turmoil was near us only; around us and afar the sea was moveless, laughing blue, picked out with whitest spots that seemed the sails of countless fleets in company with us.

CHAPTER V

AVING at hand a living gazette in the bank agent, I was not long in finding out, almost involuntarily, all about many of the first-class passengers. The next morning the agent came to sit beside me in place of the advocate, who had not left his room. Every day this gentleman made half a dozen new acquaintances. The morning before, he had got into conversation with the young couple that occupied the stateroom next to his, and finding that they were timid and embarrassed before other people, he thought he would torment them a little. Hardly, accordingly, had he taken his seat when he asked the young people sitting opposite whether they had rested well. "Quite well, thank you," they answered with an uneasy glance. "And yet," said the other, with the most natural air in the world, but looking hard at both, "and yet the sea was, I thought, rather rough last night." The rest smiled ; the young couple blushed and began to examine the knives and forks with much attention, while the agent talked quietly and pleasantly on without appearing to notice; doing, the while, great honor to the cookery of the *Galileo.* The tall priest was a Neapolitan who had been settled in the Argentine for about thirty years. He was returning thither after a short trip to Italy, made, he said (though there were doubts about it), to see the Pope. The agent had heard his story one evening. He had gone to the Argentine with what he stood in ; had been parish priest of rising farm colonies in several States of the Republic, in regions almost uninhabited, where he carried the viaticum on horseback, galloping all night long with the host about his neck and a revolver in his belt. He had, he said, been several times attacked and had defended himself with his weapon ; and it had happened, more- over, that travellers, meeting him by moonlight, had taken to flight, scared by his great black shadow. It was clear that he had had as much care for his own body as for other men's souls, and had been in the habit of accepting a fancy price for the marriage and burial services. At any rate he boasted of having got together a comfortable maintenance, and was always discoursing of *pesos* and *patacones* with a disagreeable flapping about of his hands, like a weathercock, and with a Basso porto accent which years of speaking Spanish had not been able to obliterate. The agent

knew but little of the tenor. He had, he believed,
a good voice enough; it made one think of a scalded
cat,—but no matter,—and he was, as usual, a very
peacock for conceit. From the first day he had gone
around among the passengers exhibiting a tattered
newspaper with a These-Our-Actors article and the
words underlined, "This artist has the key to the
human heart."—" Made one think of his hearers'
house-door keys," said the agent, but that might
be an error. Believed the tenor was getting up
a vocal and instrumental concert for the evening
when we crossed the Line. He knew more about
the blonde lady with the black-silk stockings,—
Italian-Swiss,—wife of an Italian professor of something or other at Montevideo. Had made the voyage from America to Genoa with her two years
previously. An excellent creature, as good as gold
(*buona come il pane*), with the brain of a sparrow,
—as beautiful and as ignorant as a dahlia,—a great
thirty-year-old girl whom the solitary condition of
single male passengers inspired with a bold and loving pity. During ten years, taking every now and
then a run over to her native country, she had been,
with her childish good-humor, the life of six or eight
different ships, and had consoled with her sweet pity
as many sets of passengers, so that she enjoyed a
kind of jolly celebrity with the Società di Navigazione. In a trip of two years previous, amongst
others, she had had a droll adventure with an Argen-

tine, a deputy, who, it did so happen, was on board
with us in the *Galileo*. This gentleman, a very good-
humored, amiable person, but exceedingly precise
and orderly in his habits, occupied a stateroom on
deck. So, while he was amusing himself in the
saloon or pacing the fore-deck, this lady and a friend
of hers would go and throw everything about in his
room, and he would storm and rage over having to
set it to rights. This had gone on well enough
several times. But one day when the sweet Swiss
had made the venture alone, the gentleman had unexpectedly come back, had flown into a passion and
had shut the lady up in the room until she should
have restored order. But this, being no light task,
lasted some time; and, a sudden squall coming up,
the lady remained shut in there for several hours,
her alarmed husband meanwhile looking and calling
out for her along the corridors, demanding that a
boat should be lowered to pick her up, and wholly
unconscious of the derisive pity of those about him.
But no further harm came of it. On this voyage,
however, the lady and gentleman made no sign of
ever having met before. I turned to look at the
deputy, where he sat at the lower end of the table.
A dark man, between thirty-eight and forty, strong
profile, eye-glasses,—the face of a man who would
not allow his home to be invaded with impunity.
As for the professor-husband, the agent said he was
a fine man, devoted to the study of nautical mechan-

ics, although he had a face rather literary than scientific, and he passed the day in grave meditation
before the engine, the wheel, the capstan; at every

"The professor-husband."

fresh order that was
given on board requir-
ing the most minute
explanation from the
officers. This he carried
forward, for the pleasure
of giving to the people
there morsels of the
bread of science, while
those on the poop-deck
enjoyed his. But I was
just then looking at the
next neighbor of the
Argentine, a pale, blond
man with a pair of whis-
kers like weeping-wil-
lows in hair, such as are
seen in the hair-dress-
ers' windows, and who
rolled his eyes around

upon the rest of us like a suspicious fish, but spoke
to no one. I asked the agent if he knew who he
was. "O, he is worth your while." Thought to be
a thief escaping. People were talking of it on board
the ship. Frenchman. One of the passengers reading the *Figaro*, which had reached Genoa on the day

of sailing, thought he perceived a striking resem-
blance between this strange, suspicious face and certain traits which the Paris journal ascribed to the
cashier of a bank in Lyons who had disappeared
three days before, leaving his safe an exhausted re-
ceiver. The agent said he had made his investiga-
tions; at any rate he hoped to find out all about it on
our arrival, when the police should come on board.
He had not asked any questions about the married
couple seated opposite this last gentleman. They
were my neighbors below, they of the *brush*. The
lady forty or so, with a pair of cold eyes and a perpetual forced smile on her thin lips. Not ugly, but
one of those whose mind has spoiled the face; such as
at first glance inspire repugnance for the ill they work
to others, and then compassion for what they must
themselves suffer. The husband had the air of a
retired major of cavalry; seemed a man of firm mind,
but mastered by a nature stronger than his, and worn
out by dull, unchanging trouble. They never spoke
to one another; they never were together except at
table; they behaved like strangers; but my neighbor noticed that she darted terrible side-glances at
him when she thought he was looking at any other
woman,—the jealousy of pride had survived affection.
An ill-assorted couple, in short; like two convicts in
a chain-gang between whom there existed a mysterious and deadly aversion. But the one my neighbor
knew best was the captain, a capital seaman, rough

and irascible, master of an amazingly rich vocabulary
of Genoese oaths and abuse, which he heaped upon
the humbler portion of the crew,—a perfect litany
of reprimand delivered with a most irresistible cres-
cendo of effect; proud, too, of the vigor of his fists,
which he had used pretty freely during his twenty
honored years of command. He had a fixed idea,
and that was an absolute severity in the matter of
morals. *Porcaie a bordo no ne véuggio*, "I won't
have any n—well, nonsense on board," was his
word. He wished to have the ship as virtuous as a
monastery, and he thought he could carry his point.
Sometimes his lessons were rather emphatic. On a
previous voyage, having found out that two persons
of opposite sex had retired to a deck stateroom, he
had caused a good stout batten to be nailed across
the door, and had left them there until the pair,
driven by hunger, had pounded furiously, and at
last had come out coram populo, *mëzi morti da-a
vergeúgna*,—half-dead with shame. But he had like
to have fallen ill with rage on the last trip, for he
brought from Buenos Ayres to Genoa a complete
company of singers and a *corps de ballet* of one hundred and twenty legs; and there were not in the ship
battens enough or nails enough to keep them in order.
In fact, all his threatening eloquence in the language
of *sci* had not prevented the *Galileo* from becoming
something of a pandemonium. Under ordinary conditions, however, when he was not borne down by

the numbers and the boldness of the enemy, he was
so rigorous as not to allow even a mild flirtation.
He boasted, too, that he kept people in order without infringing the laws of courtesy, that he could
say anything without offence. When a passenger
followed any lady about too much he took him aside
and said, respectfully: "I beg your pardon, but you
are getting somewhat nauseous (*angoscioso*). I won't
have any nonsense on board here." In other respects
a right good fellow. The majestic old person who
sat beside him, the Hamerling, was a Chilean—a real
personage. Called on board, the " Mountain borer,"
because he had made the little run over from his own
country (thirty-five days at sea) to buy tunnelling
machines in England, and had stayed in Europe, from
time of landing to time of leaving, exactly one fortnight. Grave, as the Chileans always are, and with
high-bred ways, he had chatted a little the first few
days with the Argentines; but as these had vexed
him in a dispute about the eternal question, the southern boundary of the two republics, he had drawn
away from them and spoke with no one but the captain and the priest. My neighbor knew no more of
him just then. But he was looking up a beardless,
over-dressed young Tuscan who sat at table over
against the professor's wife, on whom he kept his
eyes, so absorbed that sometimes his fork itself
stopped short on the way to his mouth, as if it were
struck with admiration. He seemed a kind of half-

starved Don Giovanni who was taking his first long
flight from home; and he had, none the less, an
amazing boldness under that guise of sucking *premier
amoureux*, for while he was prancing around the
Swiss lady, whom he seemed to have known on land,
he was all the while making little excursions forward, where he snuffed the air like a young colt,
especially at evening when he ran the risk of having
the jacket that he changed so often dusted for him
by the emigrants. So saying, the agent rolled an
orange almost into the plate of the young bridegroom, and then suddenly put out his hand, saying,
"Would you mind?" Unhappy bridegroom! At
that instant, profiting by the little confusion usual
at the end of every course, he had dropped his right
hand under the table while the bride dropped her
left. At the unexpected address the two hands
came briskly to the surface—separate; but it was
too late, a chaste blush had already betrayed the
secret. "They are too happy," said the agent in my
ear, "I must embitter their lives for them a little."
He then rose, and when I went on deck half an
hour later, I found him talking with a priest in the
second class. But the second class was nearly empty,
and offered but little food to his curiosity. There
were two old priests who were always reading their
breviaries; there was an old lady, travelling alone,
and wearing glasses, who turned over from morning
till night some old illustrated newspapers; and there

was a numerous family all in mourning who made a
dark, sorrowful group amidships, quite still for hours
together, save that the two smallest boys would now
and then race across the bridge to the poop-deck,
where the lady with the black cross would sadly
caress them with her small wasted hands.

CHAPTER VI

SPOUT of water, received full in the face as I opened my port for a little air at dawn next morning kept me in my berth the whole day with a wet bandage around my head, to meditate at leisure upon the brutality of Father Ocean. The blow was so well planted that my head was dashed against the other side of the room, and I lay there in a pool, stunned, and with my mouth full of salt water.

Owing to this accident it was not until the ninth day that I could make my visit to the emigrants. Ruy Blas, as, with dignified air, he handed the coffee, announced that the weather was fine. But it was not his decoction that aroused me so much as the warblings of the tenor and the mewlings of the Brazilian baby, accompanied on the pianoforte by (no doubt) that magnificent edition of humanity— the young person of the letter. In the midst of these

noises my ear was pained by an excited discussion
in the next stateroom, occupied by the lady of the
brush and her husband. 'T was wondrous pitiful. I
caught no more than a word here and there, but the
ring and the intonation of those two voices, in un-
regarding quarrel, and, urged by a sentiment colder
but more deadly than anger, bespoke a habit of disputing about nothing, an involuntary impulse, a
sudden swelling up of evil thoughts and wishes
which they must give vent to or be suffocated. The
dialogue was crossed from time to time by a sardonic
laugh or a half-uttered word repeated now by one
now by the other, in the same tone ; a refrain, as it
were, of abuse ; and by, " Oh, hush ! " rather hissed
out than spoken. The words seemed all torn to
pieces between the teeth so that it was impossible to
distinguish the voice of the man from that of the
woman. It was a quarrel in undertone, with poisonous blasts for weapons ; more painful, a hundred
times over, to listen to than if it had been yells and
blows. What a dreadful thing was that conjugal
hatred shut up in a dungeon out on the wide ocean ;
two creatures tied together only to tear each other,
and carrying from one side of the world to the other
the hell that was tormenting them. Then they
stopped short ; and a moment after, as I came out
they did so likewise, perfectly well dressed, and to
all appearance unmoved ; but when they reached the
stairway that leads to the deck they turned one to

6

the right the other to the left without a glance.   In
the corridor I came upon the young Tuscan, a good
deal got up and standing sentinel.   Then passing
the Swiss lady's room I
thought I saw the flash
of a blue eye at the
softly opening
door.   Next I
ran against the
agent, who re-
marked, apropos
of nothing, "Do
you know, that
young couple an-
noys me?"   He
had heard over-
night the bride say-
ing her prayers,

"Conjugating the verbs in an undertone."

and then—a variety of things.   Amongst others, at
all sorts of hours they would study the Spanish
grammar, conjugating the verbs in undertone, and
stopping every now and then to kiss each other.
Only last evening he had heard a pluperfect that he
could not stand.   He was going to change his room.
And he had accounts to give me of some new people; but, begging him to keep these until later on,
I went forward to see the emigrants and get into
talk with them.
    It was cleaning time, the forecastle was crowded,

the weather fine ; everything seemed favorable. But
I soon found it was not so easy a matter as I had
supposed. Taking the greatest care to touch no foot,
I passed among the people that were sitting about,
and I soon heard behind me, "Make way for the
signori"; and, turning round, encountered the glance
of a peasant who fixed upon me an eye which boldly
confirmed the sense of his sneering exclamation.
Farther on I put out my hand to caress a child ; but
the mother bluntly drew the little creature to her
without looking at me. I was inexpressibly pained.
I had not thought of the state of mind that many of
these people must naturally be in, all troubled as they
were with memories of the life they had left ; a life so
intolerable that to cut it short they were willing to
quit their country. Nor, again, of the resentment
they must feel against that varied crowd of proprietors
and extortioners, of overseers, of lawyers, of middlemen, of government officials ; all known to them as the
signori, the gentle folk, the quality, and all supposed
to be leagued together against them ; all looked upon as the authors of their misery. For them I was
a representative of that class ; and I had forgotten,
moreover, that to persons in their state of mind a
denizen of that little privileged world, the first cabin,
image of the country which they were forced to leave,
must be especially odious ; as if he were a vampire
following them across the sea and sucking their blood
until they reached America. So that it was quite

impossible that they should understand the really kind and respectful feelings which actuated me ; and it would have been imprudent to enter point-blank into talk with any of them. Had I done so they would have regarded my motive as one of cruel curiosity ; a desire to hear of woes and horrors : they would have taken me for some schemer, some meddling contractor who had come out in the *Galileo* to engage laborers on the sly, where he would not be troubled with competition. These reflections overthrew at once all my hopes.

So I tossed away my cigar and began walking about, looking at the rigging and the spars as if I were thinking of nothing but the ship, yet all the while listening closely. Many settled groups had already been made up, as always happens among emigrants from the same province or of the same profession. The greater part were peasants, and there was no difficulty in perceiving what was the principal theme of discourse : the miserable condition of the agricultural class in Italy, the too great competition among the laborers, all turning to the advantage of the proprietors and tenant farmers—low wages—dear food—excessive taxes—seasons with no work—bad years—greedy employers—no hope of bettering their condition. The talk for the most part took the form of narrative : tales of misery, rascality, injustice. In one group, where a kind of bitter joyousness appeared to prevail, they were laughing at the

rage which would devour the signori when they
found themselves without any laborers, forced to
double wages or to sell their lands for a bit of bread.
" When we are all gone," said one, "they will perish of
hunger too !" And another, " Before ten years are
over the revolution will break out." But those who
said the most dangerous things spoke low after casting a look around, because a great many of them, as
I afterwards learned, were afraid the government
might have on board some secret police service.
There were groups of Calabrese peasants with their
hooded cloaks, their sandals, and their leg-bands,
(*zampitti*) ; but few of them spoke. In other parties
the talk was of the sea and of America ; and it was
easy to preceive who had been there, from the high
confident tone in which such persons held forth and
the attention with which the others listened ; for it
is amazing what power vanity has over many of these
poor creatures even in their distress ; and what a
burning desire they feel to become known, to make
for themselves a pedestal even in so poor a throng, in
order to show how superior they are to the wretchedness to which they are reduced and by which they
are surrounded.

Those who seemed to talk the most were the
Ligurians, and one could almost know them by the
confident, almost defiant, way they had with them ;
an air which comes from a commercial and naval
spirit and a general sense of fifty years' successful

emigration by those of their race. They had, or gave themselves, the air of being quite at home and at ease on board ship. The mountaineers, on the contrary, were almost all stolid and taciturn, as if dazed by the sight of that flat, boundless surface, so different from their mountains, all varied with broken plains, and from their narrow cosy little valleys. Some of these people were standing upright like wooden automatons, some were crouched like wild beasts. There were, however, among them a few of those bold, light-hearted spirits whom novelty and the throng of men excite like wine. These bustled about from party to party addressing their little remarks to everyone, and laughing over the sea as if they were to find heaps of gold ready for them on their arrival. And from the many couples of men, and women too, who were sitting talking face to face, as if smoking or working at their own house doors, it was clear that not a few of those permanent friendships were being formed which, cultivated in America as circumstances permit, are always the most dear; bearing for life, as they do, the impress of that early need of sympathy and mutual encouragement to face a mysterious future which gave them birth. Women stood about with their infants in their arms as at the corners of the streets. Near the caboose, or canteen of the third class, I marked the Lombard singers chatting and laughing with theatrical ease in the midst of a group

"Women stood about with their infants in their arms as at
the corners of the streets."

of young Switzers. These all wore, probably with
some political idea, caps of red cloth, and made
good with a pantomine, perhaps a little too ex-
pressive, their lack of the needed phrases. I met
the handsome Bolognese walking all alone, with her
prima-donna stride, the cynosure of many glances ;
her inseparable satchel at her side, and looking down
at every moment with a grimace of disgust lest she
should soil her shoes. The deck was, in fact, strewn
with bits of paper, with apple parings, crumbs of
biscuit, all sorts of things, and looked as if a
regiment had been bivouacking there. In general,
too, the faces and the clothes of the soldiers agreed
well enough with the condition of the place. Many
countenances indeed had on them the dirt of sailing
day. But I did not blame them so much when
I remembered that while German emigrants at
Bremen, before going on board, have good shelter and
a bath to refresh them from their land travel, ours
at Genoa sleep on the sidewalks.

I moved on towards the water-tanks. The fair
Genoese was there in her white jacket and her blue
petticoat, between her father and her little brother,
clean and fresh as a flower, and busily sewing. But
the crowd of her admirers had grown thicker. She
had around her at different distances perhaps a
dozen passengers who never took their eyes off her ;
jesting and whispering in one another's ears with a
kind of grin and a look in their eyes which left but

little doubt about the character of their admiration. Others came up, stood on tiptoe to look at her, and then went away. She was famous already, and was beyond all doubt to be the great success of the voyage in the society of the fore-deck. But celebrity had not changed her; no, not in the least. From time to time she raised those quiet blue eyes, as if she had trees around her instead of men, and then dropped them once more upon her work, unconsciously, as she bent her head, display-ing to all those eager looks her white neck and the magnificent folds of her golden hair. Ah, poor third-class kitchen! I looked at its window and saw the red

"His eyes fixed, his forehead wrinkled."

face of the cook, his eyes fixed, his forehead wrinkled. Beyond all doubt there was a passion flaming up among the saucepans too. The public health was in danger. As I looked at him I saw his glance as it turned from the girl take a fierce expression, and following it my eye fell upon a figure in the circle of admirers that fixed my attention in a new quarter. It was a youth less than twenty years old, beardless and starved-looking; his poor wretched shoulders like coat-pegs; a sort of cross, it appeared, between the village schoolmaster and the bookkeeper; the kind of person that goes to America "to get something to do." Seated on a barrel-head, he kept his look fastened on the girl with a passion so ardent and so humble that it might have extorted a glance of compassion from a woman of marble. He seemed to be alone on board, and carried around his body a belt of yellow leather which probably contained his whole peculium. I looked at him for some time, and all the while those eyes were moist and moveless, with a faint sad smile in them as of pity for himself; the whole body quite still, like one who is content to adore, who expects nothing, hopes nothing, and is there for life. All this time the girl did not seem aware of his presence. He languished there all alone like a Stylites on his column; and the warmth of his poor unregarded flame was lost in space like the smoke from the *Galileo's* funnels.

I next repaired to the forecastle which was full of people. As I went up I heard alongside of me,

"Yes, they make this their theatre!"—*Già, vegnen chì al teater*. This *vegnen* was meant for me, of course. I was received here worse than in the other place. I met with furious glances and turned backs. Nor this alone. *Sub terris tonuisse putes*. It occurred to me, and I was not wrong, that the place was a kind of *Mountain* where all the emigrants with revolutionary ideas, all those who had to go into a corner to hold dangerous talk, came together; and where all the protests against bad food, and all the plottings against rules and regulations were to have origin. There were bold dark faces; and the general air of the men was that of the bravo in repose. They seemed to be all single men, or such as had left their wives behind them after two or three years of marriage (these last a long list) either because they are driven to emigrate by the needs of an increasing family or because, having tried married life and found it a bore, they wished to get out of it this way. In one group I found the tall old man who had shaken his fist at his country the evening of our departure; the very type of a dried-up adventurer, with fiery eyes, with cords in his neck that looked ready to burst the skin, and wearing a green jacket that seemed to have belonged to some actor. His head was bare, his gray locks free. He spoke loudly with a Tuscan accent, and gesticulated with raised forefinger. I heard as I walked about the word *pagnottisti*, and caught, flying, a furious look that made me

think it would be as well to move on. Near the
capstan a little fellow was playing on his pipe, but
the wind carried the sound away and no one took
any heed.   Some were seated on the
deck, at cards.   Right forward, on
the cut-water, stood a queer
figure of a mountebank with a
long, bony, olive-colored face
lighted up by two large green
eyes, his black hair falling over
his shoulders, his bare arms
folded on his breast, and having
tattooed on one of them the
initials, A S., with a cross.
Thus upright and gloomy in
his loneliness, now borne
aloft, now sinking with the
movement of the vessel as if
dancing in the air, he seemed
the personified idea of all the
misery brought together on
that deck; the living symbol
of the vagabond and uncer-
tain destiny of every one around.   There was but
one woman up there, an old woman seated on a
timber-head, beside her husband, likewise old; both
with arms crossed upon their knees and their heads
upon their arms, so that their faces were not seen;
nothing but the thin gray hair; and their necks,

"No one took any heed."

whose wrinkles showed them to be past seventy,
were stretched out in an attitude of utter abandonment and mortal weariness. What were they
going to do in America? Perhaps join their children. I saw nothing on board more pitiful than
these two poor, old, broken-down creatures, almost
in the grasp of death already, and yet going out
to a land where their future must be a bitter
struggle. I bent over them. They were asleep. A
short distance off, upright against the bulwark,
cowled and solitary, stood the friar who was going
to Terra del Fuego, a face as of wax, with eyes vacant, expressionless.

Coming down from the forecastle I met the surgeon, a Neapolitan, the very image of Giovanni
Nicotera, but with different eyes and a different air;
vacant, stolid,—a not unusual case of physical likeness between persons of opposite natures. I went
with him to the sick bay, a large oblong apartment
lighted from above, with two tiers of bunks round
about. There was a child here ill of the measles,
flushed and feverish, a love of a boy with bright
curly hair. Standing near him was a peasant woman from the neighborhood of Naples, a fine, handsome woman, who, as soon as she saw the doctor,
began to weep, choking her sobs with her hands.
The doctor examined the child and then said, in a
reproving tone: "The illness must run its course;
there is nothing to fear. Put that foolish notion out

of your head." He then explained to me that some silly women had upset her by saying that if anything happened to the child it would be thrown overboard into the sea; and she was in despair. Then turning another way and speaking loudly he asked, "And how is it with you?" Presently I saw thrust out of a low berth the head of a sickly old man who, in spite of the doctor, persisted in putting forth his legs and sitting on the edge of the bunk. He had his clothes on. He answered in a thin voice, "Pretty well" (*Non c'e tanto male*). The doctor examined him and shook his head. The man was suffering from a bad pleurisy, and had taken to his bed the day after we left. He was a peasant from Pinerola, all alone, and was going to the Argentine to join his son. I asked him in what part of the Argentine his son was. He did not know. His younger son had gone thither three years before, leaving him at home with the other brother, and this one had lately died. Then the younger son had written him to come out and had sent a *buono* for the trip, but without giving a precise address, the fact being that he worked on the roads, and was constantly changing quarters. But he had told his father how he might be found. So saying the poor old man thrust his thin hand into a breast pocket and pulled out a handful of tattered greasy papers which he began to run over with rembling fingers. Just then a sudden roll of the ship threw his poor bald

head hard against the upper berth. He passed his
hand over the place to see if there were any blood,
and then turned once more to his papers. There
were torn envelopes, papers with figures, perhaps his
last accounts with his padrone, a receipt, and a little
almanac. At last he picked out a crumpled half-
sheet on which was written in large characters, but
blotted with ink and almost illegible, the name of a
village in the province of Buenos Ayres in which, at
such a number of such and such a street, he would
find shelter with a Piedmontese family. Hither
would come within the month a *patriotta*, a comrade
of his son, who would take him to his Carlo. With
such a direction as this, old, sick, and ignorant, he had
set out for America. " I greatly fear," said the doctor, as we went out, " that he has set out too late."

And then I must go with him to see the " man-
ger." In a little corner in the forward part of the
ship, between a turkey coop and a huge hogshead
shoved up against the side, about large enough to
hold a sack of coals, a family of five persons had
made their lair, passing the day jammed in against
each other and against the walls so as to look as if
they had only gone in there for fun. It was a family
of peasants from the neighborhood of Mestre. Husband and wife, both still young,—she *enceinte*,—two
boys—twins—six years old, and a girl of about nine,
with her head bandaged. She was in front, knitting,
and the blond urchins were imprisoned between the

knees of the father, who was smoking, with his back
against the side of the ship, and holding out his arm
to the wife, who was mending his sleeve.   Poor but
clean, with faces that wore a certain air of serene

"Mending his sleeve."

resignation.   As the doctor approached, the man
rose up smiling, and said the "wench" was better;
she had got a cut from falling down the cabin stairs
a day or two before.   "And how about the kitchen?"
the doctor asked.   The peasant with several others
went to the kitchen every day to peel potatoes and
shell beans for the second cooks, who paid them with
a glass or so of wine.   "All right," he answered, "at

all events we get a drop of wine. But that *capo cogo* (head cook) is a queer fellow." On being asked, the peasant told his story. An uncle had left him a bit of land, enough to live on or nearly, if he worked like two. *Ma co no ghe xè fortuna,*—"When a man has no luck, everything goes wrong its own way." There was a little mortgage on the land, and then one hundred and ten lire of taxes; two bad years to begin with; in short he had worked himself nearly to death for five years and had done no good. And what if the wife did work fit to kill herself just like a man, there were five mouths and only two pair of hands. To be wearing out his life in this way, to be always in debt, to eat polenta and nothing but polenta, and to have his children starve day by day before his eyes,—this could not go on. Then the girl fell ill for a long time, and at last one of his cows was killed by lightning. That settled it. He had sold everything, and was going to try whether he could not screw out some kind of a living in America. Good-will and courage were not lacking. *Ma co no ghe xè fortuna.* Then he eagerly went on, "*Saludé putei, che vien la paronçina,*"—Make your bow, children, here comes the young lady. And greatly was I surprised to see, coming along through the throngs on deck, the lady with the black cross, in her dress of sea green, leaning on the arm of her companion, paler and more feeble than I had ever seen her. She approached the family, asked about the girl in Ven-

7

etian dialect, and put her hand on the heads of the twins; then taking out a little parcel, probably of sweetmeats or fruit, she gave it to them with a certain worn invalid grace that was infinitely touching. Meanwhile the doctor took me aside and told me she was also from Mestre, that she had recognized that family of peasants on the day of sailing as they were going on board. She was the daughter of an engineer, a widower, who had been for two years in charge of certain railway work in the interior of Uraguay, and she was going out with an aunt, who was only one year older than herself, to see her father "once more." I was in the act of asking what the last phrase meant, when the young lady coughed, and I had no need to finish the sentence. It happened, too, that the doctor pointed out to me a woman sitting near by all alone, and looking at the family with glassy, almost despairing eyes, in which there appeared a glimmer of envy and the undying memory of a lost affection. She, too, was Venetian, and was going to join her brother at Rosario, because, two months before, her husband had been stabbed in a quarrel.

And all this misery is Italian, I thought as I returned to the after-deck. And every ship that goes out of Genoa is full of it, and they are going out of Naples and Messina and Venice and Marseilles every week throughout the year, and so have been doing these ten years. And these *Galileo* emigrants, as far

as the voyage went, at all events, might well be
called fortunate in comparison with many who in
previous years were, from lack of room in the hold,
littered down on deck like beasts, living there for
weeks, drenched with water and suffering deadly
cold ; or with others who had nearly perished of
hunger and thirst in ships half-provisioned, or almost
died of poisonous fish and putrid water,—and many
did die.   And I thought of many others, again, who,
shipped off for America by rascally agents, had been
treacherously landed in a port of Europe, where they
were forced to beg their bread ; or, who, having paid
for their passage in a steamer, had been put on board
a sailing vessel and kept six months at sea ; or, who,
supposing they were to go to the Plata River, where
friends and relatives awaited them, had been put
ashore on the coast of Brazil to be decimated by the
tropical heat and the yellow fever.   And thinking
of all this foul crime and of the thousands of my
fellow-citizens who in foreign cities keep body and
soul together by the most degrading drudgery, and
of the bands of starving street performers whom we
send out to the four winds, and of the hideous traffic
in children, and of many other things, I bitterly en-
vied those who can go about the world and not find
at every turn those of their own blood in wretchedness and sorrow.

But to sweeten all this bitterness, a kind Providence had sent on board two French commercial

travellers.   One was a Parisian, a good fellow enough
though somewhat loose in talk, but, alas ! with a face
on him which I seemed to have seen before in one of
Darwin's illustrated works at the head of a chapter
on apes.   The other I have spoken of already, a
Marsigliese, fifty years old, with a Patagonian bust
and short legs, one of which was crooked and trail-
ing.   He had a face like a bloated Napoleon I.,
and he was so grave that the nonsensical things he
continually said seemed doubly ridiculous.   He pretended to be commercial correspondent of the *Journal des Débats*, though no one believed it, and he
bragged a good deal about literature, citing on all
occasions one and the same book, which was his
gospel, and of which he had most certainly read
nothing but the title, the Dictionary of Littré, " *un
ouvrage qui restera dans les siècles*."   Moreover, he
boasted of knowing Italy thoroughly, and spoke
Italian in a way to frighten the sharks.   But the
funniest part of it all was that, having enjoyed in
Italy, as well appeared from his talk, nothing but
street-corner conquests, he harangued, *ex cathedra*,
about the fair sex, making a hundred nice distinc-
tions, *à la* Stendhal, between the ladies of one great
Italian city and another, as if he had made study of
the flower of our aristocracy in the capacity of
French ambassador.   And then he had a way of ar-
guing about all sorts of things, a way common
enough among the lower French bourgeois class, by

subterfuges and set phrases, of which the following
plea may be taken as a fair sample, brought up by
him against one of the Argentines, who declared that
beer was hurtful. "*J'ai assisté à l'enterrement de
bien des gens qui n'en buvaient pas.*" But his forte
was gallant adventures, which he recounted half-
boastfully, half-comically, with actor's gesticulation,
standing up, and always making a wave with his
fingers and a pirouette on one heel, to come round
again and face his hearers with "*Et voilà !*" like a
juggler asking for applause.

That very morning he and his colleague, who sat
over against him at table, enlivened us all with a
discussion, begun I do not know how, about the cost
of a respectable dinner at one of the so-called *mar-
chands de vin.* After a few words, the attention of
the company having piqued the vanity of both, the
Parisian allowed himself to remark in a sympathizing
tone that his interlocutor did not know Paris. The
Marsigliese flew out like a shot, "*J'ai fait vingt-
cinq voyages à Paris, monsieur !*"—"*Et moi,*" answered the other, rising in the midst of a general
silence,—"*je l'habite.*"

But the look, the accent, and the gesture were so
solemn as to provoke a loud laugh which almost
drowned the rejoinder of the enraged Marsigliese:
"*Vous prenez la chose sur un ton* . . . *Nous
nous moquons pas mal de Paris* . . . *Thiers qui
a sauvé deux fois la France.*" . . .

But the other was so happy in the triumph of his *moi je l'habite* that he said no more, but turned to his neighbors with some words, among which I caught ". . . *Thiers, une vilaine figure de polichinelle.*" On which we all rose from table, still laughing.

This day, the weather being most charming, all the *beau monde* was on deck a couple of hours before dinner except the Argentines, who at that time were in the habit of having a kind of national luncheon upon their delicious preserved meats, a provision of which they had on board with them. The deck looked like the terrace of a vast bathing establishment. Some of the passengers were lolling on the benches, turning over the leaves of Charpentier's yellow literature; many were promenading two and two. The old Chilean walked up and down with the Neapolitan priest, who was shaking his long flesh-hooks in the air as if to catch bank-notes flying, and every time that he passed near me I heard some of his phrases : "*Yo creo que con un capital de docientos mil pataconse. . . . Vea Usted la véndida de las cédulas hipotecarias provinciales. . . .*" Beyond, and near the wheel the white robes of the blonde lady were seen. She had a blue ribbon in her hair and was leaning over the bulwark beside the beardless young Tuscan and it was plain that they were talking of commonplace matters,—of the sea,—of America; but though they did not look at each other it was no less plain, from a slight but constant smile which trembled on the lips of both, that this was only the exterior accompaniment of an inward and exceedingly harmonious duet.

Looking around for the husband I descried him on the piazzetta below, deeply attentive to the discourse of one of the officers who was explaining the sextant. On one of the long benches about midway was the young lady from Mestre with her aunt. I observed the latter closely for the first time. She was a specimen, not altogether rare, of a freak of nature which had enclosed a woman's soul in a man's body—broad, bony face—large hands —deep voice. All the womanhood of the poor girl was brought together into the eyes. These were small, gray, full of kindness and sweetness; and from their expression it was plain that she felt the disagreeable want of harmony between her body and her spirit; that she was resigned to her fate of being unpleasing; that she tried to keep apart from one sex as from the other, and sought in every way to pass unnoticed. But that timid resignation and the shade of something almost like shame that veiled her eyes inspired a sentiment of mingled sympathy and pity which made her sometimes seem quite different from what she was. All at once and with much surprise I saw the Garibaldian come and take a seat beside the niece. He bowed respectfully but with an air that bespoke a several days' acquaintance. It was the first time I had seen him in conversation with a

human soul. How could they have become ac-
quainted ?   The young lady spoke from time to time,
regarding the horizon with her clear, quiet glance,
he listening with an air of respectful deference, his

eyes fixed
upon the deck.   I   "Listening with an air of respectful deference."
imagined that from
that first moment the soft breath which came from
those pallid lips might be calling back to life in the
man's soul many feelings that were dead and buried ;
but no sign of it appeared upon his face, immovable

and stern in spite of its respectful expression. The
lady of the stateroom next to mine was sitting at
the other end of the bench, dressed too much for a
steamer's deck, and reading; but the unquiet movement of her flat little foot showed that her thoughts
were not on the page. The encounter of that morning, however, had not chased from her lips their usual
nervous smile, a smile that bespoke an indomitable
power in domestic strife, a power of stabbing the
heart or the brain of a husband with pin-pricks for
thirty years running. What could there be to
separate them thus? A carnal aversion like that of
the married couple in *Germinal?* No fault that I
could imagine on the part of either was a cause sufficient to account for the loathing there was between
them; for the husband, who did not look like a
villain, would have forgiven her; and she did not
seem one of those delicate souls that carry all their
lives the unclosing scar of a treacherous wound. And
yet I would have sworn that these two creatures
could never more be reconciled and that the way they
were in was leading them to crime.

But what most drew my attention among all these
people was the Brazilian family: husband and wife,
with three growing children and one infant at the
breast, carried in arms by a negress short of stature and
with a bosom like a Hottentot; all close together on a
settee near the mizzen-mast, quite silent, like statues,
and rolling their large black eyes around upon the

passers by as if all moved by one string.   The father
and the mother sat close together, as if each jealous of
the other, and had the air of being rich.   Perhaps they
had become uncivilized in the solitude of one of those
fazendas in the interior of Brazil, swarming with
negro slaves, surrounded by boundless fields of sugar
or of coffee, and only to be reached through dense
forests by many long days of journeying.   On the
bench opposite to them, with her back to the sea, and
doing fancy work, sat the young lady pianist.   I
could not but remark how deftly she handled the
little scissors, and note the exquisite art with which
she managed to get a good long look at everybody,
yet without displaying the smallest curiosity and
without allowing anyone to catch her eye.   Her
mother, meanwhile, was talking with the agent, who
was standing in front of her ; and, from the smile he
wore, it was plain that she was pulling to pieces with
delicate ferocity one or more of the company.   A
bright flash of envy which came into her eye announced the appearance of the Argentine lady, who
had not been seen for two days.   She came along,
simply and elegantly dressed and leaning on the arm
of her husband, with the step and the smile of a
convalescent who did not try to conceal the pleasure
she took in being looked at by all.   She was indeed
a noble specimen of the rich beauty of creole blood.
Hair and eyes of the blackest, these veiled by long
lashes ; complexion dark and warm, and of marvel-

lous freshness. Her walk, undulating and most graceful, set off the lovely fulness of her person. And in that walk, that look, that bearing, shone out the gay haughtiness of the *porteña* to whom is conceded the first place among the beauties of Latin America, the bold self-reliance of the woman born amid surroundings of struggle and adventure, a society which respects her for herself alone, and which educates her from a child to be ready for any change of fortune. Slowly, and with the easy, smiling grace of the hostess she made the round of the deck as if it were a ball-room, and then sat down near the compass,—the real one, which, luckily for us all, she could not interfere with as she could with ours.[1]

Meanwhile the groups were breaking up and forming again, so that I found myself for a moment near the monoculous Genoese, whose face wore its usual expression of infinite boredom, lighted up from time to time with thought of food, as a stagnant pool by a ray of sun. I asked what he thought of the cuisine on board the *Galileo*. He shook his head and considered a moment; then, in the tone in which he would have pronounced that Russia was abusing the forbearance of Europe, he answered : " Look here ! I am a candid man. We get more brown sauces than is exactly fair,—in my opinion, at least." And yet he had a respect for the cook, who had been at the Hotel Feder—very strong on sweet dishes—two hundred

[1] *Far perdere la bussola a qualcheduno,*—" To turn his head."

and fifty lire per month, and a handsome man. He
offered to present me, but I put off the introduction
until another time. "Exactly!" he said, pulling
out his watch, "I must go and take a look. We
were to have liver pie to-day." And he made way
for the haliphobous advocate who was passing at the
moment, his face twisted as usual. This gentleman
stopped for an instant to listen to the Marsigliese
who was singing the praises of the sea in the usual
stock phrases: *Mais regardez donc! Est ce beau!
Est ce imposant! Est ce grand! J'adore la mer,
moi!* The advocate shrugged his shoulders with a
vexed air, as who should say: The sea, beautiful!
That's a strange notion. People when they are all
comfortable think everything beautiful, like so many
crétins, drivellers. Mountains beautiful, plains beautiful. The sky beautiful when it is clear, beautiful in
storms,— lovely where there is vegetation, lovely
where there is none. Asses! To me the sea seems like
a great puddle, nothing more. "Ah! what now?" he
said, looking uneasily around as the screw gave a
bang rather more violent than usual. But the queer
part of it was that while he was talking of the sea
he never looked at it. The most that he did was to
send a glance around which rapidly swept the outline
of the ship; just as a nervous soldier casts a glance
towards the enemy which is advancing towards the
fort. "Never mind," I said, "we have a smooth
sea." "Ah!" he said, "I dare say; a smooth sea,

no doubt; and in less than an hour we may all be on our knees expecting death."

At this juncture along came the agent to announce a discovery. That plump lady with the red face sitting there near by, who was always so cross in the morning and so jolly in the evening. The mystery was cleared up. She drank like a fish. She was said to be a beast-tamer and had her preserves in Chili. Positively, she had in her stateroom liqueurs of every color and of every country, which she kept sipping all the time from noon on, out of a collection of little glasses which she had had made on purpose—darling little bits of glass work—with which she tried to deceive herself about her weakness. He had heard it all from the mother of the pianist. The lady and her maid got half-seas-over regularly every evening, and when they were properly primed would talk with anybody, saying whatever came into their heads. When we got into the warm regions we should hear more of them. The lady was at that moment talking with a tall passenger whom I had not yet particularly remarked, a veteran globe-trotter, who had on the nape of his neck a long red mark. And there were stories about him too. He was said to be an old sea-captain, a regular beast, and that red streak was the mark of an attempt by his sailors to hang him on the high seas many years before. We all burst out laughing, at which the "scape-gallows" looked round. The name stuck to him. And there

were other nicknames going. One passenger, who
did not talk with anyone, his nose like a beak, and
his ears like handles to a head of the *uomo delin-
quente* of Lombroso, was called the "fire-bug." The
Frenchman of the *Figaro* was called the "thief," no
less. And another, I have no idea why, received the
title of "Director of the Society-for-no-more-bad-
smelling-cesspools." On the first occasion, however,
all these people made acquaintance and shook hands
like good friends. "Stop!" said the agent, all of a
sudden. "I don't see the Swiss lady and the young
Tuscan. I must go below and have a look." I remarked that what he suspected was impossible
because the stewardesses were about. "On the
contrary," he said, "outposts to announce the ap-
proach of the enemy with an ahem!" And away
he went. I looked once more for the professor and
saw him not far off profoundly musing over the
magnetic needle; and just as the agent came back
with the face of a hunter who has brought down his
game, he moved away, placidly remarking, "There is
a little motion." "Yes," said the agent, "she does
pitch a little." With these mild, friendly jests we
whiled away the hours.

But the true time to enjoy the sea was towards
night, when the passengers had all gone below save
two or three lonely individuals. At that hour, when
on the yet faintly glimmering western sky the sea
cut a clear line, and, all black, as if of pitch, did not

attract the eye at any one point, it was pleasant to
yield oneself to that ebb and flow of tangled and
disconnected thoughts which, keeping time to the
measured cadence of the screw, seem like the passing
fancies of a dream. But the thoughts at that hour
take the color of the sea. Compared with that
boundless spread of waters which shows no trace of
man or of time, the objects of our voyage, our little
pursuits, our own country, all seem so confused, so
small, so wretched, so far off. And to think that
three days before leaving we were pained by a cold
salute from an acquaintance in the Via Barbaroux.
How pitiably small a matter !

All such things seem now the records of another
existence, which rise to view for a moment and then
sink again into that measureless abyss which is under
and around us. And then we let ourselves be carried
out over the wide waters in an imaginary ship, that
sails and sails without rest beyond the farthest land,
upon that mighty southern ocean whose continents
would, to a micromega, seem all shrunken and drawn
together into the other hemisphere as if in dread of
solitude. And then the fancy is lost and confounded
in that solitude, and eagerly flies back among the
human race, to creatures that are loved,—to that very
room where dear faces are gathered around the lamp
which shines like a sun in our inmost soul. But
those faces do not smile. On every one of them
there is the trace of pensive disquietude, and we,

too, are saddened at the thought that every turn of
the screw increases the enormous distance that separates us from them. Enormous distance! To re-
duce it in conception we think how small the planet
is in comparison with the universe, a drop of water
on a lump of mud. How far can the infusoria be
from each other? Useless! we must come back to
the comparison of the great earth with ourselves,
and our feeling of awe is born again as strong as
ever. Yes, an enormous distance separates us.

Away, then, with all these visions. Let us think
of the sea. Our soul shall be lulled to slumber
upon those boundless waters. How beautiful! what
peace! Yet what horrors has that solemn solitude
beheld! It has seen gold-greedy buccaneers pass
over it, whetting their swords for foul carnage in
the New World. It has looked upon outbreaks of
kidnapped creatures wallowing in blood in the holds
of slave ships, long martyrdoms of starving crews,
hideous wrecks in the darkness, agonized ravings of
parents and children lashed to the mast, and with
upturned faces shrieking the name of God as the
suffocating waves rolled over them. And this misfortune might happen to us by the bursting of a
boiler, this very night, in an hour, in a moment!
Shuddering, we seem to see the slow descent of our
dead body from region to region through so many
different worlds of plants, of fish, of shells, of mol-
lusks,—a vertical of five miles,—until we reach the

cold and utter darkness of that boundless stretch of
living ooze and of microscopic skeletons that con-
stitutes the bottom of the sea:

> " The enigma of life
> Murmurs and surges down there."
>
> *L' enigma della vita
> Là sotto ondeggia e mormora.*

Whose are those lines?   Ah!   My good Panzacchi.
What is he about now, I wonder? And then visions
of a festive evening at the
Artists' Club at Turin,
like a great luminous
circle which sails
along beside our
vessel, bright
with gleam-
ing, well-
k n o w n
faces;
and one
almost hears
the laughter and
the voices.   Then
it all goes out,—lamps,
dreams, friendships, all
the joys and the doings of humanity; the eternal
reality is that formidable mass of water which covers
four fifths of the earth, and that land, with the
fearful head whose crown is ice and whose brain is

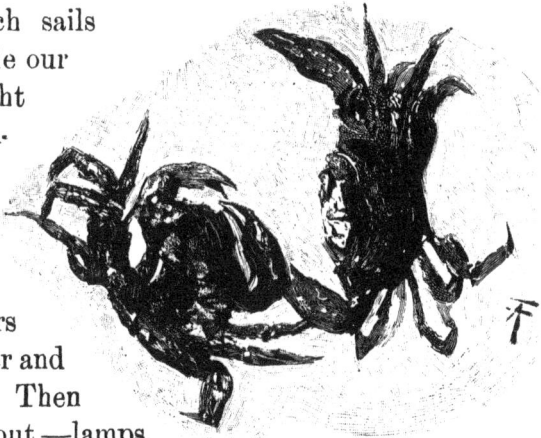

8

fire, which flies howling and weeping into the infinite. O Prodigy! O Mystery! I would stay here
on an island for centuries and centuries, my head
upon my hand, thinking and thinking, so only I
could for a single instant comprehend it all.

Duu! Cinqu! Vott! Tucc! were the cries that
roused me, coming from a group of Lombard emigrants who every evening played *mora* on the midship deck. At that hour in the cabin people were
at chess and dominoes. Those who had rooms on
deck received their friends there, and there were
lights and there was beer and Bordeaux wine.
Around the canteen, forward, was a throng of passengers who presented their order duly signed by
the commissary for a cup of coffee, a glass of rum, or
a half-litre of wine to feast the closing day. I went
on the fore-deck to range like a libertine under pro-
tection of the darkness, through which I could dimly
see groups of women with children asleep in their
arms, men who were drinking all alone, youths with
noses like beagles looking and searching in every
corner. And that evening I was present for the first
time at the separation of the two sexes, done under
the surveillance of the little, old, hunchbacked sailor,
whose business it was to send the women off to bed.
There had been nine days of monastic life in the open
air. Matrimonial tenderness had reawakened a little,
and, besides the regular relations, others not so legiti-
mate appeared to be in train. But the old hunch-

back had to separate them all alike, without regard
to rights, legal or otherwise, and every evening at
ten o'clock, punctual and inexorable as old Silva, he
appeared, lantern in hand, and began to poke in every
corner, loosing embraces and breaking off amorous
colloquies, crying at every five paces, "To bed, to
bed, you women! To bed, you girls!" Comical it
was to the last degree. The couples resisted. Separated here they came together again farther on, between the washhouse and the butcher's shop, under
shadow of the cattle-pens, in dark passages, in every
place where no light came from the lantern. And
then the poor old boy went back on his tracks,
patiently repeating his "Come, you women! come,
my children! It is time,"—*Andemmo donne! Andemmo figgie! Che l'è oôa.* Sometimes to propitiate the recalcitrants he would say, *Andemmo scignôe,*
—"Come, ladies!"

In about a quarter of an hour the women moved
in procession, just as if it were a dress promenade,
between two rows of men down through the cabin
door into the bowels of the vessel. Some came
back once more, holding out the baby to be kissed
by its papa. Some stopped to squeeze and squeeze
again the hand of a new friend; others stood and
called their lagging children: Gioanniiin! Bac-
cicciiin! Putela! Picciridu! Piccinitt! Gennariello!
and the lifted lantern shone on languishing glances
from pretty girls, on the glittering eyes of young fel-

lows, the discontented looks of husbands whom the
regulations annoyed; and still the old fellow kept
calling out, "Come, come, *scignóe*, a little faster, ladies,
if you please," until the last of the procession had
gone below. But the old boy, who knew his kittle
cattle, went back to make another tour of the deck,
quite sure of finding some lurking mischief, of un-
earthing some darkling intrigue.

And so it was every evening. I followed him at a
little distance and heard his scandalized father-guard-
ian exclamations; and male voices would answer desiring him to go to the devil, while softer tones would
be heard apparently denying something or begging
for mercy. But he had no mercy. And I could
see, amid a volley of coughs, women run by with
their hair down and covering their faces to conceal
them from the eager and curious bystanders. As
soon as he had swept up the last fragments of love-
making the old hunchback with the lantern stood
before me, and, wiping his brow with his hand,
growled out, "There's another cursed day gone!"
Ah! che mesté!—"Ugh, what a trade!" But on his
rough, good-natured old face, as he looked down
the stairway, there was a look of pity for all
that trouble, and perhaps a little sympathy with all
those yearnings which he had "only obeyed orders"
in chasing below. "Hard duty, eh?" I said to get
him into talk and hear some of his philosophy. He
raised his lantern a little to look me in the face, and

then after a moment of reflection said, sententiously :
" When a man [*ommo*] finds himself in the position,
as I find myself in the position, to judge people as
they are on board here, gentle and simple, and the
things that go on in a ship, funny and sorrowful, and
the men and the women, but the women more than
the men, believe me, *scignore*, he gets a notion that
it is no use being surprised at anything, and is ready
to put up with almost everything." So saying, he
disappeared, and the men also one after another went
below. The ship was silent and quiet, like some
enormous animal that was gliding drowsily over the
sea without sound save for the measured beating
of its mighty heart.

CHAPTER VII

THE TROPIC OF CANCER

HE next day we were to pass the Tropic of Cancer. I was told this early in the morning by the steward with his usual down-cast look, — for he practised, among other things, the affec-tation of dropping his eyes while he spoke, as if to conceal the joy that filled his soul at the pros-pect of final triumph in the quest of love. But the Tropic of Cancer. It was the despiteful harbinger of nearly three thousand miles of torrid zone which we must pass before we could feel the cool trade-winds of the other hemisphere; and with the very thought I seemed to feel two great drops of sweat course down my temples. I looked out of the port, and lo! a wonder. The ocean most placid, all silver and rosy red, covered with a transparent veil of vapor which the rising sun made look like a luminous cloud of dust; and then some miles away,

in the very midst of that boundless virgin beauty of
air and water, a large ship which seemed immovable,
her broad, white sails like the outspread wings of a
gigantic swan that was regarding us. I open the
port and a delicious waft of sea air floods my face
and breast, runs down into my very veins, and stirs
me up like a breath from a freshened world. The
ship was a Swedish sailing vessel, probably from the
Cape of Good Hope; the first sail we had seen since
Gibraltar. For a few moments she shone white
before my eyes in the clearness of that enchanting
morning, welcome as the greeting of a friend; then
she passed out of view and the ocean seemed more
solitary than before; but kindlier, too, than I had
ever seen it; as if the horizon were the boundary
of an enormous garden. It was one of those morn-
ings in which passengers meet one another on deck
with smiling faces and outstretched hands, as though
the first breath of the rising day had brought each
of them some good news.

But in a few hours all this fair prospect was dark-
ened, the sky was clouded over, the air grew heavy
and hot as if we had made a leap from spring into
the midst of summer. We had entered that mass of
vapor, terror of the navigators of old, which the
great heat of the equator draws up from the ocean
and heaps upon the torrid zone, and which those
happy creatures of Jules Verne's creation, as they
travel in the sky, see as a dark belt stretched around

our planet like the blue streaks upon the disc of
Jupiter. The smooth sea of that morning was the
last smile of the temperate zone softened by the last
waft of the trade-winds. We were now sailing in
the region of clouds, of thickest showers, of doleful
dulness. And its influence was straightway seen
among the third-class people. The agent came for
me in the saloon. "Come and see some alley squabbles,[1]" he said; "the play has begun."

A parcel of women had risen in rebellion about
the distribution of fresh water, of which, over and
above the number of litres allowed each *rancho*, a
sailor was to serve out a certain quantity to every
woman when she asked for it for her own personal
use. So some complained that it had been refused
them while the others received it. But it was an
intricate matter. It was the outbreak of a resentment they had long been brooding over against
what they regarded as an habitual and not uninter-
ested injustice. The old women said the young
ones were preferred because they played the co-
quette; these on the contrary declared that the old
ones were favored because they had money and
greased the palms of those in charge. Others again
complained that the gentlefolk, the *quality*, were
treated with more distinction; the *signore*, forsooth,
poor, decayed creatures who had nothing left of that

---

[1] "Alley squabbles," *baruffe chiozzotte. Chiozza* answers very well to
Billingsgate,—its inhabitants being noted for fluent and abusive slang.

about them but the worn dress and the sad memory. The most waspish of the protestants were crowded together in a corner near the kitchen, where the carcass of a calf was hanging up. When I got there the commissary was surrounded by fifteen or twenty slipshod women, red as turkey-cocks, all talking together in three or four different dialects, and all pointing the finger of accusation at the sailor in charge, who, with his great beard like a Capuchin friar, stood there as unmoved in the midst of all that cackle as a statue in a gale of wind. "But I do not understand a word," said the commissary, with native coolness. "Do me the small favor to speak one at a time." And the looks of some of the younger ones softened a little as they rested on the white hands

The commissary.

and rosy cheeks of the handsome fellow; but in the eyes of the rest there flashed that sombre fire which

gleams in the face of the low-lived woman whenever
she disputes even about the merest trifle with her
betters, and which arises from vague ill-will of very
old date and quite independent of the matter in
hand. *Inn balossad!* we heard some of them
say. *Pure nui avimmo pagato signurì. A l'è ora
d'finila,*—"We have paid too. There must be an
end of this." And the women's complaints were
backed up by dull murmurs from a little crowd of
men, who in their secret hearts enjoyed the show,
and moreover encouraged the malcontents from class
sympathy and perhaps from a little embryo insolence
as future republicans. At last the commissary ob-
tained a partial silence, one woman only speaking.
I had but time to see a head of tangled hair and a
raised forefinger keeping time to a flood of gutter
eloquence when an outburst of exclamations drowned
her voice: "That's not true!" *Tazé vu! Busiarda!
Che'l me senta mi! A l'è n'onta!*—"Hold your
tongue! Liar! Listen to me! It's a shame!"
Then in the press a baby began to cry, and they
were ready to tear each other's eyes out.

Suddenly a woman's shrill shriek was heard, and the
people were seen running together near the foremast.
In a moment there was a crowd there, and a loud
burst of laughter, as if at something that had happened. The news spread, and more people flocked in
from every side until there was a bustle and a laughing from the kitchen to the forecastle. But it was a

broad suggestive laugh which, with certain winks and nudges that passed, sufficiently showed what kind of event it was that had happened. And such was the curiosity to know the cause of it all that the very disputants, forgetting their quarrel, rushed off to see what was the matter. It seems that a couple of flying fish sailing across the deck had hit the rigging and fallen, one among the wheels of the donkey engine and the other right upon the bosom of a young damsel,—and headforemost, as if he meant to keep on. As soon as she could, the girl ran behind the butcher's shop; and a clown of an emigrant carried the shameless fish about, yelling something or other like the criers in the *seraglio* until the commissary signed him to be quiet. But the scurrility and the laughing went on all the same, while the two sea-swallows, shining like silver and passing from hand to hand, served to quiet down somewhat the rising irritation of the "working classes."

Meanwhile, I marked among the first-class passengers several individuals: the Marsigliese, the Tuscan, the tenor, who seemed in the habit of hunting about among the third-class people. The most conspicuous among them was the Marsigliese who, with his face like a dropsical Napoleon, went marauding around the companion-way of the women's cabin swaying his great Patagonian torso about upon his bow legs. The agent told me he had begun a regular series of visits among the emigrant ladies with

conquering-hero ideas, and liked to allude to them
from time to time with a gently closed eye: "*Il y
a quelque chose à faire par là, savez vous!*" And
he had tried to smooth his path with the men by an
ostentation of natural sympathy flavored with a dash
of socialism; but besides not getting on at all with
the many he had heard remarks from certain individuals that made him think a horse kicked him (*da
levare il pelo,*—to make the hair stand up, literally).
Those persons of education and breeding in whose
minds the innate idea of equality is fortified by
association, have no idea how general is the almost
unconscious contempt with which the democratic
middle class regards the people, and how few there
are who, even when they wish to conciliate them by
treating them as equals, can talk with them and not
make them feel conscious of it. Seeing, therefore,
the failure of his first little attempts the Marsigliese
had been less assiduous, and confined his views to a
mere " artistic search " after the beautiful. He did
from time to time discover a handsome face, and described it to me at table, boasting that he could distinguish the various Italian types. He held forth
upon the Tuscan nose, the Venetian mouth, the
Lombard contours (*attaccature*) with inconceivable
self-sufficiency; and though, as had been proved to
him more than once, he had mistaken the Val d'
Aosta for Calabria, with other similar colossal blunders, he went on undismayed, teaching everybody

" . . . *La bouche de la femme Toscane* . . . *Le type Genois, messieurs,* . . . *J'ai remarqué que l'angle facial Napolitain* . . . *Il y a là une nuance, je vous assure.*" It was delightful.

But at breakfast that morning he did not succeed in cheering up the guests. They began to feel the influence of the tropics, and their dulness was in piteous lack of keeping with the bright waistcoats and white jackets which the sudden heat had brought plentifully out. For a few moments only he waked us up with a little discussion, into which the Argentines mischievously drew him, upon the Malthusian theory, and especially upon the old, old question as to whether emigration is a sufficient remedy for over-population. Wholly unread in Malthus, but burning to show that he was a well-informed man, he rashly maintained that emigration depopulated a country, that Europe in a hundred years would be half-wilderness, with the wolves and bears at the very city gates. The others said No, *locuras* (nonsense). In every country births were more numerous than deaths; nor this alone, but that in the countries so left the species was propagated more freely, because, the means of subsistence being in more favorable proportion to the number of inhabitants, marriage was easier, and the gaps were always filled, and more; the proof of this being that in countries from which there is much emigration there is no sensible diminution of misery. " *Pas possible!* " answered the Marsigliese, boldly; *"prouvez moi cela!"* But the others, with that admirable readiness of memory for which they were remarkable, quoted Malthus to show that in the years of fullest emigration England did not cease to suffer from want. *" Malthus, n'a pas dit cela!"* "How? How?" But he, without either admitting or denying, said nothing at all. "Stuart Mill," they went on, "holds that emigration by no means releases us from the necessity of providing against the increase of population. You will allow that he has said that." Then the other, frankly, *" Pas précisément, messieurs."* And as he knew no more of Stuart Mill than he did of Malthus he backed down (*si"ncaponiva*), amid the laughter of his interlocutors, who saw the joke.

This was the only cheerful passage of the breakfast. The cloudy horizon, the gray sea, and the heat, which began to bedew our faces with sweat, kept all the rest of the company quite silent. The blonde lady only showed a countenance as cool as a rosy apple, sending a double spray of words into the ear of her husband on her left, and over the tenor on her right, now and then between whiles encouraging the little Tuscan with a glance or so not to be jealous of her new friend. And we had to thank her, moreover, for a gleam of hilarity which hovered over the yawning groups on deck during the heavy hours of chylification. A naive blunder of hers had been going the rounds all the morning, and showed how wholly confused were the ideas of geography shut up under that crown of curly gold. The agent, meeting her, had said, "Signora, we cross the Tropic of Cancer

"Sending a double spray of words into the ear of her husband on her left, and over the tenor on her right."

to-day." "O, indeed!" she cried, with enthusiasm. "Then we shall see something at last!"

But I could not understand how one could be dull on board ship—on the contrary, I rather liked seeing how bored the others were for the same reason that makes one feel so happy at being well when those around are suffering with sea-sickness. And to-day there could be no lack of diversion. Between one o'clock and four, the most trying time, I began to see

faces that half made me think : Now they will drop
to pieces and have to be swept off the deck. It was
not the *ennui* which Leopardi calls the greatest of
human sentiments, but a pitiful slackening of mental
fibre, betrayed by the drooping of eyelids, of cheeks,
of lips, as if these faces had been made of boiled
meat. Among those most tormented was the Genoese, who stood looking through the window of the
engine-room, with a face upon which there was not
even a dying gleam of intelligence. "What are you
doing here?" I asked. "Why are you not in the
kitchen?" He had just come from there. No
news. Thought there would be *tagliatelli* (flat
maccaroni) to-morrow. Could not be sure. And
then he explained why he stood so long looking at
the monotonous movement of a piston-rod. It was
his theory about boredom,—his own. "I have remarked," he said, "that a man is bored because one
cannot prevent himself from thinking of disagreeable
things. The only way, therefore, to get rid of boredom is to be like the beasts, and not think at all.
So I stand here quite still and watch that rod go up
and down. Little by little, in about twenty minutes,
I bring myself to a condition of perfect stupidity—
a very ass. So I do not think about anything at all
and am not bored. *No gh'è atro.* That 's all there
is to it." I burst out laughing, but he was quite
grave, and turned round to gaze at the piston-rod
again, his eye fixed and dilated like a dead man's.

I wanted to tell him that a better way to get out of himself would be to go right down and see the whole engine; but perceiving that the desired effect was in a fair way of being brought about I forbore. And then I went down myself.

One reflection I had made, every day, in this connection, and that was that probably not ten out of the seventeen hundred passengers on board the *Galileo* knew what the engine was like or had any curiosity about it. And so of a hundred other mechanical marvels of human wit. We make use of them and go our way regardless; not less ignorant than the savages whom we despise for their ignorance. And yet not only for those whose ideas go no farther than a huge kettle and a mysterious and intricate mass of wheels, but also for many who have read about these things in books, it is a great pleasure to get into the blue overalls of the machinist and for the first time go down into that dark noisy kind of infernal region of which they had never yet seen anything but the ascending smoke. When down at bottom one looks up at the faint gleam of day above, one seems to have descended from the roof to the deepest foundations of a lofty edifice; and at the sight of all those steep iron ladders, one above another, those horizontal gratings, that variety of cylinders, of mighty tubes, of rods and joints of every description, all driven by furious life and all together making up some kind of formidable mon-

9

ster, which with its hundred limbs occupies a third part of the enormous ship, one stands fixed in wonder and humiliation at seeming so small beside that prodigy of power. And the wonder grows when we push on into the volcano that gives life to it all, and walk among those mighty boilers,—six steel-built houses standing on four crossing streets like a district barred up and on fire,—where many black, half-naked men with red faces and bloodshot eyes, who swallow at every moment floods of water, toil ceaselessly to feed thirty-six red-hot mouths which, urged by the blast of six huge ventilators that roar like the open throats of lions, devour in the twenty-four hours a hundred tons of coal. We seem to come back to life when, issuing thence, all dripping with sweat, we stand once more before the engine, where but a moment ago we seemed quite buried. And yet it takes some time to get one's ideas together. The engineer may explain as much as he likes, but all that dizzying movement of pistons and rockers and governors and what not, among which the oilers move with such blood-chilling coolness; the stunning uproar of the cranks, the whistling of valves, the dull plunge of the pumps, the sharp stroke of the eccentrics; the spectres who, lamp in hand, climb up and down the ladders, appear and disappear, above, below, on every side, and light up with weird gleam steel, iron, bronze, brass, copper; strange shapes and movements hardly understood;

unknown depths, unexplored passages; all this upsets the few clear ideas we may have had on coming down here.

We feel reassured by the mighty strength of this machinery; but our security diminishes as we mark with what anxious care the attendants watch it, listening to hear whether in that uniform concert of sound there be the faintest tone of discord, snuffing for the merest suspicion of burning amid all those familiar smells; how they run here and there to feel if the metal be hotter than it should be, to look if there be unjustified smoke, and to keep up that unbroken rain of oil which, from fifty long-nosed cans, runs down through the joints of that colossal frame. For that colossal frame, which copes successfully with the gales of ocean, is as delicate as a human body; the smallest disorder in any of its members is felt throughout, and must instantly be remedied. It does indeed resemble a living thing. Thirsty, like the men that feed it, from the fire that burns within, it must swallow up unceasingly a torrent of water from the sea and send it out again in boiling streams; and all that complication of rods and joints is like a Titanic body, whose every effort is concentrated upon giving formidable impulse to a mighty arm of iron, driver of the great bronze screw which tears up the ocean and urges the whole mass onward. As we look, the Liburnian of old time comes into our minds with its three pairs of paddle-wheels moved by the slow tread of oxen ; and we think with pride of the wonder which would fix one of that age to the spot, could he see what we see, and the cry of amazement which would burst from his soul. But he could not imagine what that miracle had cost his fellow-creatures. A century of fruitless attempts ; a legion of great geniuses who spent their whole lives over an improvement which the next generation consigned to oblivion—the martyrdom of Papin ; the suicide of John Fitch ; the poverty of Jouffroy ; Fulton made a mock of ; Savage driven mad ; an interminable series of injustice, of pitiful struggles, of doubts, and of despair. The examples of genius and heroic constancy to be found in this great history must console the human race for the existence of that stubborn ignorance, that ferocious greed, that detestable envy which fought against them and would have crushed them if it could have done so. All this that wonderful monster, with its hundred harsh and weary voices, says to us ; and yet it may seem to our remote descendants the weak and clumsy work of groping beginners.

Going up again I met at the top of the stairs the tall priest, who, pointing with one hand to the engine, put the forefinger of the other in front of my face like a wax candle. I did not understand ; but what he wished to say was that the engine of the *Galileo* had cost a million. I thanked him, put aside the finger, and went on deck again just at the right moment to see, for the first time, my friend the commissary in the exercise of his function as justice of the peace in a most curious "case." The big Bolognese was at that instant going into his room with the face of a wounded lioness, her inseparable pouch around her neck. There was nothing to cover the entrance but a thin green curtain, so every word could easily be heard. That unhappy commissary! I was not long in coming to a sense of what enormous patience he had to exercise in these sittings. The voice of the complainant began to be raised, quivering with rage and full of haughtiness and threatening. All I could make out was that she complained of some injury which appeared to be neither more nor less than a surmise ventured upon by a fellow-passenger as to the contents of the mysterious pouch. She stated the facts, demanded the punishment of the insulter, and

called upon the commissary to do his duty. He
in turn desired her to respect his office, and to
be calm, promising to look into the matter. At
these words her voice softened a little, and she
appeared to commence a long story in a senti-
mental tone, which gradually rose to the dramatic.
Yes, it was her autobiography, the usual thing—a
distinguished family, a relative who wrote to the
newspapers and would call them all to account, a
father and mother, good bringing up; then misfortunes, the injustice of fate, a blameless life; and, in due
time, the inevitable crisis—the burst of tears. Then
I heard the voice of the commissary soothing her.

Meanwhile a little crowd had gathered before
the door, men and women of the third class, among
them that clown-faced peasant who had lost the tip
of his nose. He appeared to be the culprit, for he
was making excuses. "After all, I did n't say I was
sure, did I? It was only a sort of guess." He was
the culprit; and when he reached the commissary's
door he went in, saying, "Here I am." Straightway
came an outburst of Bolognese abuse, which utterly
belied the lady's claim to distinguished descent.
"*Caroyna d'un fastidi! At el feghet d'avgnìrom
dinanz? At ciap pr' el col, brott purzèll! brott grògn
d'un vilan seinza educazion!*" Then all three voices
together, and finally the culprit's only. If you will
believe it, the quarrel was about the supposed contents of the famous pouch, as to which all the gentle

creatures of the fore-deck had been cudgelling their brains these nine days, and making the most ridiculous conjectures. But I did not catch the fatal word. I did, however, hear the commissary give the peasant a setting-down, threatening to put him in irons, the peasant making excuses, and the Bolognese scolding all the while, until, at last, the man came out with his head hanging and the woman with her head high. Then, raising the green curtains, I went in, to find the judge rolling on the sofa with his hands to his sides, suffocated with suppressed laughter. What was the surmise? What was supposed to be in that blessed pouch? You would never guess in the world. One of the most ridiculous notions that ever passed through the brain of an impertinent clown; one which would have made the most crabbed moralist laugh in his beard, and to which the author[1] of the *Baruffe Chiozzotte*, with respect be it spoken, might have set his name. And I had to make way to the sofa, too; but straightway had to rise as another woman came to complain of "certain reports which had been put in circulation about her." "Alas, poor commissary," I said as I went out, "the day has begun badly and will end worse." "Oh, this is nothing," he said in his mild, resigned voice, and with a look at the thermometer. "Wait until we have 97°, Fahrenheit." Then putting on his judge's face he turned to the newcomer.

[1] Goldoni, *Chioggia Squabbles.* See p. 120.

But the heat had upset us in the after-cabin no
less, as might easily be perceived that evening. It
was pitiable. There were half a dozen creatures
who ten days before did not know of one another's
existence; who in ten days more were to separate
forever; who, one would imagine, had nothing so
important to think of as what they had left behind in Europe, or what they were going to in
America; who had nothing but a couple of planks
between them and the bottomless sea; and who yet
had devised all sorts of tangled intrigues, mutual
hatreds, and complicated antipathies. There was
national rancor between the Chilian and the Peruvian, between the Italian and the Frenchman; bick-
erings between the Italians of different provinces;
miserable jealousies among the ladies, mushroom
growth of shameful little spitefulnesses which broke
out in cross looks or reciprocal ostentations of
neglect and aversion. One half of the passengers
was ready to scratch the faces of the other half.
And this quite independent of other vulgarities.
Alas! If the *Galileo* had foundered on the spot
she would not have carried to the bottom many
lofty souls. The only two who, as far as one could
judge, would have deserved to survive were the
young lady from Mestre and the Garibaldian who,
even on that evening, were sitting together con-
versing. Their acquaintance, the agent told me,
arose from his having been comrade to the young

lady's brother, wounded at Bezzecca and dying in hospital at Brescia. No doubt his soul was far above the wretched little jealousies of the others, for his face expressed such an indifference about himself, about life, and about his fellow-creatures, such a cold and lofty scorn of everything that was low, that everyone avoided him as if they instinctively perceived in him a foe. And the manner in which the pair separated late that evening struck me most forcibly, remaining in my mind as the most vivid impression of the day. Yes, I can, even now, see that handsome, haughty giant rise and bend his head with its impress of attempted suicide before that pale, pale mask, that face as of the dead, in which no expression was left but the bright hope of a life hereafter.

CHAPTER VIII

A YELLOW OCEAN

T this point I find on the cover of my Berghaus *Atlas*, where I made some notes every day, these words: "11th day. Stroke of spiritual apoplexy," and I call to mind a singular psychological phenomenon, which occurred to me on that day, and which falls to the lot of everyone, I suppose, on a long voyage, so soon as the novelty of life on board ship has worn off. Some fine morning, as you go on deck, dulness comes down on your soul all of a sudden, like the blow of a club on the back of your neck. Everything has lost color; you feel an inexpressible disgust for life and all about you; there is a sense of suffocation, such as one might experience who, falling asleep in the open air, should wake up in a dungeon with the gyves upon his wrists. At such a moment you seem to have been at sea from time immemorial, like the passengers in that fantastic dis-

covery ship of Edgar A. Poe; and the idea of passing
another fortnight on that bundle of planks among
all those boredom-stricken wretches overwhelms you.
You cannot help yourself; this strange brain-sickness,
hitherto unknown, will surely get hold of you before
the voyage is over. How get rid of the torture?
Kind Heaven, how? Write! But, as many a one
has remarked before, the ship attacks the writer in
one of his weakest points, the sense of harmony;
the noise of the screw makes him write the same
word over twenty times in a page. Read! But,
with the very idea of forcing yourself to write you
have shut up all your books in the trunks that are
down in the hold. You seriously think of taking a
sleeping draught, of tipsifying yourself with cognac,
or of trying, like the Genoese, the experiment of the
piston-rod. O for something new! A hundred lire
for this morning's *Corriere Mercantile!* A pound
of blood for an island! Let us have a mutiny, a
hurricane, the wreck of matter and the crash of
worlds, so only we may for one day get out of this
horrible condition.

The sea showed itself that morning in one of its
ugliest aspects; moveless beneath a low-hanging
arch of lazy-pacing clouds of a dirty-yellow color
and looking viscid, like so much fat mud in which a
harpoon would have stood upright like a toothpick
in a lump of mastic; and it seemed as if no fish
glanced through it, but only foul, deformed creatures

of its own color.   It may be that the plains to the
west of the Caspian Sea, when they are covered with
mire from a volcanic eruption, present a similar appearance.   If this great sea, salt like the blood, and
provided with a pulse, a heart, a circulation, had
been, not an inorganic element, but an enormous living, thinking animal, I should have said that morning
that the creature was wandering in his mind and had
a headful of formless, unconnected fancies like any
half-drunken brute.   But the sea did not look as if
alive.   There was not a breath of wind, not a ripple,
not a wrinkle on the water.   It looked like that
desert corner of the ocean [1] lying between the current of Humboldt and the stream that meets it from
the centre of the Pacific—a region long unexplored,
lying out of the lines of traffic, where no ship is to
be seen, no whale, no porpoise, no gull; a place
which everything avoids, where all sign of life dis-
appears, and where the crew of any ship that should
be forced by wind and tempest to pass over it might
well feel that they were sailing the waters of a perished world.

But by the blessing of Providence these attacks
of *ennui* are like twinges in the joints,—terrible but
short.   And the captain helped us out.   At breakfast that morning he was in the vein, and chatted,
full of good-humor, though one would hardly have
thought so from his look.   As usual, this was his

[1] Known as " The Desolate Sea."

best hour. He had by that time overhauled the reckonings of his officers, pricked off the ship's place on the chart, computed what we had done and what was yet to do, seen that the *Galileo* had made good way in the last twenty-four hours; and, when there was nothing specially disagreeable going on, there he would sit at table, rubbing his hands, and keeping up the conversation. But even at these times he failed not to "rattle down" the stewards in sailor phrase, both for a salutary warning to them and by way of keeping his own hand in. To one who made vain excuses he shouted, *Va via, impostò !*—"Be off ! you humbug !" Another he threatened with *due maschae !*—"a pair of boxed ears." To a third, *Mia, sae, che se començo a giastemmà !*—"If I begin to use bad language, look out !" And he threatened with manual and pedal castigation Ruy Blas in particular, who answered with the gentlest of smiles, as one that should say, "Rage, Tyrant ! thou hast the power, but not the love." Indeed, I'm afraid that our good captain's language was a little too lurid for ladies' company. But we held him excused when we thought of the many captains of other nations who are perfect gentlemen at table and hard drink-ers in their rooms; for since we had to trust some one with our lives, it seemed better, after all, that it should be a temperate boor (*rusticone*) than an aris-tocratic drunkard.

Accordingly that morning, as usual, he called

them all ragamuffins on one side and swine on the
other, and then began to converse quietly.   His talk
was that of the blunt sailor, and I remember it well
from the torture it gave to my unhappy neighbor,
the advocate.   It was the plump lady, the supposed
tamer of beasts, who gave an unfortunate turn
to the discourse by asking the captain, with an in-
opportuneness which betrayed matutinal Chartreuse,
what was the most usual cause of shipwreck.   The
captain answered that there were more than fifty
causes of marine disaster—explosion, fire, leaks, hur-
ricanes, cyclones, typhoons, reefs, sandbanks, colli-
sions, and so on.   Half of the wrecks, however, arose
from professional ignorance ; from rashness ; from
carelessness ; from ill-built vessels ; in short, from
preventible causes.   One year with another, there
were about six thousand wrecks of vessels large and
small ; without taking into account China, Japan,
and Malaysia.

The advocate began to look gloomy from the first,
and pretended not to listen ; but it was clear that a
morbid curiosity overcame his prudence.   And it
was worse still when the same lady, making one of
those conversational leaps so common with her sex,
asked the captain how one felt and what one saw
when sinking in deep water.

" *Cose se preúva*," said the captain, " *no savieivo.*
What one feels I do not know, but as to what one
sees, it is something like this.   For a while you see

"He failed not to 'rattle down' the stewards.

the light, a dim, livid light, then it is like the twi-light, they say—a red color—rather grim, and then good-bye—utter darkness, great fall in temperature down to freezing. Still," he continued, turning to the poor advocate as if to console him, "maybe it is not altogether dark, perhaps there are chance streaks of phosphorus; but it is not cheerful at any rate."

The advocate began to show signs of impatience, growling under his breath: "Is this the way to talk on shipboard? I shall leave the table; no more breeding than so many horned brutes!"

Whereon the old Chilian, the monoculous Genoese, and the captain began to recall and de-scribe celebrated shipwrecks, each more horrible than the other, with that indifference to death which is apt to get down into the soul through the ali-mentary canal when we are seated at a well-spread table; and on they went, from the famous raft of the *Medusa* to the *Atlas*, which disappeared between Marseilles and Algiers without ever being heard of again. The captain spoke of the English steamers *Nautilus, Newton-Colville*, and another which left Dantzic in December, 1866, and vanished like ghosts without anyone ever knowing when or how.

The advocate ceased eating.

But the captain went on. With the eloquence of one who recounts a scene in which his life has been at stake, he described a terrific gale which caught him on the English coast when he was in command of a sailing ship; and, as he came to the crisis, he imitated in a head voice, but with admirable exactitude, the prolonged and despairing cry of the man at the wheel: *Andemmo a foooooondo !*—" Down she go-o-o-o-o-o-es ! "

At these words the advocate rose, and, dashing his napkin on the table, went hurriedly away, grinding out curses that would have done damage if they had reached the address. But as he often retired before the rest, the captain fortunately took no notice. No sooner was he gone than the conversation changed *ex abrupto* as if hitherto it had been carried on with purpose to annoy him; and our commander began to give the talk that varied color and

"Grinding out curses."

those strange turns which no one can impart to it like a transatlantic steamer captain, to whom the widely separated parts he visits and in which he passes his life are always present to his mind and all mixed up together. From the last representation of

10

Fra Diavolo at the Paganini in Genoa he passed over to a quarrel he had had, at St. Vincent of the Cape Verdes, with a black woman, who made flowers out of bird-feathers; then he tacked some domestic adventure or other of the coal agent at Gibraltar on to a bit of gossip from Rio Janeiro; and then passed at one jump from a breakfast to which he had been invited at Las Palmas in the Canaries to a meddlesome custom-house officer at Montevideo. I seemed to be listening to a marvellous creature who lived in three continents at once, and for whom distance and time had no existence. I remarked, too, that the people he met in the ports he visited were the only ones that remained fixed and distinct in his memory; and the numberless others who came on board as passengers passed through his mind as they did through the ship, leaving but the vaguest remembrance behind them. His knowledge, too, of countries was *sui generis*, such as is had from looking at them through the door, as it were. For instance, he would know the price of vegetables in their markets, and have no idea of their history or form of government. So too with languages. He knew only the substantives and verbs of a certain kind, the small change, so to speak, of conversation; and had only one kind of grammar for them all. His judgments of worldly matters were marked by the naïveté of a grown-up college student who goes into society once a month or so;

and his acquirements and opinions were out of date, without connection and wholly one-sided, like the views he had of the cities he visited; that is to say, sea views only. His last anecdote was about a little difficulty with a grain broker at Odessa, in 1868, resulting as usual in a handsome largesse of facers on his part. *E ghe n' ho dœte,*—"O I gave it him," he said; and he wound up by giving his near neighbors at table a serious and well-considered eulogium of his wife; a frugal home-keeping woman, full of good sense, and one whom he wished he had met and married ten years earlier.

When we rose from the table he stopped at the door of the saloon, as he always did when he felt pretty well pleased with himself, to see the guests go out, saluting them gently with an air of grave benignity. Standing close to him, I was able to catch a severe glance which he cast at the blonde lady, whose conduct, it would seem, began to shock his rigorous ideas of maritime morality; the more, perhaps, at that moment, when he was still warm from the eulogium he had been passing upon his wife. But the lady passed by smiling and saw nothing. At the next instant I was amazed to see him raise his cap and bow with an air of great respect to the young lady from Mestre, who passed by on the arm of her aunt. When she was gone he turned to the bystanders and said gravely, *Quella figgia lì . . . a l'è un angeo,*—"That girl is an angel!"

The heat being great at that hour, almost everybody remained on deck a long time under shade of
the awning; and I could mark better than the evening before the changes which the last few days had
brought about in the relations between passengers.
Such politeness! Persons who during the first week
seemed hardly able to endure one another were now
in close and friendly conversation; whereas others
who had seemed tied together now avoided each
other with disgust. A long trip is like a bit of
separate existence, where friendships are born and
ripen and die for us as quickly as the seasons follow
one another for the ship, which passes in three weeks
from spring to autumn. The certainty of parting
before many days and of meeting never again en-
courages confidence. The facility of going over to
new friends on the first quarrel, and the ease with
which we can pretend to be more than we are, or
different from what we are, is a temptation to make
new ties and to break out of old ones; because
everyone does the same by us, and we hardly have
time to see the little trick when all is at an end.
For this reason friendships on board ship dance the
contra-dance and "set" to one and to another.
Then, too, there is nothing like boredom to make
men do mean things. On the tenth day there are
those capable of humbly courting the conversation
of certain others whom they had affronted the evening before with the most barefaced manifestations

of aversion. I saw, amongst other new pairs, the Neapolitan priest walking with a young Argentine who hitherto had bantered him more openly and more impertinently than all the rest, but who now listened with visible deference to his harangues about *emisiones fiduciarias y de numerario* of some financial institution in Buenos Ayres; and on the other side of the deck was that upstart of a mill-owner, who had somehow fastened upon the old Chilian, and who complained in a loud voice of the *falta de limpieza* (lack of cleanliness) on board Italian ships, without remarking that his inter-locutor wore upon his face an expression of disgust which meant that he would before long turn his back. But the great event was going on abaft the wheel. The husband of the Swiss lady was for the first time in colloquy with the Argentine deputy, to whom he appeared to be explaining the mechanism of the patent log; and most comical was the pro-found attention which the listener seemed to pay, slowly turning his head now and then to glance at the sometime violatress of his quarters, who promenaded between the surly little Tuscan and the radiant tenor, all smiles and blandishments, but attentive the while to the other two, and well pleased, as may be supposed, at such unexpected overtures. The lady, as she walked up and down, passed before the little piano-player seated on one side; and she in her turn looked the other from head

to foot with a long piercing glance, in which there
was curiosity and sensual envy and all the imprisoned passions of a captive animal; and then her
countenance resumed its usual expression of nunlike
impassibility.   Her mother, meanwhile, seated between her and the lady of the brush, tore to pieces
with eye and tongue a new lilac dress which the
young bride had on.   It was a little creased, there 's
no denying it.   Said young lady was hanging on
her husband's arm, and standing with him before
the beast-tamer, who seemed to be jesting in a way
to embarrass her, and, lolling in a rocking-chair,
ineffectually tried to medicine her somewhat " elevated " condition with aromatic extracts.   Meanwhile the agent, commanding the whole with his
detective glance, leaned against the mizzen-mast, his
arms folded on his breast, with the air of a man who
is awaiting a crisis of some kind.   All the others,
sitting or standing about, talked in a wearied way,
yawning openly, while the yellow sea made a suitable background for those gossippy, sleepy faces.
Amongst many pictures, driven out each by the
next, which the deck presented during the voyage,
this one only, painted in mud color, has remained,
I do not know why, fixed and vivid in my memory.

But suddenly the scene became alive and the representation a real farce.   The Tuscan quickly, almost
rudely, quitted the company and went straight forward as if with a view to indemnification among the

ladies there. A moment later the Swiss lady and the tenor separated, he to sit down and make pretence of reading a book, she to join her husband, the Argentine retiring at once with a diplomatic salute. The agent appeared at my elbow like a ghost. "Now mark," he said, "there is a military movement going on. You, who are a writer, ought to note these things. The Tuscan has retreated, the tenor is held in reserve. The lady is manœuvring in face of the enemy. Oh, by Jove! they played it on me yesterday, but they shall not to-day." In fact, the lady was coaxing her husband most outrageously; she passed her arm through his; she whispered in his ear; she seemed to ask explanations of the patent log. And the face of the long-haired professor was a sight to see. There was a whole system of philosophy there, doubtless of old date with him. He half-closed his eyes like a drowsy cat, and twisting his whole face to one side, showed the tip of his tongue with a leer of indescribable facetiousness through which there shone all the while a flash of mockery, as if in his heart he were laughing at her himself, the other, the others, the whole world. Meanwhile the tenor had disappeared. The lady passed her hand over her eyes and covered with her fan an ill-acted yawn, as if to show her husband that she wished to go below and have a nap. "Look out!" said the agent, "now for the decisive movement." The words were hardly out of his mouth when the lady left her husband and, slowly, with a sleepy-looking face, crossed the deck to go below. "Ha!" said the agent, "she has chosen her time well; there won't be so much as a dog down there in that oven, but there 's a heaven above us all the same." And down he went. Not one of these movements had escaped that rattlesnake of a mother of the piano-player. She whispered her little remarks in the ear of her neighbor, the lady of the brush, and both rose as one woman. But it was of no use. The dear Swiss lady came up again, masking her vexation with a sweet smile and bringing a book, as if that were what she had gone down for; and two minutes later up came the tenor by another stairway, sol-faing and looking out at these a with an indifference that meant fury. A few paces behind him came the agent, filled with delight, and signing to me from afar with open hand and nose-touching thumb. "How beautiful the sea is!" said the tenor, ranging up alongside of me.

The sea was detestable, but he was a most diverting character. I made his acquaintance as we came up with the Canaries, and had chatted with him in the evening two or three times. He was about thirty-five, but looked younger; had the face of a tailor's foreman, little blond mustaches twisted upwards, eyes that said, "It is I!" affected utterance, Almaviva walk, clothes from Bocconi Brothers. He looked at the horizon as if the Atlantic were an enor-

mous pitful of applauders calling him before the
curtain. He held forth upon geography, literature,
politics, and art with a kind of cunning ease, always
on the brink of some hideous blunder, and stopping
short after a cautious look at his interlocutor. In
literature and politics he had a curious trick. All of
a sudden, while talking, he would, without any apparent pretext, fix his eyes on the horizon and solemnly exclaim, " William Shakespeare ! " passing his
hand over his forehead as if in thought too deep for
utterance; but it was only a name that came up to
the surface like a bubble of air; or, perhaps, the talk
would fall upon some historical personage, Napoleon
I., for example. " Ah ! " he would exclaim with a
twist of his face, " for the love of heaven, don't talk
to me of Napoleon I.," as if he had within his own
brain a mighty treasure of original, well-weighed, im-
mutable ideas upon the subject which were not to
be called in question. And not a word more would
he say. Finally, to sum up the whole vast system
of his ideas and intellectual sympathies, he used to
remark, " I keep three books on the stand by my bed
at night,—Dante, Faust, and ——." The first time
he said the Bible, but the next time he forgot and
mentioned the *Mysteries of " the People "* of Eugene
Sue. On board ship, however, I never saw any book
in his hand except *The Loves of the Empress Eugenie.*
One last trait : He said he was a volunteer with
Garibaldi ; but when it came to facts, he never men-

tioned any campaign in particular, but spoke of all those wars with a kind of misty generality, as if they belonged to remote antiquity, to the age of fable. On the whole, a jolly fellow enough. He never got angry except when speaking of a certain Bolognese impresario, the hatred of his life, as it would seem; and he always used the same phrase, "I'll have his liver!" (*Gli farò sputare il cuore!*) On the day in question he did not feel so much like it.

After two o'clock the deck was left to itself. The tenor went down to warble at the piano, the professor went on the midship-deck to hold forth upon science to the "lower orders," the Argentines to play cards, the others to bathe, to sleep, or to get their things off. I followed that day the young lady from Mestre, as she went with her aunt to make her usual visit to the peasant family, carrying her usual little parcel of fruit and sweetmeats in her hand. I could perceive the instant she set foot among them how strong a hold she already had upon the feelings of these people. The roughest peasants rose to their feet as soon as they saw her, and all looked hard at the blue veins of that fine neck, at her thin hands, and her large black cross standing out upon the sea-green dress, which marked no curves but was not without its grace. Not a trace of any evil thought was to be seen upon the countenance of the boldest and most viperous woman who talked of her when she had passed. And it was respect not so much for the lady as for the sad doom which they saw written in her face, and for the sweet resignation with which she bore it, without, at the same time, losing the kindness and innocent charm which is born of a happy love of life. One word I heard, murmured behind her as she passed, which made me tremble for her, should she have caught it,—"That's consumption." But it did not reach her ear. Some little boys came towards her, and she patted their cheeks as she gave them almonds and raisins. An emigrant inadvertently put his foot upon the skirt of her dress and tore it from the gathers. While it was being set to rights the doctor came up, and all three went down to the sick bay.

I followed them. They were going to visit the Piedmontese contadino, ill of pleurisy. The poor man was much worse. Stretched there in his dark berth, with his long, gray beard, which made him look still more gaunt, he was like a corpse lying in a coffin from which one of the sides had been taken out. As the young lady, whom he had often seen before, came near, his mouth quivered piteously, as those of children and greatly enfeebled invalids do when they are going to cry. And he murmured with a lump in his throat: *A' m rincress per me' fieul!*—" Ah, my poor son!"

It was plain that these words affected the young lady deeply. She replied at once, with assumed frankness, but in a broken voice: "No, no, don't

say that. You 'll see your son. You are better
to-day. Don't lose the address. Where have
you put it? [It was in his coat-pocket at the foot
of the bed.] Very well. The doctor will see to it.
Would you like to have me take care of it and give
it you when you get well and reach America? Shall
I take charge of it?"

The old man nodded, Yes. She bent down,
felt in the coat-pocket, drew out the little packet,
found the paper which she knew well, folded it
with great care, and placed it in a handsome snake-
skin case, which she closed and put in her pocket.
The sick man followed all these movements with
the greatest interest and satisfaction, and then murmured, in a thin little voice:

"*A l'è trop grassiosa, trop grassiosa.*"

"Cheer up," she said, giving him her hand. "I 'll
come again soon. Good-bye. Courage!"

The old man took her hand and fervently kissed
it several times, while big tears ran down his face.
He followed her with his eyes to the door, and then
let his head drop back upon the pillow in utter despair, as if he were never to raise it up again.

The young lady went with her aunt on deck
again and moved towards her friends, the family of
peasants, who were packed into their little corner
between the turkey-coop and the great hogshead
like a nestful of birds. But they had given that
nutshell of a place a sort of homelike air already

by hanging a bit of looking-glass on the cask, and stretching a towel to keep off the sun. The head of one of the twins served as a rest for the father's two hands, and the hair of the other was being attended to by the mother who, rounder than ever, wielded a fragment of fine-tooth comb, while the girl was washing a handkerchief in a little pot of water placed on a battered trunk by way of table. As the young lady came near the father rose and took his pipe out of his mouth, while the whole six faces smiled. I heard a word or two.

Sempre ben?—" Getting on nicely ? "

Come Dio vol,—" Yes, thank God,"—said the peasant. *Ma la ga paura che ghe suçeda prima de arivar,*—" But I'm afraid it will happen before we get in." And then the woman, with an anxious face: *Credela ela, paronçina, che i ghe farà pagar anca a lù el quarto de posto?*—" Do you think, padroncina, that they will make us pay for a quarter-place for him ? "

It must have been a very funny question, for I saw for the first time a smile on the face of the young lady, instantly suppressed, however, as she signed with her head that she did not think that they would; then, taking a kerchief of red wool out of her pocket she gave it to the child, saying, *Ciapa, vissare, ti te lo metterà sto inverno-quando mi*—"Take this, my pretty, you can wear it next winter,—when I——."

But what in the world was going on overhead? The sky had grown dark in a moment, the clouds settled down almost upon the mastheads, and evening seemed to have come at one stride. On both sides of the ship nothing was seen but dense clouds, and a little bit of gray, ruffled sea which set us rolling violently and covered the deck with spray. We all thought it meant a gale, but the officer of the watch shouted, from the bridge, "A rain squall; below, all of you!" He had hardly spoken when down came the roaring rain in bucketfuls, flooding the deck and drenching everyone. Then the women all began to scream; there was a mad flight to get under cover, a splashing through streams and pools and rivulets of water, a headlong rush for the hatches, as if the ship were going to pieces. But the companion-ways were narrow, and there was a jam; there were furious elbowings, struggles to get in first, a cursing and a swearing as the rain increased and sluiced them all and dashed against the glazed deckhouses, soaking and washing everything about. The hellish confusion made me think with terror what would be the consequences of a panic on board. But it was only the first greeting of the torrid zone, of that great irrigator of the world in which we had been sailing for two days. And it lasted but a few moments. The gloomy vault of clouds lifted and, breaking away here and there, let in upon the dark waters, still lashed in places with sheets of rain, the strangest spots of light, the most wondrous streaks, livid, white, green, golden, giving the ocean the appearance as of many seas joined together, each with its own luminary,—a weird and sombre image of a world thrown into confusion as its end approaches.

CHAPTER IX

HERE were more rain squalls the next day, and, thanks to one of them, I had an opportunity, for the first time, of speaking with the young lady from Mestre, by whose side I found myself in the covered way on the starboard side, where, already drenched and shivering with cold, she had taken refuge from the shower. Her first words, the first play of her features, heard and seen thus close at hand in the midst of the crowd that pressed upon us, revealed her nature to me more than any act of her's had hitherto done. A certain quivering of her pale lips and an intense trembling in her voice showed there was an ardent nature beneath her composed and gentle demeanor; deep pity for human suffering, the sight of which made her suffer in her turn, and a real love for those who suffered; giving rise to some idea of religious socialism which was confused in her mind, but flamed up clear in her heart and consumed her being. For the first time in her life she saw much suffering and many sorrows in a mass, so to speak, all real, palpitating, within her very reach; and the depths of her soul were stirred.

I did not quite follow her course of thought, for, owing to weakness, or the difficulty of expressing herself, she never finished her sentences, the last few words of which were lost as if carried away by the wind. "We do not do enough for those who suffer," she said, "and yet—there is nothing else to do in the world—there it all is." If her strength had been sufficient she would most certainly have devoted herself to some mission of charity until she died; as was plainly declared by the expression of her delicate mouth and her resolute brow, lightly shadowed from time to time by the thought of human selfishness and human woe, which in her short life she must have rather divined than realized. And in spite of wide dissimilarity, there came into my mind as I gazed upon her the white raised face of one of those Nihilist girls which Stepniak paints, eaten up by the zeal of their creed and ready to die for it. She spoke in a voice of inexpressible sweetness, with her eyes fixed on the horizon, while she gently fingered the black cross that hung at her neck; and the alternate gasps of her infant-like breath were the more pitiful when contrasted with the mighty life which the ocean wafted into her face. Did she realize her condition ? I judged that she did, from her indifference to all those about her. She lived as if in another world, confounding one fellow-traveller with another and asking constantly, Who ? Which ? as if it were an effort to remember. And was she really resigned ? I had a chance to judge of this a short time after when she was talking with the beautiful Genoese girl to whom she had given a pretty little leathern housewife as a present. I looked in her eyes, as she fastened them upon the girl, to see whether that resplendent youth and beauty were awakening any passing sentiment of envy at the sad contrast, any feeling of yearning or of pain. None whatever. She was resigned beyond a doubt. Love and the desire of life had gone before, and were already in the tomb.

At that moment I heard behind me a brisk rustling as of skirts, and a musical laugh. It was the blonde lady, dressed in blue, her face discreetly powdered, and fragrant as a nosegay. She was coming for the first time to visit the fore-deck ; in company with the first officer, — a stout, fresh-colored fellow, a couple of yards high, and with whom she seemed to be already tolerably familiar. She passed along, chatting gaily, and looking about her ; but it was plain that she saw exactly nothing ; that for her forward and aft, engine, emigrants, wretchedness, the Atlantic Ocean, and the Mediterranean Sea were all matters that concerned her not :

they did not distract her for a single instant from the gay consciousness of being a pretty, charming woman in the free exercise of her function. I could mark, too, how sharp a sense the men of the "people" have even for women who are "gentle folk." They had never seen her, but they snuffed her from afar, and took good care, the sly rogues, not to move as she passed that her blue dress might brush their knees. They made, when she had gone by, the unspellable sound with tongue and lips, that one does who swallows a delicious oyster; they kissed their palms with a meaning laugh. But they moved sullenly out of the way for the lady of the brush, who came behind alone, carrying a little parcel. For a couple of days she had taken to aping the young lady from Mestre, and, like her, would give fruit and sugar plums to the children.

But alas! alas! she looked, with her sour smile, like a schoolmistress, and, as she offered the goodies, would keep a sharp lookout lest anyone should touch her. From head to foot she was the poor little middle-class nobody, full of envy of those above her, and of scorn for those below her; ready for any mean-ness, so only she might be seen with a *marchesa*, and capable of taking the bread out of her children's mouths so that she might sweep along the sidewalk in a velvet dress. The little creatures took what she offered, but the looks of their elders expressed the most cordial aversion. As my eye followed her,

moving slowly along in the midst of the press I saw
that "decayed gentlewoman" of the third class
whom, with her daughter, the commissary had
pointed out some days before; her feeble health
now feebler, and looking most pitiably poor in her
black silk dress, all soiled and torn. There are
some small humiliations in misfortune which are
worse than misfortune itself. Both mother and
daughter timidly, after much hesitation, and looking
about them as if ashamed, went to the fresh-water
tank and bent down like animals at a trough, to
drink from the iron spigot as the others did; but,
seeing the Swiss lady coming that way again, they
drew back and, with downcast looks, disappeared
in the throng. Some emigrants, who had marked
this scene, laughed a loud, mocking laugh. The
blonde lady meanwhile, at a sign from the first
officer, stopped to look at the Genoese, whose fame
as the "virtuous beauty" had no doubt reached her
ears. She seemed to think the girl beautiful; but
I saw in her eye an expression of pity, the pity with
which a bold and fortunate operator would regard a
rich simpleton who was keeping a splendid capital
idle in his safe. Then she moved on, saluting with
a wave of her hand her husband, who was above on
the hurricane-deck examining the structure of the
red side-light.

That poor Genoese girl! The commissary, on his
way to look at a broken spigot, told me a pitiful

story. Around that good and beautiful creature
there had closed a circle of euvious aversion which
gave her no peace. All the aspirants whom she had
declined to look at or had repelled with her disgust
had become her enemies, and her firm and dignified
manner had made them fairly hate her. They said
she was too stupid for anything (*stupida come una
scarpa*), a piece of bloodless flesh, all hands and feet,
—and such teeth ! To the anger of the men was
added the jealousy of the women, furious at seeing
a hundred adoring "sapheads" about her. The
Bolognese, especially, and the two opera girls looked
as if they would like to boil her alive. They had
begun by sarcastically calling her "the princess";
then they had said that that nunlike modesty of hers
was all put on, and finally had circulated the most
atrocious calumnies regarding her. Impossible to
describe the foulness of the talk that went on, the
vileness of the remarks made upon her person, pro-
voking insolent laughs whose significance there was
no mistaking. They would have insulted her openly, perhaps have laid violent hands upon her, for no
other purpose than to humiliate her, but for the
authorities. The very cook was furious, and showed
at the window of his stronghold the countenance of
an offended sultan. For two or three days the little
Tuscan in the after-cabin had been buzzing about
her, and had at last got into conversation with her
father; whereon all that scum of the earth had said

it was a bargain, a settled matter, but suddenly had ceased their talk, and that without anyone knowing why. The only one who remained faithful, in love to the very marrow of his bones, poor fellow, was that weakly youth with the leathern bag around his neck,—a "limèd soul" that did not struggle to be free, a Modenese, a bookkeeper by occupation, to whom an ugly, red-haired, pimply, short-sighted creature in the third class had taken an open fancy, but he would not look at her. His passion, which had almost crazed his brain, was the jest of every-one. They brayed out heart-rending sighs behind his back; they sang:

> " Too small, too small
> To make love art thou ! "

and all the rest of it; but he was so dead in love that he took no heed, staying in the same place for hours, his elbow on his knee and his chin in his hand, fastening his gaze upon her as in an ecstasy; happy when those clear blue eyes, as they looked around, encountered his own by chance. He was there while the commissary was talking of him, im-movable, with a face and look which showed that for one word he would have given bag, pen, pass-port, America, the universe. It was pitiful to see. He was likely to lose his head and make an utter ass of himself before the voyage was over—that was clear.

This then was our " *innamorato* " ; a kind of person never lacking on board ship, the commissary told me ; and sometimes there is a variety of them, men really in love, that is to say ; the others do not count. But in the *Galileo* there was quite a collection of other characters still more queer and original, each one of whom had in those twelve days come to the front and acquired his own celebrity in the little republic of the fore-deck. There were jovial souls and there were serious men. These last preferred the forecastle which was a kind of Aventine Mount, where all the turbulent and atrabilious spirits got together. The most popular among these was the old Tuscan in the green jacket who had shaken his fist at Genoa on the evening of our sailing. This man was a born devil. From morning till night he harangued, in a hoarse voice, his threatening fore-finger in the air ; and his following increased from day to day. He would have liked to raise a social revolution on board the *Galileo ;* he inveighed against the signori on the poop-deck, urged the passengers to protest against the dirt of the sleeping-places and the uncleanness of the food ; sometimes by way of example hurling his ration from him and calling down vengeance upon the cookery. His audience applauded but ate their food ; while he, in a fury, cried out that they were all "slaves" and every one of them was "bought."

There was, however, one who did not bow down before him, a little, old, dried-up man, with a black tuft on his forehead and a pair of black eyes like a hawk, who said he was a smuggler. This person chose, likewise, to cherish the reputation of a great criminal, loaded with the guilt of a thousand mysterious murders, and ready for anything. Perhaps no more than a kind of Captain Fracasse in crime, but skilful in playing his part, so that he was universally f e a r e d, though he had not hurt a hair of anybody's head; and the women pointed him out, saying he had a long dagger under his jacket, and would certainly do something dreadful before the voyage was over. He walked among the throng with folded arms and head held high, and did not choose that anyone should fix an eye upon him. If anyone

did so he would stop and stare at the rash man, as who should say, "Are you tired of your life?" But from fear or prudence they all turned their heads another way. This pretence was, of course, necessary to his reputation as a dangerous man; but beyond it he did no harm to a living soul, and entertained for the old Tuscan the usual scorn of the warrior for the politician.

The third in the triad on the forecastle was that queer fellow of a mountebank with long hair and tattooed arms, whose voice no man had heard, so that everyone said he was dumb. This character would stand for five hours at a stretch perfectly motionless at the extreme fore-part of the ship, his green eyes raised to heaven as if he were gazing at a star invisible to other mortals, and profoundly immersed in superhuman contemplations.

The jolly fellows, on the contrary, assembled on the midship-deck, which offered more space for buffoonery, and was like the open square of a village; a lounging place convenient for groups and gossip. Up here in a corner on the port side close by the bridge there was chatting and uproar from rise of morn till set of sun. The buffoon of the company was a peasant from Monferrato, the one who had made that scandalous surmise about the leathern purse of the Bolognese; a quarrelsome little figure without any nose. The whole third class knew how he had lost it—in fact, a drunken carabineer,[1] whom

---

[1] Police officer—so called ; partly military, partly municipal.

he, reeling ripe himself, had provoked one evening
in the street of his village, had cut it off with a blow
of his sabre.　But the fun of it all was that, next
morning, hoping to make something out of this nasal
mutilation, he had gone to the authorities, to whom
the more prudent carabineer had carefully refrained
from making any report, and had been rewarded for
his trouble with much summonsing before the courts,
several days in jail, and a fine of one hundred lire.
This fellow had mistaken his vocation.　He was a
born clown.　He could thrust out his mouth like a
beast's muzzle; he danced all sorts of grotesque steps
of his own invention; he mimicked people in the
most amazing way; and when any officer of the ship
passed by, would salute him with a mock respect
that was altogether killing.

Next after him in renown was a little man with a
bald head and a huge sty on one eye; an ex-porter,
who always kept near him a cage with a couple of
blackbirds, of which he took great care, expecting to
sell them in Buenos Ayres for eighty lire apiece—a
common speculation enough.　He owed his popularity
to a treasure which he had inherited from some relative, a large album full of nasty caricatures, charades,
and anecdotes which, read with the page doubled,
were passages from the lives of the saints, otherwise
devilish beastliness.　He always had around him a
group of liquorish dilettanti, who read the same filth
a hundred times a day, rolling over the benches and

"He owed his popularity to a large album full of nasty caricatures."

laughing until they cried,—while he held his head
high, like an applauded actor, and was happy.

And then there was a third, a cook in a tavern; a
very usual type on board ship, the wiseacre who has
been to America and, in virtue of this, assumes a kind
of learned superiority over his fellow-travellers, ex-
plains in his own way the wonders of sea and sky,
holds forth upon naval architecture, talks as familiarly
of the New World as of his own house, lavishes advice right and left, and calls everyone who does not
go along with him a clodhopper and a blockhead.
The commissary came upon him one day as, apple in
hand, he was uttering explanatory absurdities, fit to
stop the ship, about the rotation of the earth. Between whiles he played the *ocarina*.[1]

Finally, there was a Venetian barber, who enjoyed
a proud pre-eminence from his ability to imitate a cur
of low degree (*can da pagliaia*—" yaller dog ") bay-
ing the moon in a lamentable howl which lacerated
the nerves and would have deceived any dog in Italy.
But then every specialist there had been unearthed
and forced to give proof of his skill; one old gar-
dener, amongst others, would squat down behind a
cattle pen and imitate the furious panting of one for
whom *I cannot* waits upon *I would* with unsurpass-
able perfection; he was a real artist, they said, and
they set great store by him. They played at
draughts, at cross and pile (tit-tat-to), at lotto, and

---

[1] Kind of flageolet made of earthenware.

they sang for hours together. They even played at blind-man's-buff like great gray-headed hobblede-hoys, and at hot cockles like little children. The grand spectacle, however, was when the tattooed mounte-bank, fired with professional enthusiasm, came from forward and walked about on his hands or did the wheel or the serpent trick, amidst a tempest of ap-plause, his countenance all the while quite grave and sad, as if he were doing penance ; and then went back where he came from without a word. Still, all this merriment looked rather forced than spontane-ous; these men seemed to seize with fury upon the slightest occasion to stun themselves with clatter as when one gets drunk on purpose to drive away sorrowful memories and grim forebodings. They would throw themselves, a hundred at a time, against the bulwark, or rush together in a whirling circle with shouts and cries and whistling and cat-calls and cock-a-doodle-dooing that was heard from one end of the ship to the other, making the very officers look round at them, and all this for no better reason than a hat blown overboard or a nose blackened by a fall against the coal bunker. And when an un-protected girl or woman passed among them there was a clacking of tongues and a chirruping and a general exhibition of onomatopœia which made the unhappy victim take to her heels at once. The black nurse of the Brazilian family, above all, when she went to her place in the third class to eat or

sleep, aroused, with her white eyeballs and her grinning teeth, such a chorus of brutal love-strains that
it was like the yelling of an excited menagerie.

And we of the first class had our little ways too.
Would there have been, after all, any very great difference between the fore-deck and the poop? And
if the varnish of culture and good manners had been
taken off from—those who had it—how easily could
we have matched in our part of the ship the types
and conversation of the third class. It is quite wonderful how much they knew of us, how they hit
upon each one's weak points, and how nearly right
they were in their gossip about us behind our backs.
It all came round to us again in one way or another.
They knew from the stewards and the servants something of the character and habits of everyone, and
were posted as to our daily doings ; just as those
living in the garrets know about the tenants of
the handsome lodgings below. What they did not
know they guessed, and they made their remarks
upon everything. They gave everyone a nickname,
and mimicked everybody's gait and voice. Often
enough, when walking among them, we would turn
suddenly round and surprise three or four of them
winking at one another, or composing their faces
to preternatural seriousness after a mocking grin.
These were our Caudine Forks.

This very evening the whole ship was delighted
by an exquisite joke practised upon one of these

fellows, a third-class passenger who had paid the difference and dined in the second cabin, but passed his time among the gossips of the midship-deck. He was a little man, neither old nor young, with a face as wrinkled as a roasted apple; a good fellow enough, dressed like a verger, and giving himself the airs of a well-to-do citizen, but simple and credulous as a child. He was much coaxed and petted as being the possessor of a case of wine which he was taking to his brother in America, and which he guarded most jealously as a sacred treasure against the many snares that were laid for it. That morning, going on deck, his attention had been attracted by the telegraphic dial which sends signals from the bridge to the engine-room. The third officer, who dined with him at table, being near by,

"His attention had been attracted by the telegraphic dial."

was asked what that bit of mechanism might be.

"That is the telegraph," said the other.

The little man was amazed. "The telegraph!" he exclaimed, "to telegraph with!"

The officer caught on in a moment. He was a Genoese, as sharp as a steel trap (*fino come la triaca*), a masterly practical joker, and always quite serious.

"To telegraph," he said, "of course.—What for? Why, the fact is that by means of a travelling wire we are always in connection with the great hollows under the ocean, and we send news to the owners every four hours."

The little man expressed his admiration, and then, as an idea occurred to him, timidly remarked:

"Ah! yes! I suppose that it is used only for the ship."

"As a special favor," said the officer, " passengers are sometimes allowed to use it."

"Oh, in that case," said the other eagerly, "I should like to send a despatch to my wife."

He hesitated a moment as he thought of the expense, but was told that exception would be made in his favor, and he should pay only the usual tariff. So he wrote the despatch: "Am well; sea smooth; half-way; many kisses," etc., etc. And asked if his wife could answer. Certainly she could answer. "Because I know," he went on, "she would go without her dinner rather than not send me a word." And was going to pay; but the officer said he must see how much it would all come to; he might pay that afternoon, about four o'clock, when he came back to see if there were any answer.

The poor fellow went away well pleased, leaving the paper. Came back at three—nothing. At half-past, still nothing. But at four there were twelve blessed words: "Thanks; well; God bless you; I pray for you; come back soon."

Overjoyed he reads the despatch twice over, kisses the paper, wants to pay. "Poh, poh," said the officer, "it is not worth mentioning. I 'll have it go in with the others. Just open one of those bottles of yours, and that will make it square." "Why not. By all means, we 'll open one or two and have a good time. What a thing science is, and what things it can do!" In short, a couple of bottles were opened at table and absorbed; but the poor dupe got so very happy that he opened a third, a fourth, and so on, until the case, up to that moment so carefully guarded, was quite empty. The news meanwhile had spread; and when he came out on deck for a constitutional, excited, flushed, triumphant, he was received with a carnival of yells. At first he did not make out why they were making fun of him; but when he did understand, instead of being thunderstruck, as they expected, he laughed for pure pity of their ignorance. "Fools, dolts, idiots, noodles, asses!" he shouted, as he turned away towards his friends of the second cabin, happy and quite unmoved in the midst of a perfect chorus of barking and mewing and chirping and crowing.

And this scene occurred just before we saw one of

12

the most amazing sights which sea and sky can offer
in the regions of the tropics.

The thick veil of clouds which had enveloped us
for three days had been rent a short time before sunset, and the sun went down into the sea like an
enormous ruby, sending along the tranquil waters a
long streak of purple like a torrent of lava which
was rushing to burn the *Galileo* up.   And when his
disk touched the horizon, the clouds, fired with
brilliant colors, began to move majestically ; present-
ing shape after shape so wondrous that we stood
transfixed ; and, as each dream-like contour vanished,
cried out, "Alas! that it should go!"   There were
mountains of gold, with rivers of blood that fell from
their over-hanging crags ; huge fountains of molten
metal ; mighty canopies lighted from below by a
gleam so glorious that as one gazed, the mind was
troubled with a half-sense of terror; one almost
expected to see the last vision of Dante,[1] as :

> "Within the deep and luminous subsistence
> Of the High Light appeared to *us* three circles,
> Of threefold color and of one dimension "

seeming to be "painted with our effigy " and before
which

> " Vigor failed the lofty fantasy."

[1] *Paradiso*, xxxiii., 115 *et seq.*   Longfellow's Trans.

CHAPTER X

AND still ocean, ocean, ocean! At times one could almost imagine that the land had disappeared from the face of the earth, and that we were to go on sailing, sailing, and never touch it more. The water was not yellow as it was the day before, but seemed one huge sheet of lead; while the sky was white, and the sun was white, and everything on board our ship scorched us as we touched it. But the baking heat was not the worst. There was a waft of foul and pestilential air from the men's cabin which, rising through the open hatchway, reached us on the after-deck;—a dreadful stench that moved deep compassion as one thought that it came from human beings, and hideous terror as one considered what would happen if disease broke out. And yet we were told that there were no more passengers than the law allows. Each had his allotted number of cubic feet. But what has that to do with it if one cannot breathe? The law is wrong. It allows on board the Italian steamers a whole third more of the tonnage to be occupied than in the English and American ships; and it does not have its officers constantly by to see that the report of "all right" made by the police at sailing is justified throughout the voyage; that there be not, for instance, at another port, more passengers shipped than there is room for; that healthy passengers be not put into rooms reserved for the sick; or that sleeping-places be not improvised on the open deck. How much there is still to be done for those noble boats that gleam like princes' palaces as they sail out of harbor! In most of them the foremast hands and the firemen are lodged like beasts; the sick bay is a dog hole; the places that should be cleanest turn the stomach; and for fifteen hundred steerage passengers there is—not one bath. Those hygienists who pretend to settle the space that each man ought to have, may say what they like; human flesh cannot be crowded like that, and it is no excuse to urge that things are far better than in former times. The case, now, to-day, is one that moves to pity and to indignation.

Meanwhile, as the thermometer went up, the commissary's work increased and his annoyances multiplied. The chiefest of these was the care of the women's cabin, into which he had to pass, night and day, to keep order, and to see after cleanliness. In

fact, without taking his work into account at all,
the mere sight of what he had to look at would have
been enough to disgust any man with the task this
gentleman had undertaken.   Imagine two stories
below decks, like two huge *entresols*, about as light
as an ordinary cellar; in each story three tiers of
berths all round about and down the middle; and,
what with women and children, weaned and un-
weaned, about four hundred people to occupy each
story, the thermometer standing at 90° Fahrenheit!
Here, in a lower berth would be a woman far gone
in the family way, with a two-years-old child.
Above her an old woman of seventy, and in the
upper berth a girl in the flower of her age.   Then a
Calabrese *cafona*, or herdswoman, next her a poor
lady who had fallen into poverty; farther on a city
adventuress who used cosmetics under cover of the
darkness; and not far off a God-fearing young
peasant woman who slept with her rosary in her
hand.   Going down there by night there were seen
hanging out of the bed-places gray heads and blonde
tresses, nursing children rolled up in their bandages,
the horrible shins of the old, and the shapely limbs
of the young; a foul heap of shawls and gowns and
petticoats of all imaginable and possible colors,
natural and acquired,—like banners of the unnum-
bered hosts of wretchedness; while on the deck were
orderless piles of boots and shoes and wooden sandals and gaiters and slippers and stockings, which—

it was frightful to remember—were only so many
heaps of quarrel and dispute all ready for the morrow at the hour of rising. There were many who
did not sleep.

The commissary went about amid an unbroken
hum of talk, varied by suppressed laughs, by wails,
by the sighs of girls and the groans of women overcome by the heat; and the murmurs of poor old
creatures who, unable to close an eye, were mum-
bling Pater-Nosters and Ave Marias. At times he
was called aside by a suppressed voice and had to
bend over or rise on tiptoe to hear a complaint
or a protest. "Signor Commissario," said one in
his ear, "please do something — that girl in No.
25 is a scandal and a shame. I 've two little boys
down here; do make her behave herself and remember where she is." Another begged him to tell
those above her not to stick their feet out, and to be
less foul in their talk. The old women in particular
beset him upon the point of morals ; and denounced
certain culprits furiously, but in the greatest confidence. "Think a moment, Signor Commissario ;
you others do not see anything at all, saving your
presence. There 's that blonde girl in No. 77 ; she
goes up on deck every night at one o'clock and
does not come down again for hours. It is a shame.
It ought to be put a stop to." Some wished
to move because of an asthmatic neighbor; or
(reasonably enough in this case) because that girl

near by smelt so strongly of musk that it could not
be endured. And the commissary had to soothe
them: "All right, we'll see about it—Don't mind—
Go to sleep." Then, moving on with his lantern, he
would see mothers slumbering with their children in
their arms and breathing heavily, their faces con-
torted by a sad or a frightful dream; young bosoms
left uncovered; toothless mouths gaping wide as if
yelling in their sleep; and glistening, smiling eyes
fixed upon him in the half-light. Sometimes in the
passage-way he would come upon a face that looked
suspicious and must be questioned. "Where are
you going at this time of night?" "Up on deck (of
course) for a purpose." "What, with eyes glistening like that! I'll give you five minutes and then
I'll feel your pulse." Farther on he stopped to give
a warning: "I tell you for the last time, if you do
not change to-morrow I'll—Are n't you ashamed!"
And the poor creature would reply with what was
sometimes the miserable truth: "Alas! I have no
other!"

And so from one aisle to another, now putting
back on the pillow the head of a naked infant
that was hanging out of the berth, now quieting
a couple of old tattling (*bracone*,—prying) crones,
who were quarrelling under their breath about some
difficulty arisen that morning as to a partition of
biscuit; and a few paces farther on cheering up a
poor lone creature who was weeping on her pillow

oppressed with a melancholy forboding that she would not meet her husband in America. By dint of passing and repassing among these people he had come to know each one's way of sleeping. The burly Bolognese who lay upon her side almost touched the berth above her; the pretty peasant of Capracotta curled herself up like a squirrel; those two jades of singing girls slept with all four limbs spread out, and the "decayed lady" kept that poor black silk dress spread over her like the pall of her past fortune. The fairest and most tranquil even in sleep was the Genoese, who lay supine and covered from head to foot like the statue of a queen upon a tomb of marble. But the sight of those gray un-happy heads, of all those mothers, homeless and lacking bread, asleep on the wide sea thousands of miles alike from the country they had left and the country they were seeking, kept every sensual idea far from his mind, even in view of the much expos-ure, conscious or unconscious, which he was forced to behold. He went about down there like a doctor in a hospital, as impregnable to temptation as that poor old jumping-jack of a sailor who carried the lantern for him. Unhappy hunchback! For him, not protected by the dignity of his office, the task was far harder; especially when the commissary went away, and left him alone in the place with the bucket of water and the dipper,—at the beck and call of every one who wished to drink. *Vien qua*

*vecio—A mi, omm di persi—Dessédet pivel! Acqua!
—Ægua!—Eva! — Da bev! — Da baver!* They
would all quarrel right before him, setting rules and
regulations at naught, and laughing him to scorn.
When he called them to order they stunned him
with chatter, woman-fashion, and some of them
turned their backs upon him with scant politeness.
At getting-up time especially, when the question was
whose was which in all that snarl of things, they
drove him mad, completely; and, fleeing as from a
swarm of wasps he took refuge on deck panting and
perspiring. That very morning, at the fated hour,
I found him at the door of the cabin utterly de-
moralized. "Well!" I said, "they make your life a
burden to you, don't they?" "*Ah!*" he replied,
spitting out his quid with fury, "*No ne posso ciù!*"
"Is it so every voyage?" I asked. "No! the Lord
be thanked!" he said. There were voyages and
voyages. Sometimes it was a cargo of right good
women. Sometimes, as this trip for example, *a l'è
na raffega de donne maleduchœ*[1] a real *carego d'-
açidenti!* Then resuming his philosophical calm and
raising his forefinger he whispered confidentially in
my ear: *Scià sente (stia a sentire). Scià no piggie
moggé! (non prenda moglie)*,—"Mark me, don't
you get married!" And so, turning his hump upon
me, he went his way.

---

[1] *Una raffica di donne maleducate*,—literally a squall of ill-conditioned
women.

That very morning, too, there had come to pass in the women's cabin a most scandalous thing, of which I did not hear until later. I stood with the commissary on the bridge to watch the great noon jaw-exercise (*ballo dei denti*). This was like what one sees on saints' holidays in the country where a hundred families take their food out in a meadow in the open air; a hum and bustle as of an encampment; numberless groups of men, women, and children, sitting, kneeling, squatting in a thousand different ways, above, below, on every projection and in every corner; their plates in their hands, between their knees, between their feet; their heads covered with handkerchiefs, aprons, paper caps, with their up-turned skirts, even with baskets, to protect them against the blazing sun ; and in midst of these groups, between the canteen and the kitchens, an eager running to and fro of numberless *capi-rancio* (heads of messes) with loaves under their arms, pots and wooden bowls in their hands, and followed by a thousand eyes, beckoned by a thousand hands, apostrophized by a thousand tongues. Beside the commissary was the Garibaldian, regarding group after group with slow, unkindly glance, and on his right the young lady from Mestre, leaning on the railing, both intently gazing at the Genoese girl who sat on the deck below. She was cutting up the meat for her little brother, pouring out drink for her father, and handing this thing or that to a couple of other women and a little boy who belonged to her *rancho*. As graceful as ever, but not as calm. She ate nothing and her hands trembled.

The young lady remarked that her eyes were red; and, supposing that she might have been crying, asked the commissary if he knew why.

He knew perfectly well, and told us all about it. From that vipers' nest of envious hatred which had been hissing round about her for several days, one head had at last arisen, and had stung her to the quick. Going back into the cabin that morning, after taking her little brother on deck, she had found a crowd of women around her berth, to which a slip of paper had been stuck with a lump of moistened bread crumb. It had been torn from a dirty newspaper, and had been scrawled over in black chalk and in large characters with a dozen words or so. She had hardly read them when she put her hands to her face and burst out into violent weeping. The words were crude, cruel adjectives; not to be written; hardly to be imagined. Then the women, who had never once thought of taking down the paper, had tried to comfort her after their fashion; and one of them, on the part of a third, had whispered in her ear the name of the culprit,—a vile, unclean, little wretch, who had stolen in and tacked up that horrible stuff at a moment when there was hardly anyone below. Not so quickly, however, as to escape the sharp eyes of a little fellow who seemed

to be asleep, but was broad awake, and duly told
his mother all about it. "Take the paper to the
captain," the woman had said, "have the commissary send for her—they'll put her in irons—they'll
put her in the pillory on deck. She'll be tried for
it when she gets on shore in America." Then the poor
girl had taken down the paper, sobbing, and waited
until her slanderer should appear. She came down,
sure enough, a short time after; and was no less a
person than that blear-eyed, red-faced creature who
had taken a fancy to the little bookkeeper, and was
as jealous as any animal. At the very first sound of
"There she is!" the Genoese had run towards her,
followed by the gossips, all eager for a scene. The
creature turned pale, but raised her head defiantly,
nevertheless. And the poor girl only held out the
paper to her, saying, in a trembling voice: *E ben, cose
v'ho facto?*—"What have I ever done to you?" The
quickness with which the other seized and tore up
the *corpus delicti* was an involuntary confession
which made denial worse than useless. The Genoese, without another word, had gone on deck, weeping and quite overcome, but without complaining to
anyone. The commissary, informed of the matter,
had sent for the culprit, who swore through thick
and thin (*colle mani e coi piedi*) that she was innocent; so all he could do was to threaten to put her
in irons and say, that the next time he would send
her down into the hold to be gnawed by the rats.

The young lady from Mestre, who had listened to all this without taking her eyes off the girl, repeated slowly to herself and in her Venetian accent, " *E ben, cosa v'ho facto?* " And her eyes glistened with tears.

The commissary had gathered some information about the girl and her family. She was from Levanto. Her father, who kept some kind of a shop, had not done well, and had determined to go to America, on the invitation of a relative there who was getting on; but, as he had not a soldo, he was obliged to defer his departure for a year, while the daughter put by the money for the journey, centime by centime; selling all her trinkets; helping to nurse a sick German lady by night, and ironing at the baths by day. A large black mark which she had on one hand, and which was visible from where we were, was no doubt the result of a burn.

At that moment, by chance, or otherwise, she raised her head; and, seeing at once that we were talking of her, blushed deeply; but, reassured by a kind look from the young lady, fixed her large blue eyes upon her and smiled. Then bending her head over her brother there was nothing of her to be seen but her golden tresses and her fair, blushing neck.

The young lady touched the arm of the Garibaldian with her fan; and, pointing to the girl, said, in her sweet, sad voice, " That is virtue ! "

This threw light for me upon the kind of talk these two held together and the usual outcome of it.

I was curious to see what effect she might have produced thus far upon her interlocutor, and looked
round to see his face; but he had already turned
away and fixed his gaze upon the sea; while the
whole third class, rising on tiptoe as at the word of
command, were doing the same, amid loud murmurs.

There was a sail on the horizon to the right. The
officer on watch had signalled her some time ago.
There was nothing to be seen but a little white spot,
trapezium-shaped, and faintly colored by a ray of
the sun in the midst of gray immensity. A far-off
squall of rain, making a black background, gave it
a wondrous whiteness, but made it look all the more
piteous as if the fury of the ocean were threatening
that ship alone. And it is impossible to describe
the life, the sudden gayety which that little image of
humanity aroused in the midst of our boundless solitude;—as if all at once we had got back into in-
habited regions. The officer sent for the flags of the
nautical alphabet and focused his glass. When we
were near, the sailing ship dipped her flag and the
Galileo returned the salute.

Then ensued between the ship and ourselves a
hasty dialogue which the officer translated into
words for us; and which the emigrants followed
with their eyes as if they understood.

It was an Italian ship, becalmed near the equator.

The first thing she told us was the name of the
owner—Antonio Paganetti.

Then: From Valparaiso, bound for Genoa.

How many days out?

Sixty.

How many days becalmed?

Eighteen.

Quello pittin! (Quel poco!) "All that time!" exclaimed the officer.

Then the other: Pray report us to our agent at Montevideo. No damage—all well.

Need anything?

No, thank you.

Buon viaggio!

Buon viaggio!

How large, how swift, how cheerful our *Galileo* appeared compared with that little moveless ship, which had, perhaps, a crew of ten or twelve men, and was condemned to float there, like a dead thing, who knows for how long, beneath the terrible sun of the Equator! With a kind of pity, we saw her grow smaller and smaller, become once more a white spot and then disappear below the horizon; but our pity was a little selfish; the kind of pity which first-class travellers in a thundering express train feel for a one-horse carriage floundering wearily along through the rain and mud. And from this little meeting alone there arose a current of good-humor from stem to stern, which lasted until evening.

But this day was the day of events. At dinner, before sitting down, the captain said, aloud, "*Scignori,* we have another passenger on board." There were some that did not understand. "A fine boy," he went on, "only one hundred and ten minutes old."

We all laughed and commented and wished the little fellow luck. From a slight blush that passed over the face of the young lady from Mestre, we perceived that the mother must be that peasant woman from her district.

"He was born in the northern hemisphere," the captain concluded. "He will be baptized in the southern. We cross the Line to-morrow.

CHAPTER XI

THE day after, from early morning on, nothing was talked of in the forward part of the ship, but the new baby and the crossing of the Equator; the Aquatore, the Iquatore, the Quatore, the Quatuore, as they called it; for they mangled the word in a hundred ways.

It was the women, principally, who talked about the birth; all most eager to know how the baby would be baptized; who would be the godfather and the godmother—gentle-folk, as usual,—they surmised. Would the tall Neapolitan christen it, or one of the two clericals in the second cabin, or the friar. And where; as there was neither chapel nor altar.— And the presents.—All these matters in the narrow life on board ship became as important as affairs of state, and I was told by the commissary that the peasant woman from Mestre was *the mark of im-*

mense envy on the part of those likely soon to follow
her example; for it is part of the code of sea-courtesy
to pay special regard to lying-in women. The other
ladies, therefore, seeing cups of broth and legs of
fowls, and glasses of Marsala going about, could not
but remember with some bitterness that no such
good fortune would be theirs on land. " What it is
to be lucky!" they exclaimed. Some were really
quite put out about it.

As to the Equator, everybody talked of that. But
in order properly to understand what impression the
sea really made upon all these people, we must go
back a little. In the first place it disgusted them.
Ignorance has no admiration for the sea. It has no
thought to inscribe upon that huge blank page, and
mere immensity is without beauty save for those
who think. I do not remember hearing so much as
a single admiring exclamation about the ocean from
a single emigrant. When they look on all that water they are invariably impressed by the first idea
which it raises in every human being; they regard
it as the element that drowns. I was able to assure
myself, almost from the moment of leaving the
Straits, that for the greater part of these people that
mighty ocean was a fraud. They saw, namely, no
wider a stretch of water than on the Mediterranean,
whereas they had all supposed that, on coming outside, their horizon would be indefinitely extended; as
happens when we go up from a hill to a mountain

top. Nor for this reason alone. In the mind of the lower orders there is always connected with the sea a lingering trace of those old notions coming down from antiquity and from the Middle Ages; and though they may not have thought to see winged monsters, *kraken* a mile in circuit, and singing fish, many did suppose they were to behold sea-serpents, huge polypi, fights between whales and sword-fish, and waves like mountains; but finding calm water, and seeing never so much as the back fin of a shark in a fortnight's sailing, they shrugged their shoulders and said, "I don't see anything about this sea more than any other sea." As to feeling curiosity regarding other matters connected with it or finding pleasure in them, they cannot. They either know nothing at all about them, or misunderstand what they hear, or simply do not believe.

I noticed that the talk we held on the after-deck about the ocean, about navigation, about different countries, all naturally suggested by our geographical position, and changing, so to speak, with the latitude, was passed from class to class and from mouth to mouth; and found an echo, a day or two later, in the gossip of the forecastle just as happens in a city or village. The officers brought it back to us piecemeal as they chanced to hear it in passing. And it is amazing what strange transformations our accounts and scientific observations underwent in this little tour. They spoke

in the third class of Atlantis, of which we were
talking while in the latitude of the Sargasso Sea, as
of a world that had disappeared not many years ago
and which some of us declared we had seen. On the
parallel of Senegambia the talk was of negroes; and
the emigrants declared that the *Galileo* steamed at
full speed to get by the coast where a tribe of terrible savages were in the habit of giving chase to ships
in order to devour the passengers;—and sometimes
succeeded. As to the Equator, there were those who
predicted there a heat as of an oven by day; a heat
that was to melt all the candles and soften the wax
on the letters; a sun so hot as to boil the brains in
the skull and bring on sunstrokes by the dozen. But
strangest of all it was to find that this passing from
one hemisphere to another, which might have convinced them of the rotundity of the earth, furnished
many, on the contrary, with an argument against it,
confirming them in their old unbelief; for did they
not see with their own eyes that all was a flat plain !
And even those who were convinced that the world
was round were disgusted to find that on passing the
Line the ship did not, as they expected, begin to descend and move round the globe like an ant around
an apple. In the course of the morning while the
husband of the Swiss lady (gifted with what some
great man calls the most incurable of all possible
stupidity, that which is contracted from books) was
explaining the Equator to a group of emigrants in

"Explaining the Equator to a group of emigrants in idiotically scientific phraseology."

idiotically scientific phraseology which they could not understand :—the electric heat generator of the globe, the evaporation register of the two hemispheres, the heart of the mighty main where blood is changed;—his hearers looked up and round and about with curiosity and interest; but not seeing anything unusual, glowered at him as who should say, "That's enough, we are not fools!" But what interested them most of all was that they had heard a day or two before how, on crossing the Equator, new stars would be seen, and that one of these, Alpha of the Centaur, was of all the stars the nearest to the earth. They thought perhaps it would be as big as the moon. From early morning of the much-expected day, and in full sunlight, men and women kept an eye on the heavens so as not to miss the miracles. One woman asked the commissary whether in the new world they were about to enter, the sun and the moon would be the same as they had been accustomed to. What was that line, that straight mark (*riga*), that divided the earth into two parts? Was it true that no one would have the correct time there? And was it true that in the year when one went to America a season was lost, and what became of that season?

The commissary tried to set the matter forth, but some paid no attention whatever to the explanation they had asked for; as if that were time lost; or else brought the whole force of their

minds to bear upon what he said in the hope of com-
prehending it, but at last gave it up with a gesture
of despair. The conclusion reached by most of them
was a strong suspicion that all these wonders were
nothing but a parcel of stuff got off by the signori to make a show of learning; or at all events
that these explanations were made out of whole
cloth by persons who knew no more about it than
anyone else. A large majority would rather have
believed in the three legendary monks of Asia who
have for fifteen hundred years been walking straight
forward to find the place where the sun rises. It was
not, indeed, inspiriting to reflect that a thousand perhaps out of those sixteen hundred citizens of one of
the most civilized countries of Europe had no broader
or more correct views about the earth and the heavens
than an equal number of their own class would have
had five hundred years ago; and that, after all, it may
be that in this world there is a certain irreducible
quantity of ignorance which, though kept in bounds
and shaped in a hundred ways, like a mass of water,
cannot be lessened in amount.

Be that as it may, the crossing of the Equator was
a holiday for everybody; that the more because of a
special dole of three litres of wine per *rancio* which
had been announced, and because the captain had
given orders to open the hatches and let everyone
get at his baggage. It was a great treat for them to
have out some fresh things in place of their old rags,

so miserably used up by the rains of the tropics. And, more even than this, the announcement of fireworks put the boys and girls in a fever of expectation. The important operation of matutinal ablution was performed with unusual vigor; and at breakfast time the young women were seen with new kerchiefs on their heads and fresh ribbons on their bosoms; the mammas with hair brushed much more sedulously than usual; the men with amazing cravats, shaven faces, clean shirts, and a good deal of the dirt scrubbed off their necks. It was like a crowd on a holiday. The women out of respect to the new saint did not work, and most of the men, gathered in large talkative groups, gave premonitory tokens of the grand times they meant to have that evening with their wine. Many, meanwhile, were thronging round the caboose to make timely interest for some bits from the first-class cabin, and even in the third-class kitchen there was a movement, an unusual agitation, calculated to induce a suspicion that contraband traffic in eatables was going on. Two heavy showers that fell at an hour's interval only served to heighten the good humor of the multitude, for the sky cleared, and the sea, rolling in long, smooth billows, now blue, now violet, seemed to promise not to disturb the festivities.

And there was feasting for us also—commencing, for me, right after breakfast in the first officer's state-room, where I passed a delightful hour in company with two other officers and the Marsigliese, drinking good

champagne—thanks to a discussion about James
Watt. For, speaking of the ill hap of inventors,
the Marsigliese rashly remarked that Watt had died
in poverty. The first officer denied this, saying that
he had died wealthy and surrounded by illustrious
friends. "*Dans la misère, monsieur! Dans l' indi-
gence la plus affreuse!*" "Rich! I assure you, rich!"
"*Sans le sou! Sans le sou!*" So there was a bet;
settled beyond appeal by reference to *L' Histoire de
la Machine à Vapeur*, a copy of which was on board;
—written as chance would have it by a Marseillais.
And the author most unceremoniously refuted his
fellow-citizen. Good-natured originals, these three
officers, not excepting the clever dark-complexioned
hero of the telegraphic despatch. All younger in
mind than might have been expected from their age,
and of a certain hermit-like simplicity rarely seen
even among hermits. Each had some study or some
art with which to beguile the time on those long
voyages. The first officer was studying German, the
second was a marine painter, the third had lately
begun to learn the flute; and each had an endless
fund of stories about his voyages, which he told
slowly in a peculiar way; recounting the most as-
tounding things in the most natural way in the world
as people do whose lot it is to pass their lives among
the wildest and most adventurous of the human race,
when exceptional circumstances afford these the fullest scope for thought and action. They had made

voyages full of incident when the record of births and deaths was constantly being added to; they had been wearied of their lives because of quarantine;

" The second officer was a marine painter."

they had stood watch in nights of storm fit to turn the hair gray; they had seen suffering, intrigue, ter-

ror; there had been on board families of gypsies;
faces unlike any other faces. And very curious was
the confusion or rather lack of connection in their
ideas regarding the politics of the two countries between which they were always passing. When they
reached Genoa they were a couple of months behind
hand in Italian matters; and before they could catch
up with these they set out again for the Argentine—
reaching it once more after a fifty-days fast from all
its affairs. But strangest of all was their attitude
toward their own families. The first officer amused
us mightily, setting forth, glass in hand, how he had
been married a year and a half, and was like one
married a month or so before. He had left Genoa a
week after the wedding. Since that time had seen
his wife at intervals of two months, and that for such
short periods that the two had had no time to
become intimate; so that when he went home he
was received with emotion and treated with a sort
of modest respect and delicacy, almost as if he were
a stranger. The honeymoon never came to an end.
He even showed us the likeness of his wife as if exhibiting, in confidence, the photograph of a young
lady to whom he was paying court. " *Type Genois!* "
said the Marsigliese as he looked at it. " But she is
from Palermo!" " *Pas possible!* " What a roar!
Such a roar that this time he had to pretend he was
jesting.

All were in good spirits, though the captain had

given out that there was to be no ducking of the
passengers who were crossing the line for the first
time.   A nuisance, he said it was, and always made
trouble.   Moreover, there were no persons who were
proper subjects for that sort of thing.   Even the Genoese stroked his clothes-brush beard with an air less
bored than usual.   He would stop, from time to time,
one passenger after another, fix his single eye upon
him and solemnly enunciate, "Chicken breasts in
Madeira!"   He had extorted a whole batch of se-
crets from the cook, and declared that there was to
be a splendid dinner—and speeches.   The agent,
with whom I took a turn or two, said the Marsigliese
was to propose a toast—he had heard him rehears-
ing it in his state-room.   And he told me, moreover,
that the evening before there had been a scene.   That
viprous-tongued mother of the piano player, namely,
having hinted to the so-called "thief" that he would
do well to contradict the slanders that were going
about regarding him, this gentleman had been to
the captain, loudly demanding to know what these
slanders were, and threatening sword and pistol.
But it seems that, on earnest entreaty, he had promised to be quiet until we got into the next hemisphere.   We went on deck and found that detestable
spitfire apparently much pleased at having at last
succeeded in raising a disturbance.   And we both
remarked an unusual animation in the dull face of
her daughter, like the reflection of some secret com-

placency; but it was in vain that the agent, suspecting some more scissors' work, looked round for
the cause with his long, searching glance.   As we
passed the pantry, there were the bride and bridegroom drinking rosolio and water.   The agent bowed,
and the young gentleman modestly remarked : " We
are having a little celebration over the Equator."
" H'm," said the agent rather sharply, " I think you
have a little celebration over all the parallels,"
whereon the pair hastily concealed their faces in
their glasses.   Then we went to have a drop of
Chartreuse at the door of the " tamer's " room.   This
lady received her friends with swimming eyes, she
felt so kindly; and declared she wished the trip
would last a year; such capital company, so well
bred, so polite, so pleasant—a whole string, in fact,
of honeyed phrases which had, I am afraid, their rise
in the many many-colored glasses she had sipped
during the day.   Thence to the deck, where we found
something new; the Argentine lady, queen of the
ship, with her court of admirers about her, in a
vanilla-colored dress which set off her warm, florid,
creole complexion to a marvel, and all radiant as if
she were glad to get back to her own half of the
world; and the Swiss lady promenading with her
old friend, the deputy, though nobody had seen
when or how she had managed to make it up with
him.   A half-hour of her bald, unjointed chat, all
little rose-colored bits of nonsense and silly laughing,

like a slightly tipsy serving girl, convinced me that
she was not ill pleased, after all, to put her little,
white foot back into the Parliament of Buenos
Ayres. And her husband, too, seemed well pleased
at the result of his professional excursions among the
emigrants; for he was seen with his spectacles fixed
upon an outspread chart getting new geographical
notions from the first officer. In all eyes there
appeared to beam a kind of confused glimmer of
hope such as is seen in people's faces on New Year's
Eve; as if they believed that better fortune was
awaiting them in the other hemisphere than had
attended them in this.

Our cheerfulness was still greater at dinner, where
all chatted eagerly like a great tableful of good
friends—save only and excepting the Garibaldian,
and the lady of the brush, who, apparently for no
other purpose than to vex her husband, held her
tongue and ate nothing. And we had, moreover,
the agreeable surprise of hearing the Brazilian pair,
who, drawn into talk by the Argentines, and gradually aroused by love of country, described, with a
noble eloquence that amazed us all, the beauty of
their native land, from the great bay of Rio Janeiro,
crowned with sugar-loaf mountains and set thick
with islands of palm trees and gigantic ferns, to the
vast forests, like cathedral colonnades, close-crowded,
endless, dark, alive with apes and panthers, with
llights of parrots green and red, with overhanging

clouds of floating gems and winged flowers and fire-
flies without number. The conversation branched
out upon this theme, and all who had been in Brazil
began to recount what they had seen, all speaking
at once, and the Brazilian fauna and flora were exhausted, and tapirs and crocodiles and mighty rivers
passed in review; huge toads that bark, monstrous
bats that suck the blood of horses, and horrible
serpents that suck the breasts of women, and frogs
that sing in the tree-tops, and tortoises two yards
long, and enormous ants of St. Paul, which the na-
tives fry and eat. And as they added harmonious
mimicry to their descriptions, there was such a mingled clamor of roaring and bellowing, and cackling
and hissing, that one seemed in the midst of a tropical forest, and felt at times a sense of horror. The
only ones that took no heed were the bride and
groom, who, profiting by the confusion, gently passed
their arms around each other's waists, under the
burning gaze of the piano player, and the blonde
Swiss lady, who dealt out sparkling glances to the
Argentine, the Tuscan, the tenor, the Peruvian, with
a freedom that was, perhaps, a little too evident, so
that the captain could not refrain from his warning
phrase : *Quella scignôa a me comença a angosciâ* (" I
shall not be able to endure that lady much longer.")
But he was soothed by the toast of the Marsigliese,
who rose up, swelled out his Patagonian chest, and,
raising his goblet of champagne, said in solemn tone :

"*Je bois à la santé de notre brave Commandant* . . . *à la Societé de Navigation* . . . *à l' Italie, Messieurs.*" All applauded save only the mill-owner, and I pardoned him in that hour the hash he made of my native language, and which he thought he made of my fellow-citizens.

We rose from the table and went on the hurricane deck, preceded by the third officer carrying an armful of rockets, Catharine wheels, and Roman candles. There was hardly room for us all, and I was shoved over to the port-side in front of the commissary, and right between the "scapegallows" and the "Director of the Society-for-no-more-bad-smelling-cesspools." The bow was already crowded, but as the sky was covered with a dense cloud and the three lanterns, red, white, and green, which burned like three great eyes, at either side of the ship and at the mast-head, gave but a faint light, all that mass of people were in the dark, and from that darkness there floated up a hundred confused sounds of drinking songs, of women laughing, and of children crying, making the multitude seem ten times as large. It was like being on the roof of the Town Hall when a carnival demonstration is going on against the Syndic. As the first Bengal light went off there was a burst of *vivas*, and sixteen hundred faces were lighted up; a vast mass of people standing on the hatches, on the bulwarks, on the top of the deck-house, on the live-stock pens, astride of the backstays, on the shrouds, standing up on chairs, on the bitts, on casks, on the deck-troughs, everywhere; not an inch of the deck could be seen, and as the outlines of the ship were concealed by human forms, all this throng of persons seemed suspended over the sea like a crowd of spectres. In midst of an admiring silence we heard a mocking voice or two: *O-o-o-o-h! Baciccia! Dagh on taj—Cadìa monsù Tasca!* Then a great silence, and the rush of the rocket was heard, and the throb of the engine. Showers of fire fell upon the glassy sea, unruffled by a breath of wind; the rockets burst and vanished in the vast, dark heavens, noiseless as if in vacuum. At every shower of fiery light I saw in the crowd some well-known countenance. Now it was the bold face of the Bolognese standing high above her neighbors; now the intense look of the poor bookkeeper; now the negress, the nurse of the Brazilian family, surrounded by eager faces; farther down the round visage of the peasant woman from Capracotta; near the slaughter-house the impassible face of the friar; and far forward the mysterious mask of the mountebank. Here and there were seen couples which the sudden illumination forced quickly to move into more conventional positions, while suppressed giggles and reproving words and little shrieks broke out every now and then, to show that a good deal was going on in the way of bold pinching and persistent pulling about. "This evening," said the commissary, "that poor old hunchback will have his

14

hands full." Meanwhile the Bengal lights tinged all these faces with purple, with white, and with green ; and at every bursting rocket there arose a cry of *Viva l'America! Viva il Galileo!* and now and then, but rarely, *Viva l'Italia!* Above the crowd hats, handkerchiefs, and glasses were seen to wave ; babies, held up by their mothers, flung their little arms about—all a true type of the people which could for a moment forget so much trouble in thoughtless hilarity. At last the fireworks came to an end, and the ship, dark once more but full of feasting as ever, plunged amid songs and shouting into the blackness of the other hemisphere.

But the causeless joy of that throng of people at the confines of a new world, on the lone ocean, and at night, was to me more pitiful than their sadness. It was like a sinister gleam that brought out their misery all the more. Unhappy exiled children of my country,—blood drawn from the arteries of my native land,—my ill-clad brothers,—my starving sisters,—sons and fathers who have fought and will fight again for the soil on which they could not, or cannot, longer live ! I never loved you as I did that evening, never as then, thought of your suffering and of the blind mistrust with which we sometimes regard you. We are not free from stain. We are to blame for the faults and shortcomings with which the world upbraids you. Our hands are not clean in this matter, for we have not loved you or labored

for you as we ought. Never did I feel such bitterness of regret as in that hour for having nothing
but words to give you. The last dream of Faust
was in my mind. To open a new land to thousands
upon thousands, to see smiling harvests and happy
villages upon the onward path of an industrious,
free, contented people. For this only is life worth
having! You are our country, our world; and so
long as your mother earth sees you weep and suffer,
so long will all our happiness be selfishness, and all
our boasting, lies.

CHAPTER XII

LITTLE GALILEO

FTER that day of frolic, as is usual in such cases, a more leaden dulness than ever settled down upon the ship. The heat was dreadful and was enhanced by the sight of a repulsive-looking sea which gave an idea of what the ocean might become if no bounds were set to the multiplication of its inhabitants—a hideous and pestilential charnel of dead herrings and putrified codfish. Oppressed by the monotony, and still quivering after the disorder of the day before, the greater part of the steerage people would not even move when the sailors, washing down the deck, as usual, with the hose, sent streams and spouts of water in every direction; but just closed their eyes and let themselves be sluiced like worn-out dogs. For many hours the whole ship seemed plunged in profoundest lethargy, and even after an interval of time the remembrance of that day is as dismal as that of a dead face. I think I see now in the sultry afternoon the counte- nance of the Genoese as he comes to my stateroom and asks : "Shall we go and see them kill ?" "Kill ! Kill what ?" I said. A steer of course. He always knew about it the day before, and went to look on and massacre the time. O ! the endless hours passed at the air-port, staring out at that sluggish, melan- choly sea. They say that time is money, and yet I would have given a whole century full of such hours for five centimes. Sea ! sea ! and still more sea ! That little Mediterranean yonder ! Why, I thought of it as a blue lake suffocated between mountains, and far away beyond the bounds of thought. Water, boundless water ! There half flashed across my mind a horrible suspicion that we had lost our way and were heading for the Antarctic Pole, to crash into the eternal ice. Ah ! happy chance ! Ruy Blas came to rouse me. He gazed at me with a lack-lustre eye meant to suggest a night passed in aristocratic excess, and imparted some good news. The christening was fixed for four o'clock that afternoon.

Everything was arranged. The baptism and the registration were to be held in the chart-room, near the wheel under the bridge. The Neapolitan priest was to administer the so-called private baptism, for which he must have been in great practice, since he had travelled during his early years over the lonely plains of farthest Argentina, where there were no churches, and where the inhabitants, preserving rude tradition only of the Catholic religion, and hearing of a priest, would come hastening to him for the rite; young fellows even sometimes demanding it as they sat on horseback. He had politely offered his services without question of *patacones* and a steward had seen him that morning get out a cope and stole which bore unmistakable signs of long and adventurous service. The child was, as usual, to have the name of the ship; and the *Galileo* had already a dozen homonymous children scattered about the world. The young lady from Mestre was to be godmother. The captain had offered to be godfather; but had been induced to resign his place to the Argentine Delegate, that gentleman having cogently urged that the child ought to have, for sponsor and welcomer to the citizenship he was adopting, a representative of the Republic.

This graceful act as I afterwards learned, made his peace with the other passengers; for they had before accused him and the rest of being rather distant with the Europeans, and of holding themselves aloof. I had, however, known them for several days, and had observed them with the liveliest curiosity; for they were the first I had seen of a people which is, or ought to be, more important for an Italian to know than any other. The delegate was the oldest of the party and seemed to take the lead, as having the most level (*quadra*—square) head among them all.

Tall, with the fine, firm face of a man inured to the ways of the world and the strife of politics, he sent through his eye-glasses the bold conquering glance of one that swayed the votes of men, and the hearts of women. The husband of the blonde lady, was a light-haired little counsellor, secretary to some minister plenipotentiary of his own country, with a pair of lively gray eyes, as sharp as bodkins, which seemed, when they looked at one, to pierce through brain and bosom, down to the very memorandum book. There were two dark youths, very elegant, and rather insignificant, who seemed to think of nothing but the dainty white linen of which they made such show, and of their thick hair, so artistically built up: hair of that deep, sheeny, Argentine —Andalusian black which is neither more nor less than a flout to grizzled heads. The most original of all was the fifth, a large fine man of thirty, with a bold face, and a rough voice; type of the horse tamer, proprietor of a vast *estancia*, in the province of Buenos Ayres, where he passed two years out of three, among thirty thousand cows and twenty thousand sheep—leading the life of the *gaucho;* going to Paris for a change; and expending there each time a thousand head of cattle or so.

A trait common to all was the fineness of the mouth and the smallness of the head; which they always carried high; but the hereditary habit which others have observed in the Argentines of coming down upon the toes rather than upon the heel, I did not, to say the truth, remark. Notably elegant and dainty in their personal habits, every one of them. Courteous, but of a courtesy, so to speak, more flowing than that of the Spaniard, less ceremonious than that of the Frenchman; joined to a lively ease of manner and conversation altogether usual with men who go out into life as soon as they cease to be children, and who, in the midst of an immature, unsettled, disorderly society grow up untroubled, unrestrained; full of confidence in themselves and their own good fortune. Their turn of mind was expressed by a kind of look, which is best likened to the bold glance of a man on horseback with a free horizon before him. Withal an amazing readiness in pronouncing opinions upon the nations, the institutions, and the manners of Europe,—seen in passing;—opinions which displayed a perception rather acute than profound, and a great variety, not so much of study as of reading, —quoted readily and aptly. And they showed, not so much perhaps in their opinions as in their preference for certain subjects of conversation, a strong sympathy with nature and with French life, arising from an indisputable analogy in the features of their mind and intelligence. They all had Paris at their fingers' ends, and their trunks were full of boulevard newspapers and photograph likenesses of *artistes* from the Opera and the Comédie. In other countries they knew well enough the gambling houses and the baths, and above all the music halls ; about which they talked with all the fire of youth ; but it was plain that they had nothing to ask of us in this respect, for they had Europe over to dance and sing for them in their own place. As to Italy it was impossible to find out, under the necessary courtesy of their phrases, what their real sentiments were. They were well pleased with the immigration from our country, regarding it as an influx of excellent laborers and would say, pointing to the emigrants : " All that is so much gold for us ; send us all Italy, so only you leave the monarchy at home."

It was clear, also, that they, like the revolutionists of the last century, regarded a human being subject to monarchy as a poor creature worthy of all commiseration, and that they looked upon us Europeans as a sort of beings born old, dragging ourselves about among the miserable relics of a dead past, and half-starved,—as matter of course. Beneath all this there flashed out a lively national pride, the pride of a small people that had conquered great Spain, humiliated England, and enlarged the borders of the civilized world ; sweeping out barbarism from an enormous region, so that men of every language and of every race might find shelter there. In fact, they celebrated at least twice a week, with floods of champagne, some glorious event of the Argentine revolution ;—admirable proof, of course, of the good results flowing from those victories. But between

their national pride and that of Europeans there
was this remarkable difference; that, while we base
ours upon the past, and always pique ourselves upon
that, and boast of that, they seldom, if ever, spoke
of it, but looked to the future with the child's constant phrase, "When we are grown up!" And in
them all there was evident, not the hope, but the
certitude, bright, deep, unshakable, of becoming in
time an enormous people, the United States of Latin
America, swarming from the valley of the Amazon
to the farthest confines of Patagonia. And their
consciousness of being called to this pre-eminence
was evident, moreover, from their anxiety on every
occasion to show themselves original, not only with
respect to the old Spanish ancestors, of whom they
spoke in a slightly mocking tone, as of a race of
which, in happy hour, they had outgrown every
trace, but also with respect to the other Latin peoples
of America, the Chilians, the Peruvians, the Bolivi-
ans, the Brazilians; pointing out the moral and
intellectual shortcomings and the absurd character-
istics of all these with a facetious irony which
betrayed a supercilious rivalry tempered by no
brotherly feeling whatever. All these remarks they
made in eager, fluent language, broken by hearty
laughs and outbursts of almost involuntary sincerity,
revealing natures capable of violent but generous
passions, and a great fickleness of emotion born of
an ardent desire and determination to enjoy life in

every possible way. One thing I could have wished
to see, and that was, something more like human
pity in the eyes and voices of one or two of them
when telling of certain inhuman episodes in their
history; something a little sadder and softer, to dis-
pel the suspicion that the long tradition of wars in
the desert and wars among themselves, horrible all,
had left a trace of evil in their natures. But, on the
whole, the first impression was most agreeable, such
as to make one doubly eager to scan their characters
more closely.

For the first time I found myself with people
wholly new to me,—a thing which had never happened in Europe. In the midst of a vast mass of
ideas and attainments common to us all, I vaguely
recognized the traces of a moral and mental education wholly different from ours; the peculiar notions
of a race encamped upon the confines of civilization
at the extremity of a thinly populated continent, in
the solitude which an invading army would find,
and impressed by scenery beautiful in another way
from ours; more vast, more primitive, more awful.
And I was amazed at that Spanish language of
theirs, no longer hide-bound, as it were, but worked
loose, and lighted up, accentuated, in a way altogether new to me; starred with blooms of speech
most strange and wondrous, and rolled out with a
far-off touch of Indian melody which made one think
of copper-colored faces and plumed head-dresses.

But more than by their language I was struck by
their incredible flow of words, and by their mimic
powers of gesture and intonation; especially when
they grew warm in describing their mighty mountains and their boundless plains. The blond counsellor, in particular, described the hunting of wild
horses as an actor would recite a classic extract, with
a vigor of movement and a melody of speech almost
beyond belief, and all without art or affectation. I
noticed in all their voices the charm of a metallic
ring and a natural gift of modulation. The lady,
especially, had a clear voice, with certain delightful
head notes, which sounded, to one who listened
without looking, like the tones of a child.[1] Observing, one evening, the strange effect she produced
upon me by pronouncing in this way the name of
the state of Jujui, she went on saying over other
Indian names of mountains and rivers to amuse me,
fairly laughing at my wonder:—"Ringuiririca,"
" Paranapicabà," " Ibirapità-Miní." It was like the
warbling of a nightingale.

To them the voyage from America to Europe was
as is to us the trip from Genoa to Leghorn; and
they had made it many times. For whatever conceit they may have of themselves, and whatever they
may think of us, Europe is always the mother country, the great country of their souls, and they are
attracted to it. The delegate, accordingly, could

[1] *Voce bianca.*

count up eight transatlantic voyages, and the net of
his love affairs must have been spread over a forest
of masts. Still young, he had a long life behind
him even in a public capacity; for, being about forty,
he had been at thirty editor-in-chief of an important
journal, a high ministerial official, director of a bank,
and government envoy to Paris on a financial mission. And his was no exceptional case among the
youth of his country. He said, and truly, that his
country was in the hands of young men, since the
Republic desired that the early spring sap which
boiled in its veins should run in those of its servants.
"You others," he said, "crowded into a narrow
space, loaded down with history, with laws and with
traditions, must go slowly, and let the old men take
the lead; while we young fellows of three hundred
years date, with a third part of South America for
our country, and bound to make up for the time
lost in fights with the savages and in wars of social
revolution of which we are only just now clear, we
must take bold impatience for our guide, and drive
on at full speed." So he went on pleasantly about
the "misuse" of old age in Europe. "It would
seem," he said, "that with you gray hairs are a necessary qualification for certain trusts. There are
some diseases which confer the right to certain
honors. Gout, for instance, might almost seem to
be all-powerful. Your youth is worn out in endless
waiting; you reach a place which requires a clear

mind and steady nerve exactly at the time when these qualities fail you. You use up all your powers in climbing, and, by the time you are up, the clock strikes the hour for retiring."

At this juncture the stewardess came to say it was time for the christening. The delegate ran to his stateroom to change his silk travelling cap for a covering something more formal. I moved towards the chart-room. In the forward part of the ship there was already a commotion, especially among the women, who all wanted to come up on the main deck to look on; so much so that guards had to be placed at the ladders to prevent their overcrowding the place. There was a murmur of curiosity as great as at the baptism of a crown prince; and no one remarked the threatening rain squall which had already begun to darken the air. Entering the chart-room with two or three others, I had some difficulty in finding standing room. Before a table stood the captain, who represented the general government, together with his first officer and the commissary as witnesses. Round about against the wall were the blonde lady, the Argentine lady, the brush lady, the pianist and her mother, the Brazilian lady, with her black nurse; and about a dozen men, among them the Garibaldian, with his sad, stern face. The end window, which opened on the deck, was full of heads of steerage women, each above each, and beaming with delight at having secured good places.

"After them came the mother, held round the waist
by the hunchback sailor."

Behind them was heard the murmur of the crowd. On the table were the ship's muster-roll and log-book lying open; a tray with a glass of water and a salt cellar, together with some printed birth-certificate blanks. All wore an air of thoughtful composure. That strange room, hung with charts and gleaming here and there with nautical instruments, those twenty-four capital letters inscribed as an epitaph upon the signal-flag lockers, that group of persons so different and so unusual, those grave, immovable officers, that hum and stir of an invisible multitude, the dark sea line cutting across the open door, evoked a feeling at once of amazement and respect which declared itself in a suppressed whisper.

In a few moments the tall priest arrived in a cope and stole which looked as if they had served to baptize the early Atlantic navigators; and the attention of all was at once fixed upon him. He entered with bowed head, looking at no one; then, approaching the table, and making the sign of the Cross, he began to mutter, with closed eyes and in the midst of a profound silence, the usual exorcisms [*sic*] over the salt and the water. Then putting a spoonful of salt into the water, he stirred it up, and dipping his finger therein, blessed those present. The women made the sign of the Cross, and the whispering began again.

The baby did not immediately come, so the captain sent the commissary to see after it. As the old man ill of pleurisy had grown worse, the new-

delivered mother had been moved from the sick bay
to an empty stateroom in the second cabin. It was
but a step, and the commissary reappeared at once
saying: *Vegnan*—" Here they are."

Up the ladder then came the father in a high
state of triumph, in a clean shirt, freshly shaven, and
with the little creature in his arms ; then came the
young lady from Mestre, in her usual sea-green dress;
the Argentine supporting her by the hand. After
them, to the surprise of myself and of everybody,
came the mother, pale but smiling, held round the
waist by the hunchback sailor. "There was no help
for it," he growled. She would come in spite of the
doctor's warnings, stubbornly determined to do here
as she used to do at home, where *dopo do zorni la se
gaveva sempre messo a far le so façende :* "She always
went back to work after a couple of days." Last
came one of the twins with a bit of candle in his
hand.

A kindly murmur of pity and of sympathy greeted
the small Galileo who, with his little red face in a
little white ruffled cap, a medal round his neck, and
rolled up in a blue wrapper, slumbered placidly.

The young lady, as soon as she entered, took the
child from the father's arms, and with her own
sweet sad smile showed him to the captain ; and I
doubt if a single one there present failed to note the
mournful contrast between the little creature that
was just entering life and that excellent and noble

15

being that was so soon to leave it. All looked for a moment at her alone, as with bent head she gazed into the baby face and gave token in her eyes of how great a treasure of motherly love was to be carried with her into the grave.

The captain, in the curt tones of the Quartiere di Pré, and with the frown of one who is setting forth an indictment, read the birth certificate inscribed on the muster-roll of the ship:

Before me, captain commanding the steamship *Galileo*, duly registered in the port of Genoa, this such and such a day of so-and-so, in the year eighteen hundred and so forth, at the hour of whatever it may have been, personally came and appeared so-and-so, doctor on board said steamer, accompanied by so-and-so, and so-and-so, did show to me a male child to which the woman so-and-so had just given birth. And a smile was on every lip as we heard him read out that the native place of that poor little baby was lat. 4° north; lon. west of Paris 28°, 48' (26°, 28' W. Greenwich).

In witness whereof, the captain went on to read, we have drawn up this present statement in writing, and placed it on record upon the muster-roll of this ship. Signed by —— ——

And then the captain with two of his officers signed the record, and three certificates, one for the Italian Consul at Montevideo, one for the Recruiting Bureau of the port of Genoa, and one for the father.

"Last came one of the twins with a bit of candle in his hand."

He then handed the pen to the father who, with the sweat of that unusual toil upon his brow, managed to scrawl his name three times.

At this moment the ship gave a slight roll, and the godmother staggered. The Argentine caught her arm to support her, and I could read in his eyes the pitying astonishment he felt at touching that fleshless limb. The sky had grown dark, the sea was of a livid color, and raindrops were falling on the deck above.

The priest stepped forward.

The child was named. He crossed himself; and, placing his large, hairy hand under the head of the sleeping infant, while the Argentine placed his hand on its breast, he duly made the three aspersions from the glass of water saying:

" *Galilee, Petre, Johannes, ego te baptizo in nomine Patris et Filii et Spiritus Sancti.*"

Then: " *Galilee Petre, Johannes, vade in pacem, et Dominus sit tecum.*" All the women at the window answered, *Amen.*

Then he said the *Agimus.*

I was looking the while at the mother who rolled her large eyes upon the baby, upon the officers, the instruments, upon that strange chapel; and who listened to the creak of the wheel and the distant whistling of the wind in the rigging, casting from time to time a furtive glance at the dark sea. She seemed to be greatly troubled lest there should be

something profane and ill-omened in a ceremony
performed thus in haste in such a place in such
weather.

The priest ended with : " *Ave Maria, gratia plena
Dominus tecum.*"

"*Sancta Maria, Mater Dei, ora pro nobis,*" responded the women.

At that very moment a most vivid flash lighted
up the place, an ox gave a long bellow, the ship
lurched and the mother began to weep.

" *Amen,*" said the priest.

" *Amen,*" was answered from without.

All turned to the poor woman asking what was
the matter, and bidding her take courage. She
wiped her eyes with the back of her hand and
asked : *Parché no'l ghe ga messo el sal sula boca ?*
"Why did they not put salt on his mouth ?"

They had to reason with her, to explain. It was a
private baptism ; some things could not be done because it was not in church—all could be completed
in America—she must compose herself, the sacra-
ment was valid all the same.

Then she cheered up, kissed the baby fondly,
made her acknowledgments and so went out. It
was raining hard ; but the little train, followed by
the Garibaldian, could hardly make its way to the
second cabin. The hunchback had to make room
with his elbows, and the twin had his candle-end
snatched out of his hand. Everybody wished to

see, not the baby, but the sponsors; and have a notion of what presents the happy mother was likely to get. When they saw the young lady there was clapping of hands. Suddenly, a loud, harsh voice was heard:

"That's right! Truckle to the gentle folk, will you! They stand sponsor at his christening to-day, but they will let him perish of hunger when he grows up! Idiots!"

It was the old tribune in the green jacket, standing upright on the hatch of the women's cabin. At once several persons left the crowd of gazers. Some cried shame; some echoed him. But the joyous shouts of the children drowned their voices.

The mother had hardly reached the stateroom when she sank down upon a box, exhausted. The father placed the infant in a berth, and the godparents brought out the presents. Then began a duet of voices in wonder and gratitude: "But what is this! You give yourselves too much trouble. You make us blush! How good, how kind you are! Is that for me, and this too? The Lord be praised!" And the father, in an access of gratitude, bent over the new-born in the berth, exclaiming: *Vorò strussi-arme, vorò suar sangue per ti, vissare mie.* "I'll work myself to death for thee, I'll sweat blood for my darling," and this in a heartfelt tone which promised a life of labor and sacrifice for the little creature, born between heaven and earth, and halfway between the country he had left and an unknown land; with no dependence in the world but the courage and the muscles of his father. And then:— *Tazi, vecia mata*—"Be quiet, you old fool," he harshly cried to his weeping wife and flung his arms around her neck.

The young lady then turned to the Garibaldian, who was looking out of the door, and, calling his attention to that embrace,—"Family affection!" she said with a reproving gesture of her forefinger and a kindly smile.

He made no answer.

CHAPTER XIII

UT the christening, like the festival of crossing the line, gave only a brief truce to the irritation which was creeping over the emigrants by reason of the increasing heat; particularly over the women, who were growing hour by hour more sick and tired of a mode of life so foreign to their habits. Several days since, the disorder of petty larceny had broken out, and with it a general fever of suspicion. Towels, slippers, clothes, disappeared as if by enchantment; those who were robbed thought they recognized their property in the hands of one or another, and at every moment a couple of scolding slatterns, leading their children by the hand and with the *corpus delicti* under their arms, followed by their husbands and their witnesses, would be coming to the commissary to demand justice. Then there was trial and pleading in due form. Perhaps it was a

handkerchief, from which some thievish woman had
taken the mark, or a shoe with the maker's label
torn off. The accused party denied everything, in-
voking the Saviour and the Madonna; the accuser
obstinately persisted, calling down the rest of the
Calendar; then a couple of experts had to be called
in to examine the handkerchief, or a cobbler to pro-
nounce upon the shoe. But the Piedmontese would
have none of the Neapolitan experts, the Neapolitan
utterly repudiated North Italy; the husbands took
the part of their wives; the witnesses and the bystanders were for their own provinces. There were
interminable disputes between stolid mountaineers,
who urged a hundred times the same argument in
exactly the same phrase, and voluble men of the
plains, who belched forth words in torrents. Often-
times they did not understand one another, and an
interpreter was called in. Sometimes search had to
be made. Then the accused began to weep, the children to whimper, and the men to threaten: "Wait
until we get on shore, you scum of the earth!" "Do
you want me to pitch you into the boiler, you accursed gallows' bird?" "I'll throw your insides to
the fishes!" "You! why, the whole ship knows
you!" "And as for you, the whole Atlantic Ocean
would not wash you clean!"

The poor commissary racked his brains to understand and to do justice; but in whatever way he decided there was always a cry of "partiality." If he

pronounced against a Neapolitan or a Sicilian these
said, " Of course ! the other is your countryman ! "
If he gave it against his own countryman all the
north country people cried out : " Yes, yes, no doubt.
Those creatures have ways—such ways—of making
friends." It was useless to argue with them. " But
listen,—don't you remember how I decided in favor
of one of your friends yesterday because she was in
the right ? " No use. He had done so because she
was pretty, or all alone, or because—in short there
must have been some other reason. And on both
sides a chorus of growls : " I wonder if we are not
Italian as well as they, though we don't speak
Genoese. They are the ones to give orders now."
And it was the more pity to see these people, so far
from their own country, betray in every little dispute family rancor, race antipathy ; to hear with
what devilish ingenuity they wounded each the other
in his pride of citizenship, digging up old-time griev-
ances and reproaches and nursing them back to life
as it were, so as to carry them to America in their
full vigor. After every dispute the parties separated full of spite and enmity which they in-
stilled into their friends and country people of both
sexes when they went forward again. These gradually divided into two factions, which glowered at
each other, and insulted each other—moving out of
the way as if from fear of vermin or making a great
show of buttoning up their pockets so as not to lose

a wallet or a handkerchief.   Alas! alas!   The commissary with all his diligence could not hear every
cause, and with all his patience had sometimes to
plant his teeth in the second joint of his forefinger.
The tall Bolognese, whose haughtiness rose with the
temperature, would have had the whole ship searched
because somebody had carried off her tortoise-shell
comb ; and threatened the Società di Navigazione
with vengeance at the hands of her brother the
journalist, as soon as she landed in America.   The
poor lady of the black silk dress, was in despair because someone had stolen from her a silver pin, the
gift of her sister she said ; but she did not dare have
recourse to the commissary for fear of some *vendetta*.
And there were women who, not so much from fear
as from a desire to exhibit a spiteful mistrust of their
neighbors, slept with all their property under them
or in their arms—at the risk of being misunderstood,
all the same.   In short it was maddening.

    And yet the disputes about thievery, real or
invented, were not the most difficult to deal with.
The worst was that all this irritation had induced a
most extraordinary touchiness which broke out on
the smallest occasion, so that they were constantly
coming to the commissary to complain of some lack
of due respect ; and that gentleman had to sit in
judgment upon questions of manners and breeding.
The poor hump-backed sailor said he could stand it
no longer : *Dixan che gh'è de ladre !* (dicono che ci son

delle ladre)—he never spoke of any but women. "Thieves among them! of course there are; what do they expect? But if we refused to carry thieves we should not make enough to pay for coal—Sink the whole set of them!" As things stood, a serious scuffle might break out at any moment. The evening before, as soon as the christening was over, two women had had a fight in a corner of the cabin,— quite quietly, like ladies. And this evening the poor bookkeeper came to worse grief still. Having ventured to remonstrate with a couple of emigrants who were making gestures behind the Genoese girl and raising much vulgar laughter, these fellows fell upon him and would have handled him very roughly had not the Garibaldian, passing that way, rescued the poor creature, but not before his neck-cloth was torn to pieces. "All due to the electric centres of the globe" said the commissary. "And," he went on to remark, "worse remains behind."

The Garibaldian, when he had released the book-keeper, returned to the midship deck—from which he had seen the disturbance—and passed near me. I was inclined to ask for particulars, but his stern, cold look repelled, as usual, every advance. During the first few days he had exchanged a word or two with me; now he hardly made a sign by way of salute, sometimes he made no sign. It seemed that the ever-increasing tedium of forced companion-ship in that life on board ship embittered still more the aversion for his kind which he cherished in his heart. The more his familiarity, always taciturn and respectful, with the young lady from Mestre increased, the more solitary and self-contained he became for the rest of us, as if that gentle intercourse had made his philosophy more gloomy rather than more cheerful. He now spoke to no one. He would pass hours leaning over the taffrail looking at the wake of the *Galileo* as if it were an endless written scroll unrolled before his eyes to tell the history of the world. And his haughty bluntness had produced its usual effect upon the others; at first antipathy and a show of equal scorn; then, when the steadiness of his demeanor showed that all this was the effect of habit and in no way personal, there ensued a feeling of respect and awe which showed itself in the readiness with which the look of any fellow-passenger turned to the sea or the rigging when he cast his eyes upon them to see if they were contemplating him,—and if so, how.

It seemed as if a kind of sympathy had arisen for the haughty creature that not only did nothing to attract such a feeling but spared no pains to repel it. It was because sadness, joined with beauty and strength, has its own charm as indicating a noble scorn for the easy gratification which the one and the other can procure; and because, moreover, there shone out of his eye that dark light which comes directly from the soul and gives token of the virtue which is so much admired and feared—courage. As for myself, the more I kept out of his way the more I desired to know him. I felt for him that affection, born of esteem and awe, which renders the carelessness of its object quite intolerable, and which would almost make a man debase himself so only he could overcome it. This the more on board ship where one must constantly be thrown in with the person, and where his indifference may be remarked and commented upon to our disadvantage. When he was not by I tried to persuade myself that his soul and his life did not correspond with his aspect, or my idea of it ; and that, if I had known his inner soul, I should only have had one more delusion to add to the thousands out of which the history of our friendships is made up. But when I saw him again it was all in vain; I could have sworn that the man could never have done a base thing, that he did indeed scorn all human vanities, and that even now he would be ready to give his life, at once and without a thought of ambition, for a generous idea. I submitted to his superior spirit as to a magnetic force ; and, while I felt a certain annoyance and even humiliation, I should have liked to let him see it or even to have confessed it frankly. But his face was a walled-up gate for every one.

He seemed indifferent to the great shows of nature. I did not perceive even a gleam upon his countenance at sight of one of the most splendid

and amazing sunsets that we had seen since entering
the tropics. The sky was clear from east to west,
and the sun just ready to dip his rim in a sea as of
red-hot coals; and, huge, as if he had come a million
leagues nearer to the earth, was streaked from side to
side with a single thin black cloud, which made him
look divided as by miracle into two burning hemispheres. And there rose at the same time to an
amazing height in the air eight wondrous rays, of
veiled light but liveliest color, passing from white
to rosy red and so to softest green, which lasted
after his disk had disappeared ; and, covering a third
part of the vault of heaven, seemed like an immense
glowing hand that was to grasp the earth. But we
wondered more when, turning round at a sign from
the captain, we saw eight other rays over against
and reflected from these upon the heavens; less
bright, but with the same vanishing tints, as if it
were the dawn preceding a second undreamed-of
sun that was to rise as the other disappeared. And
the white sea took all the colors of the sky and
glistened as if with millions of floating pearls.

But that animal of an advocate—he only—never
looked. He turned his back to the sunset, he never
raised his eyes to the reflection. He hated nature,
and wished to show it; for that sun that went down
into the sea was going into bad company, and he
was not going to be answerable for either. In the
midst of our admiring silence he was peevishly be-

moaning himself to the first officer about the crim-i-nal
carelessness of the company, which did not keep up
with the life-saving inventions of the day. "Eighty
per cent. of those who suffer wreck are drowned,"
he said, "through fault of the owners. Why did

"The turned his back to the sunset."

not the company provide the proper number of life-
preservers? Why were there but ten boats, hardly
enough to save one passenger in four? Why were
not the men exercised in improvising life rafts?
Why were there no 'Gwyn' pumps? Why not
adopt Captain Hurst's double deck? Where were
the Peake life-boats and the Thompson safety chairs?
They, the gentlemen of the company, drowned thousands of worthy men and let inventors starve, shrug-

ging their shoulders and laughing in their avaricious
sleeves at every new means that was proposed to
save the pre-ci-ous life of man ! "

This timorous little dotard knew a wondrous deal
about such matters, and was a master of knotting.
The agent, who found out everything, imparted to
me his suspicions that the poor old man had some
stupendous life-preserving machine in his room—perhaps several; keeping them in a huge chest which
no steward had ever seen open. He himself, too,
going there to make a little visit, had been rather
abruptly refused entrance, and shrewdly suspected
that the old fellow was at that moment trying on
one of his amazing gutta-percha contrivances.

Meanwhile the advocate was warming up, and
going on more volubly than ever. "It is these
companies," he said, "that give us to the sharks.
The marine code is a farce. There ought to be
something like a law enforced to send them off to
rot in the galleys."

The first officer objected; and the advocate re-
joined more hotly than before; so that there soon
was a little group about them, teasing and making
fun of the poor scared valetudinarian, whom the hot
night was quite driving from his propriety.

But the talk was suddenly cut short by a cry
from an emigrant on the upper deck—"The sea is
on fire ! "

All turned towards the water. The ship was in-

deed sailing over a burning sea, splashing from her
sides myriads of topaz lights, handfuls of diamonds;
and leaving behind her, like a street of molten gold,
a long streak of liquid phosphorus which seemed to
issue from her stern as from a flaming mine.　Here
there was gold; there there was silver; the luminous
space extended far and wide, softening down into a
whitish glow, making one think of what the Dutch
call the milky sea, often beheld by sailors on the
Pacific Ocean, in the Bay of Bengal, and among the
Molucca Islands.　But close by us the water lived
and burned, a beauteous thing to see, a coruscation
of intertwining flakes of fire, a quivering sweep of
little stars and suns that rushed at the ship and
tumbled back again, that leaped and fell but disappeared not, giving the wave transparent splendor as
if lighted from below by the fabled stars Pluto and
Proserpina, that gleam at the centre of the earth.　It
was easy to imagine how this resplendent sea should
have turned the brain of those mariners of old time
who were the first to see it.　The dazzled eye was
fastened upon it and could not turn away; as if all
the riches of the universe were floating there.　One
longed to thrust in a hand and draw it out full of
pearls, to plunge down and come up again more re-
fulgent than an Eastern monarch.　We all were
incited to say queer things, to make strange com-
parisons; the imagination seemed to wallow in that
boundless surging flood of treasure which sparkled

round us in tempting mockery. But what was our
wonder when after an hour of this there came a
school of dolphins, swimming and darting in the
midst of this fire, and leaping around the ship as if
to vie with us in joy. Then it was nothing but one
whirl of sparks, of fiery foam and blazing spray, a
dance of constellations, a madness of splendor, which
made the emigrants shriek with delight as if they
had been so many children.

One man alone was ill at ease—the husband of
the Swiss lady. He made his appearance on the
quarter-deck with flushed face and sullen mien.
But he had brought it upon himself. He had gone
up on the midship-deck among a crowd of peasants
and had begun to set forth how all this phosphores-
cence was occasioned by a mass of microscopic creatures called by some unearthly name; in other words,
that every one of these sparks was an animal. This
time, however, he had piled it up too high, and his
audience had scouted him.

But now a new spectacle attracted our admiring
gaze. The sky had cleared on every side and we
saw for the first time on the horizon the four lovely
stars of the Southern Cross, unknown to the

"Lonely region of the North,"

and twinkling amid the black solitude of the Coal
Sacks, those deserts of the Antarctic sky. On one
side glowed the Alpha and the Beta of the Centaur,

on the other that stupendous sun, Canopus, in the constellation of the Ship. The spacious firmament was cloudless, still, and brilliant. The Northern Pole Star had sunk beneath the ocean.

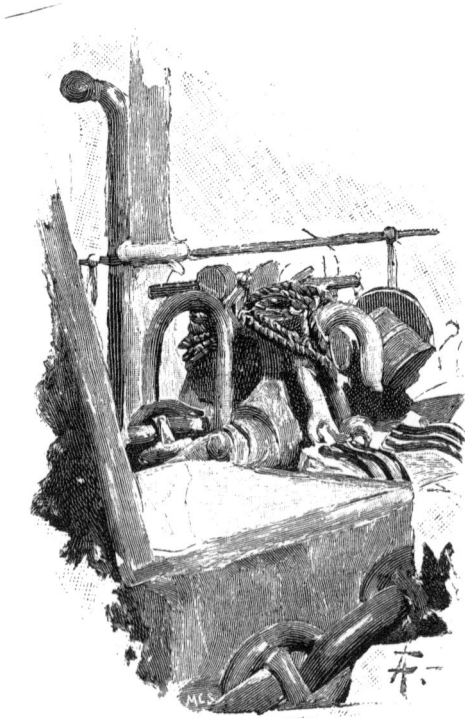

CHAPTER XIV

A BLUE SEA

T this point, the 17th day, I find noted on my Berghaus map that we are to pass the famous line drawn by Pope Alexander VI. to divide the world between Spain and Portugal; and then these words: "Fine weather in the house and out of doors." In fact, the humor of that multitude of emigrants did follow the changing complexion of the sea with wonderful fidelity. Just as when we are speaking with a powerful personage from whom we are asking a favor, and who can do us an injury, our countenance involuntarily reflects every expression that passes over his, so the thoughts and the talk of all those people were bright or dark, yellow or gray or blue, according to the color of the sea. Most rightly do we talk of " the face of the waters," for its smooth or wrinkled surface, the shadows that glance over it, the pale or sombre tints that cover

it on a sudden, do resemble to a marvellous degree
the movements of a human face in which are shown,
as in a glass, the stirring of an unstable, treacherous
soul. How many changes there are in a few hours,
and yet fair weather all the time! The ocean would
look old and wearied out, and then in a few instants
would grow young again; a thrill of life would run
through it, and change all in a moment; then it
would settle down once more,—be thoughtful, pensive, tired of everything, go to sleep; then up it
would start as if disturbed, angry, affronted by that
nutshell full of ants that was passing over it; frown-
ing as if it meant to strike, and then subside into
scornful, smiling indifference once more, as who
should say: "There, there, pass on; I forgive you."

And the aspect of the ship changed with these
changes, as if those sixteen hundred persons had had
one and the same nervous system. At ten o'clock,
all lying about, speechless, and with the look of
those who have nothing more to hope for in this life,
they gave the *Galileo* the appearance of a floating
hospital; an hour later, by reason of a breeze that
cleared the horizon, or a ray of sunlight that darted
down upon the forecastle, all on foot, all in motion,
amid such a hum of joyous talk as was amazing even
to themselves. Then, too, their disposition towards
us, and the reception they gave us in their part of
the ship, would vary as phase succeeded phase upon
the sea. In the morning, sour looks, backs rudely

turned, words growled out that meant a rooted hatred
of the signori. And then, in the evening of the
same day, kindly glances, children bid make way,
and even friendly words thrown out as if with a desire to get into conversation. And in this respect
we of the after-cabin did just as they did. Sometimes we would look at them with pitying eye, and
say within ourselves: "Poor worthy creatures!
They are our blood after all. What would we not
do to be of service to them! How excellent and
admirable to be loved by them!" And when, a
little later, the clouds shut down and the sultry air
oppressed us, we would think: "Brutes! They
would strike us dead where we stand if they could.
And, like idiots, we go and try to coax them!"

But that day the sea was blue, and through the
moral transparency, so to speak, of these people's
good-humor, there was many a new psychological
observation to be made. For please observe; beneath the rough web of mere spite and hatred there
had been woven in these sixteen days another, made
up of sympathy, of love, of intrigue, far more intricate and far more highly colored than the first. The
commissary was cognizant of everything, or almost
everything; and this either by direct evidence or
from what was told him, whether he asked it or no,
by fifteen or twenty gossips, who knew every bit of
scandal, and who filled the same office in the steerage that the mother of the piano player and the

agent did in the after-cabin. It was a joy beyond
price to hear this gentleman, as he stood on the
bridge with his eye upon the throng, run over the
gamut (*sfilar la corona*) of the passions, and point
out one by one the persons he alluded to, his speech
slow and measured, like a justice of the peace; and
he most grave and reverend in appearance, but most
comical in fact. The fore-deck, all black with people, was spread beneath like a vast roofless stage,
fanned just then by a gentle breeze, in which the
clothes hung out to dry, and the kerchiefs and caps
of the women, were flapping to and fro.

And he told us about it. There were not a few
flirtations, and these, being forced to keep within the
bounds of the strictest propriety, had burned and
blazed up, if one may say so, visibly, as they never
do in the city or in the country. There was no
young woman, married or not, but had her wooers,
some timid, some bold and pressing, all more or less
in love, and all more or less encouraged openly or on
the sly. This enforced continence and the constant
propinquity of so many women, the disorder of their
dress in the morning or during the long midday
slumber, and the frequent exposure of maternity,
had even roused passions for peasant women who
had seen a half century of life, and who on land
would hardly have been noticed at all. The young
girls, if they were not absolute frights, had each
her circle of adorers, some of whom, after a while,

grew tired, and went off to dangle after a new
beauty, leaving place for somebody else, if he chose
to occupy it, and so the groups were always changing.
There were passing fancies and Platonic contemplations whose object was to kill the time ; and there
were comic flirtations got up to amuse the company.
But there were men who fell in love so seriously
and so deeply that their brutal boldness almost defied the light of day and the regulations of disci-
pline ; who were as jealous and resolute as Arabs ;
who would brook no rival; and who threatened
right and left with naked knife. These had all
their posts of vantage, from which, during the day,
when they were forced to be discreet, they sat
glaring at the fair author of their pangs like falcons
at their prey ; and even cursed and menaced those
who passed in front of them. There were even
some grizzled heads, some fifty-years-old plowmen,
rhinoceros-hided, who might be supposed to have
outgrown the passions of youth, and who were yet
amorous. One of these, a North countryman, with
a muzzle like a boar, had made a spectacle of himself over the peasant woman of Capracotta, whose
round face, like an ill-washed Madonna, flushing
under the reflection of a rose-colored kerchief, proved
attractive to many others ; her own tall, bearded
husband to the contrary notwithstanding. The two
singing girls, who went about all day laughing with
everybody, and pulled about by everybody, seemed

to take a special pleasure in flirting with well-be-
haved husbands. The women hated them with a

perfect hatred, and apostrophized them without stint
or measure before their faces and behind their backs,
threatening to go to the commissary and have the
place cleared of them.

But these were not the only ones. There were certain "bold-faced creatures from the city" who went about in a most shameless manner. The women hated above all others that ape of a negress that belonged to the Brazilians. She only came to meals and in the evening; but she had roused a perfect volcano of repulsive passion. "How on earth did she do it," they said, "with that flat nose and general ugliness?" A couple of husbands had already come to blows about her. The wife of one had made a scene that was heard down in the engine-room; and the wife of the other had given him a sounding backhander, for which, however, he had reimbursed her on the spot, undertaking to pay the interest when he got on shore. The big Bolognese, it is true, did preserve a certain decorum. "She wished," said the commissary, "to carry intact into another world her name of *ragaza unesta*." It had got about rather freely that her heart had been touched by a Swiss emigrant; she put on the dignity of an archduchess, all the more dignified and scornful as those facetious surmises about the contents of her mysterious pouch grew more frequent and more insolent.

There were at the same time many others who in love matters did set a good example; girls well brought up, or at all events modest, properly courted by decent young fellows who did the bosom friend or the serious wooer in all form, and who, with languishing but respectful looks, spent the day tied to the fair one's apron-string under the eyes of her parents. But gallantry in general took a tone and mien calculated to educate, rapidly and altogether badly, the crowd of young boys and of girls from ten to fourteen who were on board, and who in that promiscuous throng saw and heard everything. The lowest instincts, kept under at home by hard toil, or dormant in the quiet solitude of the fields, were awakened little by little like adders in the bosoms of all that crowded company, idle, and heated by the tropical sun. The result was vile in its form, but in substance it was much the same as is handed round and swallowed like gilded pills in many a highly respectable drawing-room and nobody shocked or scandalized. * . * *

Just as we were talking of him, my good crook-back came by with a flask of oil in his hand ; and, following perhaps the course of his own thoughts, he said to me : *Scià sente ; l' è pezo una bionda che sette brunne.* "One blonde is worse than seven brunettes.——But what now ? "

It was the boys on the bow that were clapping their hands, as the topsails, sky-sails, and spencers, fore and aft, were set, and the ship with her white wings spread, sailed through the blue sea in all the majesty of her beauty. At the same moment, as if to greet us, a flight of Brazilian water birds came, made three circles round the topsail yards, and then disappeared. The *Galileo* had never seemed so beau-

tiful. Huge she was and powerful, but the fine lines
of her hull and her great length gave her the grace
of a gondola. Her lofty masts with their network
of cordage seemed trunks of gigantic branchless
palms entwined with leafless vines, while the wide-
open purple mouths of the wind funnels gave the
idea of colossal flowers, attracted by America instead
of by the sun. Her sides were rough and black with
tar, her deck bristled with ironwork, a dense cloud
of smoke hung over all, and the place looked like a
vast manufactory; but it was relieved by the pale
blue boats made fast above the rail, by the white,
swelling wind-sails, by the light bridge swaying
against the sky, by a hundred gleams from metal,
wood, and glass; by a thousand objects, strange in
shape, but every one a useful implement, an orna-
ment, a power, an industry, a defence. And the jar
of the engine, the dull stroke of the cranks, the
plunge of the screw, the clanking of the rudder chains,
the hiss of the log line, the dry rattle of the shrouds,
the tinkling of glass and china in the racks, all made
up a strange, vague sort of music which charmed the
ear and entered into the soul like the mysterious
voices of invisible beings that were hovering over us
and urging us to labor and to strife. The deck rises
and falls under our feet as if it were a body with
life, the huge frame makes unexpected and incompre-
hensible leaps, like the strivings of fear, rude un-
graceful jumps, as if from vexation, and movements

of the bow like the shaking of an enormous wondering head ; and then, for a long space scarcely seeming to touch the waves, will move so still and evenly upon the slow ground-swell that an ivory ball would hardly roll about upon the deck.

But on she goes and never stops, through cloud and darkness, right against the winds and waves, with a whole people on her back, with five thousand tons within her bulk—from one world to the other, guided without mistake by a little bar of steel that might serve to cut open the leaves of a book, and by a man who moves a wheel of wood, with a turn of the hand. We go over in thought the history of navigation, and as, rising from the log to the raft, from the canoe to the row galley, and so up through all the forms of the ship, with the improvement which centuries have given it, we stop before the last development to compare it with the early germ, our hearts swell with amazement and admiration, and we ask ourselves what marvel of human skill is greater than this. More wonderful is the ship than the ocean which she cleaves and leaves behind ; and to its ceaseless, unrelenting threats she replies with the tireless clank of her brazen joints : " You are vast, but you are a brute. I am little, but I am a genius. You separate worlds, I bind them together. You surround me, but I pass through. You are might, but I am knowledge."

Alas for poor human pride ! While I was yet in

the midst of these reflections a thrill ran from stem
to stern; and, straightway, there were a hundred

"Moves a wheel of wood with a turn of the hand."

scared faces and a hundred eager voices in mutual
inquiry. The ship was coming to a stand-still. Many

rushed to the bulwarks and looked over, they knew
not why; some ran to the captain; some ladies got
ready to faint. The ship stopped. Impossible to
describe the grim effect of this sudden quiet, and how
like a broken toy seemed that enormous vessel immovable and silent in the midst of the ocean! How
quickly did our confidence in the strength and power
of man vanish away. And at the same time was revealed that evil trait in man's nature which delights
in another's suffering, as some passengers spread a tale
of how the boiler was going to burst, and the keel
was broken and the water was coming into the hold.
The women screamed. The relieved firemen, coming
on deck, stripped to the waist and black with coal,
were surrounded and besieged with frightened in-
quiries. The officers went about saying things which
were lost in the outcries of the crowd. At last the
reassuring news was known fore and aft that it was
nothing;—one of the bearings of the main shaft was
hot—it was being put right—we would go on again
in an hour. We all breathed again and some who
had turned pale shrugged their shoulders and said
they had thought so from the first; but the greater
part continued thoughtful, as after a wound or an irregular beating of the heart. That engine, which no
one had noticed before, became the theme of talk for
hundreds, all full of an anxious respect for it that
was almost ridiculous. For after all it is the heart
of the ship, is it not? The officers are the brains,

and if the brains go wrong the man may not die, but if the heart stop, good-bye. And what was the engineer's name. He looked like a clever, experienced man—never spoke—must have studied a good deal —he would pull us through—no fear. All praised him without knowing anything about him. But the mill-owner wore a pitying smile and shook his head as he swaggered about the deck with his great stomach.—"Italian machinists! Well that it was no worse! American or English, yes; but the national screwiness would not hear of them."—*Faltan patacones*, said the priest. "Too poor." But in half an hour the conversation languished. That promised hour never would come to an end, and uneasiness supervened once more. "Does it take all that time to cool a bearing?" said many who did not even know what such a thing was like. "What on earth are they about down there? Did ever anyone see such a lot of good-for-nothing———!" Ah! at last the machine gives sign of life, the screw turns over, the sea foams—Heaven be praised, we are moving again!

And yet to me the most remarkable thing in this episode was a look exchanged by two persons. So true is it that the manifestations of the human soul constitute the most attractive spectacle which man can contemplate. At the very instant of the unexpected stoppage, while yet no one knew the cause of it, and there was good reason to fear some serious

accident had happened—and every one did fear it—
I happened to be on the piazzetta and saw my next-
door neighbor below turn to look at his wife, who
was above him, leaning on the rail of the poop-deck ;
and she, as if she had expected his glance, fixed her
eyes upon him. It was one of those looks which
reveal the soul as the ray under the spectroscope
reveals the chemical nature of the substance that
yields the flame. It was not anxiety, it was not fear,
not even a hesitating curiosity. It was a cold, tranquil glance, which showed the utter indifference of
each for the other, even in the face of an unknown
danger which might end in death. Each had said
to the other with the eyes: " I know that it would
be nothing to you to lose me. You know that I
would care just as little about parting with you."
After which the wife moved from the rail and the
husband looked another way.

This would have been their last farewell if a mis-
chance had separated them forever. But what could
have come to pass between these two that they
should hate one another thus and yet remain united ?
This question kept coming back to my mind in spite
of all that I could do. And I reached the conclusion
that there must be children in the case that forced
them to keep together ; most probably an only son,
a bond more powerful than when there are several.
That eternal, forced, almost trembling smile that she
wore inspired everyone with more or less repug-

nance, although she, divining this sentiment, strove
to give her countenance a look of kindly sadness as
if she were in grief but resigned to misconstruction.
He spoke with hardly anyone. He appeared embarrassed and ill at ease, as are all those who know
that their trouble is plainly enough to be seen, but
are ashamed of it and angry at being pitied. One
could see, moreover, by a certain fleeting expression
in his eye and mouth, that he had been in times
past of a frank, open disposition and inclined to
cheerful friendliness—perhaps even a really good
fellow; but that all the springs of his nature were
broken or worn out in this long contest with an adversary stronger and more obstinate than he. It
was easy in fact to see that he feared his wife and
that she did not fear him. This was discernible in
the uneasy glances which he cast around whenever
he exchanged a few words with the Argentine or
the Brazilian lady, with whom he was on those terms
of sad and kindly respect which a man not happy
with his own wife is apt to observe towards those
of other men; perceiving in each of them the image
of a happiness, or at least a content, which cannot be
his. And this shrinking as of an ill-treated child
was all the more piteous when seen in a tall, strong
man, who even yet bore in his countenance the traces
of manly beauty. A close look at him showed that
frequent trembling of the lip, usual in men accustomed to subdue anger, and the long, fixed look at

vacancy, which means deep melancholy and contem-
plated suicide. And he never displayed weariness
or vexation, like the other passengers; he seemed as
indifferent to time as a condemned criminal. I
should not have wondered to see him, at any moment, fling himself under the crank of the engine.
Perhaps at home some occupation, or some work, or
some vice, if you please, may have served as a diversion and enabled him for a few hours, at all events,
to be out of sight of his wife. But there, on those
half-dozen square yards of deck, forced to see and
be in constant contact with her, to hate and to be
hated in open view of everybody, to breathe her
breath in a dark and airless dungeon,—this was solitary confinement, the oar, the pillory, all in one.
And not a soul to speak to. He had not confided
anything to a single individual, or it would have
been known; for everyone was devouringly anxious
to penetrate his secret. And she, too, said not a
word. They were two sealed sepulchres, in each of
which there was a living monster that writhed, but
asked for neither aid nor pity.

That night, however, I thought I was about to
penetrate the mystery. The breeze had fallen, the
sea slept; so that late in the evening, when we went
below, the ship moved on without strain or creak;
and the slightest sound could be heard in the next
stateroom; just as in those queer little inns with
wooden partitions in certain cities on the Rhine, in

which, as travellers are warned by their guide-books,
"it is as well to be discreet." When I entered my
room I heard the muffled voice of the lady speaking
rapidly in a harsh, monotonous tone, recalling the past,
and mentioning facts and names as if she were overwhelming him with reproach; and then the husband
saying in a low voice from time to time, "Not true,
not true, not true!" But as her upbraidings grew
more bitter, his denials too became more fierce and
hurried. The unhappy man, unable to cope with
her, and not caring any longer, as it would seem, to
preserve his manly dignity, was reduced to the
miserable, womanish defence of saying the same
thing over and over again, lest his silence should
bring worse upon him. But suddenly he started
up and poured out a flood of words, unintelligible,
furious, outrageous, desperate; ending in a snarl like
a mad dog that made me shudder. He was biting
his fingers; and she only laughed. I stood a moment expecting the sound of blows or the gasping of
the woman as he seized her by the throat. But I
heard instead his voice in humble supplication, pronouncing over and over again a single name—Attilio
—the voice of a man who acknowledges himself
beaten, who begs for mercy, who yields everything,
so only one favor may be granted him. Attilio must
have been a son, and his father one of those men,
otherwise strong of mind, whom paternal love makes
timid, and bows with pinioned arms beneath the

scourge of a woman capable of stabbing him to death
at that one weak point.   It seemed impossible that
the woman should not have responded with some
affection to that piteous cry; and I listened closely;
but there was no answer.   A berth creaked;—the
lady wife had gone to bed without a word.   Then I
heard a noise as of a hand searching in a valise; and
I thought, perhaps, he might be getting out a revolver.   But she was silent.   The poor wretch had
not even the sorry comfort of being supposed capable
of doing anything desperate.   While I was anxiously
awaiting the end of all this, there came someone to
the door of the stateroom, and by the swinging lamp
I recognized the agent.

I did not properly catch what he said at first, for
I was attending to my neighbors; but no report was
heard; perhaps the man's courage had failed him as
it had often done before; and I caught, instead, a
sound as of one that sinks down overpowered, and
the slap of a hand upon a forehead.   The agent took
no notice.   He had something else to think of.   He
had come to me to blow off his vexation.   That
stateroom of his had become uninhabitable—for a
man.   He had slipped on an overcoat and paced the
corridor for half an hour in slippers, hoping that his
neighbors would go to sleep.   "Spanish Grammar?"
I ventured.   Exactly—Spanish Grammar, that, and
nothing else, but they came to the interjection chapter
too often.   He wished that the wife, ridiculous little

Lucca image that she was, would have done with saying Ave Maria. The worst of it was that for the first few days his coughing and banging with his elbow against the bulkhead had kept them some-what in order; but now they had got used to it and did not care a bit. They went on as if they were in a "private room" at the restaurant, munched sweet-meats brought away from the table, and sipped rosolio. It seemed as if they were having private gymnastics, with their jumping and tearing about. Who would think that such demure little wretches as they seemed above on deck, could behave so like imps. He meant to be revenged the next day; he was going to make their lives a burden to them from one end of the deck to the other; and at table make them as red as two turkey cocks at every mouthful. The little hypocrites. And he must do the walking. But he had not lost his time. Coming out of his room he had seen a white figure disappear at the end of the cross corridor, and had recognized the Swiss lady. Had not made out at what door she slipped in. Could not have been that of the gentleman with the eyeglasses, for the Argentines were all together in the *gaucho's* room, whence issued a clink-ing of tumblers;—nor that of the little Tuscan, since he for a couple of evenings had been, at this hour, going forward, where he had a beat. Suspected the descendant of the Incas, but was not sure. As to the professor he was probably on deck looking for

falling stars; for whenever he was in her way, the lady
would find the stateroom very close indeed for two
persons, and then up he went to study the heavens.

In short it was a busy night; no one was asleep,
and there would be plenty of material for gossip in
the morning. He had already seen the mother of
the piano player putting her head out of her room
door, and peering up and down with a viperous curiosity. Ah! apropos; he had his eye on the daughter, whose face lighted up when somebody passed
by; but who that somebody was he could not make
out, because just when he had seen that lighting
up several people had passed by, and the foxy
creature was so quick to veil her regard that he
could not catch the direction. Yes, a fruitless little
passion, a suppressed fire; she was tied fast; it would
all end in a letter, and a snip of her scissors. But
there really was something going on, and he meant
to find out more about it. Oh, yes! Had I not
heard? The Neapolitan priest had been sent for in
a great hurry. He had rushed out like a great
dromedary, putting on his cassock as he went. Some
one must be ill among the emigrants. "Basta," he
said, in conclusion, "I 'm going up to the pantry to
have a glass of beer and then I 'll come down and
see if they 've got quiet. May they die without
benefit of clergy (*accidenti*)! Good-night."

It was a dreadful night. Twelve o'clock, and
almost everyone awake. The sultriness oppressed

us all. And because that was not enough, the
cabin seemed turned into a great whispering gal-
lery in which every sigh sounded loud and was
heard from one end of the corridor to the other.
In the stateroom behind mine the mill - owner
was snoring away, every now and then groaning aloud and exclaiming: "*Ah! povra Italia!*"
which seemed to be the dirge of his hope. From
time to time I heard the feeble cough of the
young lady from Mestre, whose room was on the
other side of the ship. The youngest child of the
Brazilian lady, a little ailing, would cry and then the
doleful lullaby of the black nurse would be heard—
a kind of hoopoe sob which made me think of the
lamentable wailings of African slaves shut up in the
hold of sailing vessels becalmed under the Equator.
Opposite me, on the other side of the corridor, the
advocate and the tenor were chatting without the
least consideration, and I made out that they were
talking of Greece. "George Byron!" I heard
someone say, and then the advocate cried out,
"So you do not believe in the power of panslavism?" "Oh!" said the other, "don't talk to me
of panslavism. For your guidance, you need never
men-ti-on pan-slav-ism to me." I caught fragments
of conversation between the Neapolitan priest and
the Chilian, each at the door of his own room:
*Cuando se produce un movimiento de baja en el precio
del oro sellado. . . .*

At last they were all quiet. But if one do not go
to sleep at once in these sultry nights in those close
staterooms it is useless to hope for anything better
than a dreadful kind of doze, in which sight and
hearing are dulled but not dead, and dreams, if they
can be called dreams, take us in dizzy sweep from
where we are to our house at home, and from our
house far out to sea again, with a vividness and a
rudeness of disenchantment which is a real torture.
And how often, years after, when we are at home
again, we have these same dreams, as if they were
glimpses of another world stamped indelibly upon
our brains like real events, distinct from thousands
of others in this life. And there comes back to me the
noise of the water against the ship's side, a few in-
ches from my ear; and which, in the unusual silence
of the ship, sounded clearer than ever; a long, steady
murmur, which broke sometimes into words, into
suppressed laughings, into low hissing, and then died
away into the faintest rustling; when, whack, there
came a furious blow, and then once more a voice, as of
prayer, as if the monster were entreating entrance,
swearing that he would do nobody any harm, promising to be good. Ah, the hypocrite! And still, without
rest, he scrapes and strokes and rubs and rasps and
licks and flaps and taps and searches for a hole,
and fumes and frets to find all tight and sound, and
bemoans himself, and wonders that he is not trusted;
and then, losing patience, he begins once more to

rage and threaten and beat at the door like an angry
master of the house.

And with this ceaseless babble there are mingled
all sorts of suspicious sounds, the door-knob, the
water-jug, the swinging lamp, and every now and
then you would swear there is somebody in the room
rummaging your trunks. You rouse yourself and
find that there is indeed some one coming in. It is
the watchman who is making his rounds to see if
the air-ports are closed. He gives a look and goes
out again. And then you hear other sounds on deck;
hasty steps, as of people running at an alarm, unintelligible noises which, in the silence of night,
seem tremendous, and make you think some accident
has happened. Passengers get up, look out, go on
deck, and then come down again. It is nothing at
all. A couple of sailors hauling a rope. You shut
your eyes and begin to doze once more, and wake
up with a start at a stunning, terrible din. What
has happened,—a boiler burst? Quarter smashed
in? No, a rain squall. Ah! at last, then, we can
sleep! But through the port a pale, ashy streak is
seen. The day glimpse glimmers. *Maledizione!*
—Five days more!

CHAPTER XV

IVE days more! This was the exclamation of everyone that morning; and the five days that yet remained seemed longer than the eighteen that had passed. For it must be remembered that, in virtue of some psychic law or other, the slow growth of tedium and general weariness had been going on unperceived even in the intervals of fine weather and of good humor. When these were at an end, the pressure of the hateful burden, far from being alleviated, was felt once more just as if it had constantly been bearing on us, and all the heavier for the time that had elapsed. That eighteenth day, too, gave promise of ill. Clouds, gray and black, made a low, hanging vault over the ocean, which had in some places the color of well-shaken oil, in others looked like moistened ashes, or now and then like a sea of blackish bitumen which rose and sank

like the pitch in the tank of the barrators.[1] Forward
and aft, groups were formed and news was circu-
lating. The old Piedmontese peasant had died during the night, of pleurisy. The death certificate had
been drawn up and signed by two witnesses that
morning, at dawn, in the chart-room, after due verifi-
cation by the doctor. This event, though well known
to be not infrequent on that long voyage and among
so many people, was, nevertheless, a source of disquietude, as if everyone were threatened. The doctor was detained on the piazzetta by the ladies who
wished to hear about it; and, with that placid face
of his, like a mild Nicotera, he told the story. It was
a piteous scene. The old man had wished to see
the young lady from Mestre before he died, in order
to give her his papers and the little money he had,
to be sent to his son. But his last moments were
an agony of despair. No efforts of the priest could
induce him to be resigned to death. In the looks
he cast upon those near him, and on that strange
hospital where he was lying, there was an immeas-
urable anguish, the terror of a child at having to
die there in mid-ocean where there could be no burial
for him. He clutched with both hands the arm of
the young lady, saying at the last only, *Oh me fieul !
Oh me pover fieul !* "O my son ! O my poor son !"
and rolled his head from side to side in utter desola-
tion. His face after death remained bathed in tears

[1] Dante, *Inf.*, **xxii.**

and distorted with terror. The young lady had
almost to be carried on deck, and could hardly drag
herself back to her room.

I went forward. Here there was the little commotion that may be seen in the square, of a morning
when some crime has been committed overnight; a
gathering and a low, eager whispering of women,
who showed under the mask of sadness a certain
satisfaction at having something unusual to discuss,
a satisfaction that is always greater when it is news
of death. They talked about the funeral and when
it was to be, how performed, on which side he was
to be thrown over, and whether feet foremost or no.
And there were the most extraordinary conjectures.
He was to be thrown overboard naked, with a cannon-ball at his neck; they were to leave him floating in a chest, tarred as the law prescribed to protect him from the fishes. Some said there were
sharks already about the ship, attracted by the smell
of the body; and some looked to see if it were so.
There were crowds at the door of the sick bay, wish-
ing to go down and see the corpse, but a sailor was
posted there to prevent them. Meanwhile, on the
forecastle, the old man in the green jacket, with his
usual circle of hearers, harangued and cursed, with
his finger in the air. "One less! We are getting
on. The flesh of the poor flung to the fishes! They
meant from the first that this one should die. It 's
my belief they did not give him anything to eat."

He declared, moreover, that instead of good soup they
sent the man dish-water; and that they had let him
die without a pillow under his head.   Moreover, certain telltales whispered that evening how he had in-
sinuated a suspicion that this was not the first death
that had happened this voyage; but that the others
had been kept quiet, and the bodies thrown overboard at dead of night from the poop-deck.   "But
the day of reckoning will come," he loudly declared,
and he with his hearers flashed such glances at me
that I desisted from trying to hear more just then,
and went to get news of little Galileo.

I found the father at the door of the stateroom in
the second cabin, seated on a box, with one of the
twins between his knees, and a pipe in his mouth.
"The lad is quite well," he said, with a smiling face;
and then, with a wink towards the forecastle, whence
voices were to be heard, he said in an undertone:
Ghe xè dele teste calde—"There are some hotheads
there."   And he went on in his northern dialect:
"For my part, when once I am in the new world,
why should I trouble my head because things go
badly in the old?"   This question was a feeler.   He
wished to know whether I were a wrong-headed
signore, or such a one as could be reasoned with.
But without any other answer from me than a nod
of the head, he went on eagerly and frankly, as if
my look had inspired confidence:

Per conto mio de mi. "You gentlemen, saving your

presence, are wrong to spread such idle reports about
America, and how they die of hunger there, and how
they come back more miserable than ever, and how
there is the plague there, and how the government
is a set of traitors and despots (*e cussi via*) and so
forth. What is the next thing? The next thing is
that when a letter comes from someone over there,
how they are getting on and making (*bessi*) money,
why nobody believes any more what the *siòri* say,
even when it is true; they suspect that it is all a
trick, that the contrary is true, and *i parte a mile a
la volta*—they go out by thousands."

I told him he was quite right, and that if nothing
but the truth were spoken it is probable that fewer
would have gone over. "And you have pretty
good prospects, I suppose?"

"*Mi?*" he answered. "This is the way I look at
it. I can't find anything worse than I leave. The
worst that can happen is to starve, as I did at home.
Dighio ben?"

Then, refilling his pipe: *I ga un bel dir: No emigré, no emigré.* "It's no use their saying, Don't emigrate, don't emigrate." The Cavaliere Careti made
me laugh. [Who should this Cavaliere Careti be?]
'You're wrong,' he said, 'you're wrong.' He told
me that every emigrant who went over took four hundred francs capital with him. 'You are going,' he
said, 'to produce and to consume out of your country.
You do it wrong.' *Cossa ghe par a lù' de sta maniera*

"It's no use their saying, Don't emigrate, don't emigrate."

di razonar, la me diga.—I only ask you what you think of an argument like that. He said, too, I was wrong to complain of the taxes, for the higher they were the more the contadino worked and the more he produced. *Piavolœ, la me scusa, digo mi.* All nonsense, saving your reverence, say I. I do not know anything about these things. I only know that I work the flesh off my bones and do not get enough food for my wife and myself. I emigrate to get something to eat. You advise me to wait until you have reclaimed Sardinia and the Maremma, put the Roman territory under cultivation, and opened co-operative banks and bakers' shops, and then the government will go right on to help agriculture. But what if I have nothing to eat the while?—*Oh crose de din e de dia!* How can a man wait if he is starving?"

Encouraged by my approval, he branched out a little, and began setting forth those general ideas with which everyone of his class has his head more or less confusedly filled as to why things go so badly; everything spent to keep soldiers; heaps of millions for guns and ships; and then *zo tasse*, the taxes, the poor not considered at all; the usual thing, but then it never sounds so true or so sad as when we hear it from one who has experience in his own trouble of its effects, and to whom we can offer no consolation, not even words. And while he told me how, after a day of toil, he found on the table nothing but onion broth, and was kept awake at night by hunger, and did not "venture" to eat lest he should take the bread out of the mouths of his children, who had not enough as it was, I reflected how little, had his case been my own, I should have cared for historical necessity and the sacrifice of the present for the future, and for national dignity and all the rest of it. Society, which demanded such sacrifices of him, had not even taught him to understand them; and it would have been insulting his misery to try and explain. And I listened to him with that feeling of shame which is justly ours when we are told of the troubles of the poor; for does not our own conscience tell us that this great injustice, though we cannot, even in imagination, devise a remedy for it, is nevertheless an inherited responsibility.

"O, no," he said, shaking his head. *Come che xè el mondo adesso, la xè una roba che no pol durar— La ghe va massa mal a tropa zente.*—"Things cannot go on so. It is too hard upon too many people." And then he told me of misery that he saw around him; pitiful stories which he heard in the steerage, —so pitiful that his case seemed fortunate by comparison. There were some who for years had not eaten meat; who for years had not worn a shirt except on festa days; who never slept in a bed; and who yet toiled grimly all the while. There were some who when their passage was paid would reach

America with a couple of scudi ; and who every day put by a bit of biscuit in a bag that they might, on landing, if they did not soon find work, have a morsel to eat without begging for it.   He knew, he said, not one but many who, that they might not be barefoot when they reached America, kept their one pair of broken shoes tied round their feet with strings, and slept with them under their pillow at night, lest they should be stolen. *E la senta*, he added, *ghe xè de quelli che i gh' ha fato tanto cativa vita, che i xè partii tropo tardi, e i va in America a farse soterar*—"There are some who have led such evil lives that it is too late, and they are going to America only to be buried."   Then he pointed out to me a peasant of about forty years old, a short dis- tance off, bareheaded, dripping with sweat, and holding his head in his wasted, trembling hands. He had a bad fever which never left him, caught in the rice fields, and he could keep nothing on his stomach.   One night (but no one must know) he himself had seized the poor fellow when he was nearly overboard.   He had tried to throw himself into the sea, and since then his wife never let him out of her sight.   Poor woman.   She was more to be pitied than he. *La varda ela, che robète!* Just think of that !

All this he said sadly, but without bitterness ; not at all to propitiate me, but simply from that vague notion, partly religious, partly intuitive, but

common amongst his class, that the wretchedness of
the masses is the way of the world, like pain and
death ; that it is a condition necessary to the existence of the human race, and that no social adjust-
ment can change it.

"Ah, well," he concluded, "God be good to us !
If I could only find in America such *brava zente*
as I have found on board here ! For hark ye, *sior
paron*, if that poor sick lass (*putela*) do not go to
heaven it is because they do not let anybody in any
more. Why, she sends broth to the nursing mothers,
and money (*bessi*) to the poor people, and linen to
those that have not any. She is a blessing to us all.
*Ma co ' ghe digo mi che el mondo va mal.   Un anzolo
compagno, che tocarà morir zovene.* Did I not say
that there was something wrong in the world ?   An
angel like that to die so young !   I 'm coming, chat-
terbox," he cried turning to the stateroom. " *Con
parmeso, paron.* My wife is calling me. *La se
varda, che a momenti se verze le catarate !* Look
out, we shall have a torrent of rain in a moment ! "

And, sure enough, there came, all on a sudden,
from the gray sky, a shower of huge drops as large
as grapes, and then a roaring downpour of thickest
rain, veiling everything as if the ship had sailed
into a cloud. A crowd of passengers surged noisily
into the covered way where I stood, and, driving
me forward a dozen paces, surrounded and imprisoned me, darkling, and in the midst of wet

jackets and a strong smell of poverty. And then occurred a memorable scene. It was not ten minutes before a movement of the crowd and an outbreak of hooting and laughing bespoke a quarrel; and, rising on tiptoe, I saw a hand in air falling with rapid and regular movement on the bowed neck of some invisible form, like a sledge hammer on an anvil. "Who is it? What is it?" Everybody was clamoring; nothing could be made out. A couple of sailors ran up, the commissary followed, the combatants were separated and led away amidst the shouts of the bystanders. Supposing, of course, that they would be taken to the "hall of judgment," I ran there, too, and making a short cut through the third class reached the place just as the culprits did, and was amazed to see in these the father of the Genoese girl, panting with rage, and that poor little Modenese bookkeeper, hatless, exhausted, with a countenance that was a plainly written receipt for a merciless thrashing. A concourse of grinning faces followed them. The accused entered the commissary's room; the crowd surged outside the door.

It was thus. When the rain squall came the bookkeeper had run with the others into the covered way and had been packed in there by the crowd like a pilchard in a cask. It was his hap, good and evil at once, to find himself close behind the Genoese girl, his face against her hair, and just behind him, alas, unseen, another, the father-in-law of his dearest dreams. The poor young fellow, dead in love these eighteen days, and tempted by the darkness, had lost the guiding lamp of reason, and had begun to imprint kiss after kiss upon the neck and shoulders of his idol, with such vehemence, such a frenzy of passion, that he did not even feel the first paternal man-handling that he received. At the second he had come to himself, as from delirium, and could hardly believe his head was on.

The trial was too funny for human endurance.

The father, beside himself with rage, was cursing and abusing him: "*Mascarson! Faccia de galea! Porco d'un ase! Ti veuggio rompe o müro!* Ragamuffin, jail-bird, and so forth! I'll break your head against the wall!" And out went the threatening hand again to seize him by the hair.

The other was pitiful to see. He denied nothing; said he had lost control of himself, begged for forgiveness, declared he was honest, tried to show a letter from the syndic of his village (Chiozzola, I think) and, taking his head in his hands, wept like a beaver (*sic*) and made gestures of despair like Massinelli in the holidays. "But I forgot myself I tell you. I acted like a brute. I give you my honor. . . . I did not mean. . . . Kill me if you like." And under all his grief and shame shone out the not ignoble passion which had driven him to such extravagance ; one of those violent emotions which do sometimes blaze up in such poor little creatures, like an explosion of gas in a lamp chimney.

But the father would not be pacified. He was thoroughly angry. His paternal pride was offended at such an audacious act having been committed by so wretched a creature, by a poor little half-alive skeleton (*quel mezz' uomo che reggeva l' anima coi denti*) that after all abased itself so utterly. He kept on yelling and screaming, *Brutto! Strason che no sei atro! A mae figgia! E ghe veu da faccia!*—and tried to get at him again, whereon the other stretched out his arms disconsolate, as who should say, " Here I am, do what you like with me." And then he declared once more that he was an honest man and again presented the letter of his syndic.

The commissary was greatly puzzled what to do. I saw in his eyes a smile which meant that, struck by the theatrical notion of a wedding on the spot, he was half inclined to propose it. But the father did not seem a man to be trifled with, so at last he got out of it by giving the young fellow a long lecture upon the respect due to women, and ordering him not to be seen on deck for a while. Then he soothed the other, saying that the " occurrence" in no way prejudiced the reputation of his daughter, who was greatly respected by everybody— and so on. Then he put them both out, desiring the father to go forward first. He did so, turning, however, to shake his fist and send back a few suit-

able Genoese adjectives, assorted.   The young fellow, left alone with the commissary, placed a hand
on his bosom and said in a dramatic tone, "Believe
me, Signor Commissary, on the word of a man of
honor, it was my misfortune—a moment of——" But
here his heart swelled, his voice was choked, and,
raising his eyes to heaven with an expression comical, but most sincere, which told the whole story of
his sea-sorrow, he exclaimed, "If you but knew!"
He could say no more; and so departed with his
head hanging down and the arrow in his side.

The figure of that poor lovesick young fellow as
he passed through the covered way is connected in
my memory with the heavens in their new aspect
after the clearing shower.   Huge rifts of bluest sky
fresh washed, swept over by flying clouds.   The
sea great tracts of green with long streaks of purest
azure, looking like a mighty meadow with endless
intersecting canals full of water to the brim.   We
seemed to have reached a region, half land half water,
abandoned by its inhabitants by reason of an inun-
dation; and the eye sought on the far horizon towers
and steeples as on the great plains of Holland; and
when the waters were a little ruffled, giving the
green expanse a look as of larger vegetation, the
illusion changed and I thought of that vast ocean
tract covered with a carpet of seaweed which for
twenty days entangled the ships and frightened the
sailors of Columbus.   Some white birds swept across

the distant sky, the sun seemed reflected here and
there from islands of sparkling emeralds, and in the
air was balmy spring, the fragrance of the shore,
speaking to the soul like an echo of far-off voices
wafted to us upon the breeze of the pampas.

But the emerald sea and the little episode of the
unhappy lover lightened for a few moments only the
gloom of that day on board the *Galileo*. The blonde
lady alone carolled for joy as she paced the deck on
her husband's arm, caressing him with voice and eye
and face, like a seven-days bride, perhaps to make
up for some grievous treachery she had in store for
him, and of which there was a premonitory twinkle
in the blue pupils of her childlike eyes; while he,
as usual, drooped his shoulders, made with the
tongue's tip and half-shut eyes the light smile that
seemed to mock himself, and her, and the rest of us,
and all the universe,—a sneer symbolic of his cool
philosophy. On all the rest, the idea of the dead
body we had on board and which was to be cast into
the sea that night threw a shade of sadness; and
eyes glanced forward from time to time as if in fear
that the man would rise up and come out again to
curse his hideous burial-place. The talk was all of
him. It grew gloomier and gloomier, as if with
coming darkness that body would grow longer, and
at dead of night reach aft and rattle with its feet at
the stateroom doors. The dinner was dull enough.
There was some grim discussion between the old

Chilian and the captain as to whether a body cast overboard with weight fastened to its heels would reach the bottom whole, or whether the tissues would be torn and stripped off by the tremendous pressure and only the skeleton get so far. The captain favored the latter idea. The Chilian, on the contrary, maintained that the pressure of the water from without was neutralized by that from within and was the same in every direction, so that the body would sink unharmed. And then, agreeing about the initial velocity of the descent, its regular acceleration and the extreme depth of the Atlantic, they settled it that the body would occupy about one hour in its vertical descent. "Wait a moment," said the Chilian, "the body might come across currents which would send it up again."

At this notion of the body coming once more to the surface I saw my neighbor, the advocate, shudder; yet he stood his ground like a man. But the Genoese was ill-advised enough to speak of a description he had read in a New York newspaper of a diver who went down into the hull of a wrecked steamer and found the drowned corpses hideously swollen, upright in the water, their eyes out of their sockets and their lips hanging down; so horrible to see by the light of his lamp that his blood froze in his veins and he fled like a madman. The advocate could bear it no longer; he sprang up, dashed his fork into his plate and crying out, "Gentlemen, bethink yourselves!" made for the door. The captain, annoyed by this scene, spoke no more; and the dinner came to an end in silence. As we rose from the table the Genoese came with joyous visage and whispered in my ear, "At midnight!"

The burial had indeed been secretly fixed for midnight in order to prevent a throng of steerage passengers; and the commissary, moreover, had put it about among them that the ceremony would take place at four in the morning.

At midnight it was overcast again and there was a long narrow streak on the western horizon as if the huge dark cowl of the sky had not yet fully settled down upon the earth to make black night. The sea was of an inky hue, the air lifeless. But for a lantern or two on deck we should have had to grope our way as if we had been in the hold.

Moving towards the forward part of the ship, I heard in the darkness the voice of the Marsigliese holding forth in eager accents upon the poetry of being buried in the ocean and of being laid to sleep in that enormous solitude:—*J'aimerais ça, moi!* said he. Some passengers came out of the third class, all silent and glancing about them. In the covered way, I overtook the Neapolitan priest in cope and stole, walking with long, slow steps, and preceded by a sailor who bore the holy water in a dish.

When I reached the bow, I found a group assembled near the women's cabin. A lantern held by the humpbacked sailor lightened them from below. There was the captain and the commissary and several first-class passengers; farther on some sailors; a dozen or twenty emigrants were crouched down along the canteen, and one or two figures were dimly seen upon the forecastle. When the priest arrived, all moved so as to stand in semicircle, and on one side appeared the waxen face of the friar. At the same moment I heard a rustle near me and saw the young lady from Mestre with her aunt in the half-light under the bridge.

Supposing that they would, as usual, launch the body from the forecastle I was at

"On one side appeared the waxen face of the friar."

a loss to imagine why they all stopped there; but at a sign from the captain, two sailors opened the entering port in the bulwark, and I understood.

Meanwhile it seemed that the ship was moving more slowly, and in a few moments, to my surprise, she stopped altogether. I was not aware that the ship must not be in motion when the body is thrown over, lest it should be sucked under the screw.

Then all were silent, and I marked the red, sleepy face of the captain, somewhat annoyed, it seemed, at having to get up and take part in this ceremony. He kept his eyes fixed upon a long plank at his feet right in front of the entering port.

A voice was heard. All turned and saw three sailors come out of the steerage carrying a shapeless mass like a heap of bedclothes.

All made way, and they came forward as if to place their burden crosswise upon the plank.

The captain said in undertone, *Per drito! brüttoi*, "Longwise, you lubbers!"

They made the change, and softly arranged the body with the feet towards the sea. The huge bolts of iron, fastened to the heels, made a stern jar upon the deck.

The body was wrapped in a white sheet sewed like a sack and covering the head, then laid upon the mattress, which was doubled round it and bound about with a cord. The iron bolts protruded from the wrapping. The whole had the piteous look of a bundle of stuff tied together anyhow for a hasty move. The body seemed so shrunken and shortened that I could have believed it a boy. From a rent

in the sheet, at one end, stuck out a naked toe. The
hooked nose and the chin seen under the winding
sheet recalled the eager expression the poor man had
worn on my first visit to him in his berth when he
was fumbling for that address of his son. Perhaps
that son was at the moment asleep in some shanty
of his railroad and dreaming that he was soon to see
his poor old father. All kept their eyes upon that
face as if they expected to see it move. The silence
and quiet of all around was so profound that we
seemed the only living beings in the world.

"Now, your reverence," said the captain.

The priest, dipping his hand in the dish the sailor
was holding, sprinkled the body, and said the bene-
diction.

All uncovered; some of the third-class people
kneeled down. I looked round and saw the young
lady on her knees in the darkness, her hands over
her face.

The priest began to recite in a hurried manner: *De
profundis clamavi ad te, Domine; exaudi vocem meam.*

Many responded, "Amen."

The two lanterns held by the sailors cast a reddish
light upon still, sad faces, with infinite darkness for
a background. Amongst others I saw the Garibaldian, and I was pained to see his face as hard and
stern as ever; not the faintest ray of pity,—no more
than if a sack of ballast were being thrown overboard. Could it be possible, I thought, that that

saintly creature yonder had made no impression whatever upon him, and was I once more shamefully deceived in supposing there was a great soul in that man,—but not a heart!

The priest mumbled still more rapidly the remaining verses of the *De profundis*, and the *Oremus—Absolve*. Then he sprinkled the body once more with holy water. At the *Requiem æternam* all arose.

"Over," said the captain.

Two sailors took the plank by the ends, and softly raising it placed it on the sill of the entering port, so that about a quarter of the length projected over the water. As they raised it, I saw something move on the bosom of the corpse. It was the black cross which the young lady had been wearing.

The lanterns were held up.

The two sailors slowly raised the plank at the head, until the body began to slip downwards.

Then I heard within me those despairing words of the poor dying wretch, as if someone had cried out with an exceeding great cry that reached the shores of ocean : *Oh me fieul! Oh me pover fieul!*

The body slid off the plank and disappeared in the darkness with a hollow plunge. The sailors closed the port and dispersed like shadows. Before we reached the quarter-deck the ship was once more in motion, and we were already far away from the poor old man, as he pursued his solitary journey down through the gulfs of night.

CHAPTER XVI.

DEVIL DAY.

IF it be true that in the course of every long voyage there is a so-called "Devil Day," in which everything goes wrong and "the ship is made a hell of," I think the *Galileo* had her Devil Day on the morrow after the burial; at all events, three-quarters of it, for, by the blessing of Providence, it did not end as it began. There were reasons for trouble in the death which had taken place on board, the knowledge that for two days we had not been making good time, and the constant sight of a sea, ugly and vast, like a huge sheet of platinum, which reflected a vault of colored clouds and on which sheets of fire seemed to rain down, as on the blasphemers in Dante's *Inferno*. But even this was hardly enough to account for such a day as ours was; and I fear I must admit some kind of mysteri-

19

ous influence exerted by the Tropic of Capricorn, which we were to pass within twenty-four hours.

No sooner was I awake than I became aware that the moral atmosphere was charged with electricity. The Genoese stewardess had broken out in such a passion of jealous fury that she screamed and railed upon the false Ruy Blas in the open corridor, calling him a hundred times by a name that was not nice at all, with no more consideration than if she had been in a back slum of Turin. The agent threatened to send for the captain on the spot; and so succeeded, with some trouble, in stopping the flow of her abuse. I went out and found the captain himself given over to the furies; brandishing a document, questioning the commissary, and threatening to go in person *a piggiali a pé in to cu* the whole forty-seven of them. A letter, it seems, had been handed him a short time before, signed, after a fashion, by forty-seven steerage passengers, complaining of the food and demanding very particularly a "greater variety in the dressing of the meat-dishes," which was always the same, "and which," the paper writing went on to set forth, "should be discontinued " (*sic*). The protest was got up by that old Tuscan in the green jacket, and written out on a sheet of paper which betrayed an instinctive horror of the wash-hand basin on the part of all the signers. The captain was inconceivably exasperated by this nastiness; and, suspecting it to have been done on purpose, declared he would give

them a lesson they would remember. Meanwhile
he ordered an inquiry. The commissary reported,
moreover, that during the night some passenger
had, out of pure spite, snipped with scissors the
black silk dress of that poor lady already spoken
of ; and that this time the unhappy creature could
bear it no longer, but had run to demand justice,
sobbing, choked with grief and rage. How to find
out the guilty party was the problem. Nor was
this all. Some persons, not choosing to put their
mouths to the fresh-water spigot, as the custom was,
had smashed all the spigots of the tanks so as to
force the men to give them their drink in cans.
But the culprits were in a fair way of being discovered ; and the question was how to punish them.
A bad beginning.

I went on deck, and found there almost all the
passengers looking like people who had passed a
night of utter misery (*sui pettini di lino*),[1] and it was
easy to see that reciprocal aversion had risen to a
point where it was ready to pass the line which
separates contemptuous silence from open abuse.
They did not say " Good-morning," and they
brushed against one another without any apology.
The beast-tamer herself, she who had lived so many
days in a kind of effervescence of maternal love for
everybody, kept aloof as if all the Chartreuse of her
secret repository were dead within her. The Genoese

[1] " On tenter-hooks " is the parallel expression.

met me with a sour visage, and, fastening his single
eye upon me, said: "Sir, do you know what the
news is this morning? No ice! The machine has
broken down, and the man in charge has smashed
his hand. This is the second time! It is outrageous!" He was dreadfully put out, that is the fact.
He was moving off, but turned round and, eying
me askance, said with a sneer, "What do you think
of that fry they put upon the table last evening?"
and so departed. My friend of the next stateroom,
too, was leaning against the mizzen mast, more woe-
begone than usual, and with all the signs about him
of having passed the night on deck so as to get rid
of his tormentor below. Even the bride and groom,
sitting side by side on an iron bench, had a stolid
look, as if, for the first time, that Procrustean bed
on which they had been learning Spanish for a fortnight had been too much for them. The only ones
who smiled were the Argentine lady, in a charming
dark green dress, whose color was reflected, as by a
mirror, in the face of the piano player's mother; and
the young lady from Mestre, who went round with
a sweet, melancholy face and a paper in her hand to
collect some money for the poor fever-stricken peasant and his wife, so that they should not reach
America without clothes and shoes. And it was a
pity and a shame to see what scowling faces were
turned upon her, and with what scant courtesy the
greater part of them at last wrote down their names.

But few spoke, and those who did so made it plain
by their venomous glances that they were speaking
ill of somebody or something, as we are all apt to do
when our nerves are upset. Amongst others, I heard
the mill-owner, who audibly thought it was "rather
strange that in a steamer like ours a man was per-
mitted to come up on deck in slippers"; and he
glanced at the Neapolitan priest, who certainly was
shuffling about in a regular pair of barges, and so
could come up close behind one unperceived—a
thing which not everybody was disposed to take altogether kindly. The impudence of this renegade
grinder of corn disgusted me; I turned my back on
the whole tedious set of them, and went forward for
a while.

But here it was worse still. The closeness and
the foul air had driven everybody on deck, and I
never had seen so many people there. It was one
dense crowd from the kitchen right forward,—all
uneasy, as if expecting something, all tousled
and frowsy, as if they had not been to bed for
several nights. It was easy to perceive that they
had had more than enough of the sea, the kitchen,
and the ship rules, and were ready to break out at
the merest nothing. Nobody played cards; no one
sang. Even the light-hearted group of the midship-
deck was mute; the noseless peasant was asleep; the
encyclopædic cook paced up and down alone; the
album of the ex-porter was unread; the Venetian

barber only raised from time to time his moon-baying howl, as if to express in those doleful strains the general sentiment of the company. And the emigrants crowding toward the stern looked at the doors of the saloon and at the first-class passengers with a fiercer eye than usual, as if they would have liked to offer something more than insolence;—for why did we take up so much of the ship,—why should we, a hundred or so, occupy nearly as much room as they, a people? Did n't we eat up all those nice dishes that they saw carried across the piazzetta twice a day, and of which they got nothing but the smell. Did n't we have servants in black to do all this running about for us, while they had to rinse their pots and pans at the deck trough, and wait for their food at the kitchen door like beggars. Why should this be?

And they were not so much to blame, after all. We should have looked with equal—perhaps with greater—jealousy upon a superior first class of millionaires, gorged with quail on toast, and tipsy with Johannisberger. They were tired to death of this long-enforced contact with careless ease; of feeling themselves crammed up with their own wretchedness in that huge pen full of rags and evil smells. And as they could not fall foul of us they fell foul of each other. As early as eight o'clock the two peasants who were jealous about the negress had come to blows; and the captain had sent them both

to the lock-up under the bridge, forcing them to
stand up face to face with their noses touching; but as
they could not keep their hands off one another so, they
were confined separately.   And then the Bolognese,
offended at a rude remark on the part of the ship's
baker, had given him a slap, one of those with a capital S—and was duly had up by the commissary.
As always happens, moreover, example being conta-
gious, there had been other difficulties and several
women had scratched faces and torn hair.   Then the
boys began,—fighting and tumbling about the deck
eight or ten in a pile, while the parents ran to separate them, showered down blows and kicks unheeding
where they fell, and heaped abuse on one another.
The general irritation had penetrated the kitchen,
where, owing to competition in contraband traffic, a
fiery interchange of choice expressions was going on
between the cook and his assistants, accompanied
with a terrific clatter of saucepans.

For us in the after-cabin things went wrong from
the first.   The breakfast was bad, and it was not im-
proved by our silence, or by the truly tragical frown
of the captain, who had on his mind an affair—not
the one of the forty-seven, but a really serious matter.   An hour before, the mother of the piano player
had accosted him with much dignity, brandishing a
protest in due form against the nocturnal meander-
ings of the Swiss lady, who, at all sorts of impossible
hours, passed her stateroom in the lightest possible

costume, to the great scandal of her daughter; but
this was better than many other things that she did.
The whole poop-deck was talking about it, it could
not go on, something must be done. The captain,
touched on his weak point, had breathed out flame
and fury, had promised, on his oath (*in so zuamento*),
to say a soft word in the ear of that old horned-owl
of a professor; and even to the lady, if need were,
and to some others too;—and what did they take
his ship for,—and people must behave themselves,
perdy, if he had to put sentries in the corridors;
and he ended solemnly with his never-failing speech,
Porcaie a bordo no ne veuggio. There was to be a
scene, evidently. All through the breakfast he
darted Torquemada glances at the blonde lady,
while others also looked and whispered;—but she
was unconscious,—wholly. Squeezed into a dove-
colored dress, fresher and more sprightly than ever,
she chirped and warbled in her husband's ear, smil·
ing on all her friends with those sweet, thoughtless
eyes,—just like the windows of an empty room,—
and showing off in a hundred ways her white teeth,
her little hands, her rounded arms, her amiable soul.
After the meal, she began walking the deck once
more, every now and then disappearing suddenly
and reappearing unexpectedly, unconscious—poor
creature—of the sword of Damocles that was hang·
ing over her blonde tresses; in fact all the more gay
and lively as the weariness around her grew greater,

and, like an ardent heroine who cheered the belea-
guered defenders as they fainted at their task, seemed
with her eyes to say that she did all she could for
suffering humanity, and it was not her fault that she
could do no more.

But about three o'clock she went below and was
seen no more; and when this one joyous face was
gone, gloom settled down upon the deck more blight-
ingly than ever.

The advocate helped us along a little by a comical
adventure that befell him. Overcoming his instinctive repugnance to salt water, he had gone to have
a bath; and, stepping into the tub, had let it run
full of water up to his breast; but putting out
his hand to turn the spigot, it did not work, or
he turned it the wrong way, or broke it, or something; at all events he let on the stream harder
than ever,—a perfect spout of water that flooded
him in a moment, soaked all his clothes, and inun-
dated the room. We saw him fly across the piazzetta, shouting to the stewards to go and shut the
deluge off before the ship filled and went down. But
only five or six passengers had strength enough left
to smile at this gleam of fun. The heat grew greater,
the foul smells from the steerage waxed pestiferous,
and the greater part of us dragged our worn-out
bodies from the deck to the saloon, where we sank
down at the tables, or round about on the sofas.
Oh, what a tiresome set! I knew every movement

of theirs, every gesture they would make, the tone of
every yawn, the books which they had for a fortnight been pretending to read.   It was like the
hundredth time at a puppet show.   It was not weariness, it was utter prostration of soul.   Nothing to
be seen but long faces, heads leaned upon hands,
eyes filmy and motionless.   The pianist played some
funeral march or other.   The Brazilian respectfully
begged her to desist, as his wife was in her berth
suffering horribly with nerves.   The girl closed the
piano with a bang, and went away.   The agent said
the plump lady was sobbing in her berth; why, he
did not know.   The Tropic of Capricorn, he supposed.   One young lady of the family in mourning
was weeping.   A sharp discussion arose between
the Marsigliese and one of the Argentines, the latter
observing, and correctly, that from the Observatory
of Marseilles only two of the stars of the Centaur
could be seen, the head and the shoulders; while the
other maintained that they were all visible.   *Toutes
les sept, Monsieur, toutes les sept!*—"But that is
absurd!"   *Mais, Monsieur, vous avez une façon. . . .*
The captain, coming in and looking around with a
ferocious glance for some one, cut this contention
short, and the silence of the tomb settled down upon
the cabin.

I could bear it no longer and went out to go up
on the bridge.   But I had not yet reached the end
of the covered way when I heard a cry of terror and

saw a crowd of people rush to the foot of one of the
deck-ladders. A child that had clambered to the
topmost step had rolled down, striking its head on
the deck.   The mother, supposing it dead, had seized
it in a frenzy, and, clasping it in her arms, began to
cry out like a madwoman, *Me lo jettano ammare!
U peccirillo mio! A criatura mia!* " Ah ! my poor
little darling, they 'll throw it into the sea ! " and
with frantic gesture gnashed her teeth, drove back
the throng, and defended, as it were, the little body.
The doctor came and took both mother and infant
to the sick bay.   This accident raised a great cry
against the ship, which " was full of danger everywhere," and against the captain for not posting
guards at the ladders.   The old fellow in the green
jacket began to declaim most furiously, his forefinger
up and his gray locks bare.   But there had been
trouble just before this.   The poor little bookkeeper,
whose credit was raised among those forward by his
kissing escapade, which was looked upon by them
with complacency as " a flout for the princess," had
been besieged for a couple of days with mocking
congratulations, as if the thing had really gone much
farther.   He took it seriously, denying everything
with fury.   At last, however, on receiving a congra-
tulation more brutal than the rest, his blood boiled
and he began to strike and kick, right and left,
like a maniac; but to no purpose, poor creature, for
four or five got round him and held him while others

drove his hat down over his eyes, and the best he
could do was to escape with a scratched countenance
into the cabin.

I looked for the Genoese girl. She was in her
usual place, at work, as calm and fair as ever, but
with a sparkle of anger in her eye, for she divined
the foul insolence of the talk around her, and understood what hatred there was in the looks she saw.
Her father had been keeping guard over her for two
days, ready and anxious to break someone's head.
But everyone's fingers were itching, for that matter.
Every half-hour there was a crowd around a couple
of quarrelling passengers. If an officer were by to
prevent their coming to blows, they defied one
another in due form. " On the forecastle ? "—" Yes,
on the forecastle ! "—" After dark this evening ? "—
" Yes, after dark this evening ! " The forecastle was
the fenced field always chosen by these doughty
champions. Three or four times, moreover, for no
conceivable reason, first two, then three, then half a
dozen had fallen by the ears, causing a surge and a
rush in the whole crowd ; while men and officers ran
up to quell the tumult. Two drunken fellows, quarrelsome in their cups, had flown at one another's
throats like wild beasts, and, falling over the cogs
of the donkey engine, had got damaged ribs, both of
them. This time the captain came up, raging, with
the evident intention of keeping his hand in by giving both some *mascá* that they should remember the

longest day they had to live. But he was too late.
Things had got to such a pass that I half expected
to see, before evening, all that crowd grapple with
and get piled on top of one another in a formless
heap of heads and limbs, like one of Doré's battles,
and then topple over the bulwarks into the sea.
But instead of aversion I felt nothing but compassion for these poor people and their trouble,—a kind
of sad yearning over them; for beneath the truculent
looks of all these faces I seemed to perceive an
abandonment, for some dreadful hours, of all hope,
an utter weariness of life, a secret grief that broke
out in anger. It was clear that they were suffering,
and that they had an infinite pity, each for the other,
and for himself. Those poor old peasants on the
forecastle, man and wife, were the living image of
this state of mind, for even then they were sitting
there, as usual, on the bitts, their arms upon their
knees, and their heads upon their arms, in utter
abandonment; while their poor bare, wrinkled necks
told of fifty years of unrequited toil. As I looked
at them, a pregnant woman fainted upon the glazed
and grated cover of the companion-way, her white
face falling amidst the outstretched arms of the
women near her. There was a cry from a hundred
voices, "She is dead, she is dead!"—and I came
away.

Where should I go! It would not be night for six
endless hours. I went back to the saloon and began

turning over the ship's album. But it was full of
commonplaces, of nonsense, and of lies. As a last
resource I went to my stateroom and tried to sleep.
But the room was smaller, more confined, more choking, more detestable than ever I had known it. The
passengers seemed all to have retired like myself,
but not a sound was heard, as if those hundred
rooms contained nothing but corpses. Not a sound
save the doleful ditty of the negress, like a solitary
chant in a street of the city of the dead. And I
seemed weighed down, not by my own weariness
only, but by all the tormenting dulness, the bitter
memories, the bruised affections, and the sad forebodings crowded together above there on deck,
among those sixteen hundred children of Italy who
were going to seek a new mother beyond the sea. It
was useless to reason with myself, to analyze my
state of mind, and try to be persuaded that there
was no good reason why, on that day, I should feel,
like the rest, a horror of great darkness, while on
other days, unlike the rest, I found all bright and
smiling. My sombre thoughts, kept for a few
moments at bay, came rushing back the instant I
slackened in my effort to repel them and overflowed
the inmost recesses of my soul. I do not know how long
I was a prey to these imaginings, but at last I fell
asleep, and dreamed a horrible dream. I was in my
own house, and it was night; it was a confusion of
lights and of faces that I did not know; someone

with the death-rattle on him, in some room of which
I could not find the door;—then, in a flash, a change
of scene, a fearful cry of "Save yourselves!"—and
all the mad disorder of a foundering ship.

At this moment there was a great noise and I
awoke. I don't know whether I had slept three
hours or five minutes. A ray of light gleamed in
the stateroom. The noise above increased. There
were voices of people calling one another by name,
there was a sound of hurrying feet and of confusion
as at a sudden cry of danger. I sprang out of my
stateroom, while from all the others the inmates came
running, and hastened up on deck, where was already
a crowd of people. Looking forward, I perceived
that every living thing from every hole and corner
of the ship had come out into the light, the ship was
black from stem to stern with people, and everyone
rushed to the starboard side, clambering on the bulwarks, the cattle pens, the benches, the shrouds, and
looking out over the sea. I saw nothing; a rampart
of backs concealed the horizon. I questioned two
passers by; they rushed on and took no notice. Then
I went up on the bridge. Ah! blessed sight! What
a lovely thing I saw! A huge black smoking steamer,
covered with flags and crowded with people, was
coming majestically toward us under the clear sky,
her high bows cleaving the blue sea, her sails swelling, all festive, all gilded with the sun like some
wonder-creature that had started out of the bosom

of the ocean. It was the *Dante* of the same line, coming from the Plata River, bound for Italy, and full of emigrants returning to their own country. It was the first large steamer we had met since coming out of the Straits, and it was a sister ship. At every puff from her huge bestarred funnels she grew larger, and the thousand forms that covered her stood out more and more distinctly. The two throngs of men each crowded forward and looked at one another, in silence,—but all trembling. The *Dante* came so close that an unexpected surge made us roll violently. When she was at her nearest and showing us the whole length of her magnificent side, there was a frantic waving of hats and handkerchiefs; and a great shout, long suppressed, broke out at once from the two crowds,—a long-drawn cry of good wishes and of adieux in strangest accents, different from any cry I had ever heard coming from a throng of men; an outburst of loud quivering voices in which the sorrows of the voyage, the yearning for home, the glad expectation of seeing it again, the hope of one day beholding it once more, and kindly joy at meeting brothers and hearing the voice of Italy away out there upon the Atlantic were confusedly mingled. But only for an instant. In a few moments the *Dante* was but a black spot upon the blue, hardly roughened at the edges by the thousand heads of her crowding passengers. But that rapid vision had changed everything on board the *Galileo*,

"The two throngs of men each crowded forward."

had reawakened hope and courage, had aroused the song and the laugh, had brought us all back once more to kindly feeling and to life.

"Signore!" I heard a voice say, near me. I turned. It was the young lady from Mestre, who touched the Garibaldian with her fan. He turned towards her, and the girl, with a face illumined by a flash from her inner soul, pointed to the vanishing ship, and said, in her sweet voice, "Our country."

CHAPTER XVII

HE next morning all met on deck with the same cheerful greeting: "Three days more! Almost run out (*Siamo agli sgoccioli*)! Day after to-morrow!" Strange enough. This unusual kindness among the passengers arose in great measure from the thought that they were, before long, to get shut of one another for good and all. The weather was fine, the air soft. The forecastle was like a village on a holiday. On the way thither I met the old hunchbacked sailor with a pair of shoes in his hand and deep thought on his countenance. He stopped and said, softly, *E donne, l'è brutto quando cianzan, ma l'è pezo quando rian.*—"These women! It's bad when they cry, but it's worse when they laugh." And he explained me his idea, which was founded upon experience. Whenever there was, namely, as yesterday, great cheerfulness on board, there almost

always followed that evening, or night, some dire-
ful trouble—for him, that is to say, and naturally
enough.   The night before, for example, "there was
such a time *lasciù*, down there."   "Great doings,
hey?" I asked him.   He rolled up his eyes, then
said, rather sharply, "*Son stüffo de fa o ruffian*," and
so moved off as he saw the agent coming.   This
gentleman, also, was very thoughtful, tormented by
two mysteries which he could not penetrate; one
already set forth, namely, who it was that that
dried-up little bit of a piano player was sighing
after, for he caught her leering all the time, and
never could see at whom, "like making love with
a spirit, you know"; the other was that he had not
marked the slightest sign on anyone's face of the
"scene" with which the captain had threatened the
Swiss lady.   Comical enough it was to find this
white-haired old fellow seriously occupied with
trifles like these, just as a minister of state might be
with the threads of a conspiracy.   Yet they say that
the sea enlarges the thoughts.   But then, he went
on, the captain knew what he was about, was not a
man to threaten to no purpose in such a matter as
that.   Who could have charmed away the tempest?
Oh! he would rack his brains and find out all about
it if he had to stand on watch three days and three
nights, like a tiger hunter.

The happy mood of the passengers favored his in-
vestigations.   Shortly after nine nearly all were out

on deck; and the groups and their movements are
stamped on my memory like those seen in the family
circle just before some domestic crisis. The Argentines were gathered around the wheel; the Marsigliese lounged chatting before the Porteña lady,
who listened to him with a fine equivocal woman's
smile of blended mockery and courtesy. The Brazilian family, in its usual place, rolled its twelve
slow eyes around as if it saw all present for the first
time; and at the mother's feet the negress was curled
up like a dog. By the mast stood our "thief," our
"scape-gallows," and the "Director of the Society for
no-more-bad-smelling-cesspools." They had been
several days in each other's company without saying
a word, like so many deaf-mutes. The advocate was
dozing on a deck chair with a book upon his stomach. The blonde lady was sitting chirping between
the tenor and the Peruvian, whose knee was covered by her spreading skirt, and on the settee farthest off was the young lady from Mestre, paler than
usual, save for her cheek bones, which were burning.
She talked with feverish eagerness, but with a smile
of inexpressible sweetness, to the Garibaldian, who
sat near, his powerful face bent like a thoughtful
man listening to music that brings back memories
but no illusions. The rest were promenading with
the brisk irregular pace of cheerful creatures.

The horizon was veiled with a light cloud, and
there was a kind of heaviness in the air that made

one feel from time to time the need of drawing a long breath. But the heat was mild compared with that of several days past. The Argentines declared they smelled the *aires* of their own country. We were in the latitude of Santa Caterina, on the coast of Brazil—there or thereabouts.

A moment more, and the Genoese came on deck, rubbing his hands, and remarking as he passed, "The barometer is falling."

The fact is, he longed even for a hurricane, so only he might get rid of the deadly dulness that was preying upon his mind. But was he a bird of ill omen, after all? The mercury had fallen all of a sudden before this, and the billows had not raged. We say of the people, as of the ocean, that when it is calm one wonders how it can be otherwise; when we see it in a fury the marvel is how it can ever quiet down again. But now the veil of the horizon was growing thicker and higher, a huge mass of grayish vapor stood ready to obscure the sun; the ruffled sea was of a dull, leaden hue. And yet I was so far from expecting bad weather that I amused myself with watching the advocate. He sat up very straight, and cast around upon the great enemy a slow glance of increasing disquietude, looking also from time to time at the captain's stateroom and the bridge beyond. A screaming of birds made me look up. Gulls circling around the mast. A bad sign. And more impressive than all was to see a weird-

looking cloud appear suddenly upon the horizon,
thick, black, edged with white from the pale sun;
and, rapidly rising, cast a dark shadow on the already boiling ocean.   It was almost cold.

The passengers were already, all of them, aware
of the change.   The readers had closed their books,
had risen, and were studying the horizon with that
look which we fix upon the face of a person we do
not know and who comes, as we surmise, to discuss
an important matter.   A flash of lightning and a far-
off growl of thunder, followed by a sudden rolling
of the ship, provoked an exclamation or two—" Now
then!   What's this?   It looks squally."   The ladies
glanced at the captain, the advocate had already disappeared.   Others also retired, English fashion.   This
was enough to cause in the rest an extraordinary
flow of spirits.   They swaggered in the face of old
ocean, like so many gallant admirals, looking the
while at the ladies out of the corner of an eye.   The
Marsigliese passed from group to group, saying joyously : " *Ça se brouille, ça se brouille.   Nous allons
voir un joli spectacle!* "   And in fact we were not
to be kept waiting for the play.   The heavy cloud
was nearly down upon us, others came swiftly on,
and certain long, thin streaks of vapor swept so
closely over us as almost to touch the spars.   The
wind was rising, the sea was getting up, the steamer
was more uneasy than we had ever known her to be
before.   We had to cling to the bulwarks and the

seats. Still there were some who would not believe
we were to have a storm. "It's only a squall," they
said; but those who had made the passage before
shook their heads and looked knowing.

I perfectly remember that, watching myself more
carefully than I did the others, I awaited with a certain psychological interest and curiosity the moment
when the feeling which we are all ashamed to confess should come over me; and I flattered myself
that I should be able to mark its slow advance. I
did not know that it was to spring upon me all of a
sudden; at that moment, namely, when the instinct
of self-preservation should be thrown into the bal-
ance and the scale of curiosity kick the beam. In
short, while yet on shore, I had often desired to try
what a storm at sea was like, and lo! a happy chance
for the artist to record. But as I looked at the piazzetta and saw officers, engineers, sailors, and stewards
throng around the shouting and gesticulating captain and then scatter in every direction to double
lash the boats, to nail up the pigpens, to batten down
the hatches, to secure the air-ports; plunging with
furious haste through the crowds that were rushing
for shelter from the spray; then, if you must know,
I looked for the artist within me and found him
not. In fact he seemed to have been gone about
a quarter of an hour.

The lightning flashed faster, the thunder growled
more loudly, the oxen bellowed. I looked about

me upon faces already pale. But in some curiosity, in others dislike to be shut up in their staterooms still prevailed. The ladies clung to their husbands' arms. The men looked at one another with doubtful glance, each gathering pride and courage from seeing the rest look more pale and wretched than he supposed himself to be. Suddenly a shower of spray on deck, a suppressed *Nom de Dieu!* and a forced laugh. The Marsigliese had lost his hat, and was sluiced from head to foot. At the same moment four sailors came running up to carry off the benches and the chairs. Then the commissary: "Go below, all of you! We are going to batten. Quick, if you please!" Then was heard a wail from the bottom of a soul, "O my God! my God!" It was the young bride. Try to imagine the deep echo in everyone's nature of that first cry, that irrepressible confession of the fear of death, that violently unmasks a state of mind which everyone has been disguising from others and from himself. Then ensued a disorderly and precipitate flight through the sheets of spray that dashed across the deck, a confusion of excited and discordant voices: *O Pablos, Pablos!*—Quick, if you please!—Blessed Virgin, our time has come!— My God!—*Accidémpoli!* [1]—Courage, Nina!—Good God! *will* you make haste there! I had but time to see the masts sweep in enormous arcs across the sky

[1] *Accidémpoli*, wholly untranslatable. "Damnation!" suggests the same idea—the result of dying without absolution.

and to mark a frightful jostling of people at the companion-way of the third-class when I was violently hurled into the saloon. A lady stumbled and fell across the entrance. I had a glimpse of the commissary on the quarter-deck, wrapped, as it were, in a sheet of water, and I heard the far-off neighing of a horse. Then we were shut in. A flash of lightning, an instant and terrific roar of thunder; and, as a frightful lurch of the vessel dashed us to the deck and against the sides, the last doubt which anyone could possibly have entertained was dispelled at once. It was a full-grown hurricane.

The greater part, grasping the firmly fastened dining-tables and staggering as if half-stunned, made for their staterooms. Some threw themselves on the sofas. The ladies wept. The noises of the ship drowned all voices. It seemed to be nearly night. Persons, places, everything, appeared changed; for at such a moment, when all disguise drops off and the human animal is left bare, prostrate, wholly swayed by furious love of life, the countenance is drawn, the voice is strange, and look and gesture reveal traits of character before undreamed of. In the half-light of the corridors, where all were falling over one another as they groped each for his own stateroom, I caught sight of faces that were agonized,—distorted almost beyond recognition, as of men condemned to die. As I turned into my own lair, the retchings of the sea-sick began to be heard, lamentable voices called for the stewards, the doors slammed loudly, trunks and boxes, breaking away, were hurled against the bulkheads. It was the hurly-burly of strange cries and dismal sounds one hears on going into a madhouse, where life and its ways are all confounded. A sudden lurch tossed me into the stateroom like a gripsack, a flash of lightning dazzled me; the door swung to. I was in an immense and hideous solitude as if shut up by my own hand in my own living tomb; and a sudden thought froze my blood: What if I should never get out of this place again?

Yes! there is the truth, told honestly. This one thought, stern, cold, sharp, immovable, fastened on my soul with its hooks of steel; the idea, a hundred times repelled and a hundred times rushing back upon me, of the noise the water would make when it broke in, of how many seconds it would take to reach my door, of the sudden darkness, of the choking, of the drowning. . . . And then the besetting, horrid fear that my suffering might be prolonged. Confusedly I tried to recall what I had heard and read to confirm me in the hope of a short agony. And well do I remember that the idea of having desired, from mere curiosity, to try what a hurricane was like, seemed senseless, incredible, unnatural, monstrous. "Fool!" I thought, "you wished for this, did you?—and now you have it."

But these phantasmal shapes were all routed, as it were, by the vigorous bodily efforts I was forced to make, as, falling on my knees upon the floor, I clung with might and main to the side of the berth; the only way to prevent my being dashed about as the rat is shaken in the trap. My brain, too, was stunned by the uproar in the saloon above, where the glass of the sideboards was being smashed to pieces and piles of plates hurled in fragments to the floor; while the piano, breaking from its fastenings, was thundering to and fro among the stanchions of the deck. But worse than all this tumult as of a sacked and plundered palace, worse than human groans or the uplifted voice of the raging sea, was the noise of our laboring ship,—a dread shrieking, a concert of pound, and crack, and crash, as if a house were being torn from its foundations; a dire lament as if the mighty giant suffered and cried out as thrills of terror and of anguish sped through the wrenched joints of his living body. Vain to try and gather courage from statistics, and what not—one wreck to a thousand voyages, or whatever it may have been. Useless to recall the firm structure of these ships that could set at nought the fury of the sea. That ceaseless dirge scattered all statistics to the winds, and laughed to scorn all consolation. Meanwhile, the sea rose higher, the rain came down in cataracts, the lightning flashed fast and faster, the thunder roared almost incessantly, and the ship gave such bounds that when my eyes were closed I seemed to be upon a gigantic swing with a sweep of half a mile. I lost my breath with every rush, and caught it as best I might between the whiles. And thus to be at the mercy of a prodigious power which left me free neither to move nor think brought on an inexpressible sense of physical dread, as if I were a beast bound fast and whirled in mid-air at the end of a stupendous well-sweep. And then, to think this torment might last ten hours, a day, three days, confused the soul like trying to grasp the infinite.

Up to a certain point I kept my mind clear enough to remember what my thoughts were; but after two or three hours, as I conjecture it, the fury of the storm increasing beyond all measure, my brain was stunned, and I can tell but little of what was passing in my mind. I remember the tremendous tones of the sea, more strange and frightful than any imagination can conceive, a voice as of all human creation crowded together, mad and shrieking; with this the yells and howls of all the beasts of earth, the crash of toppling cities, the hurrah of countless armies,—whole peoples bursting into savage, mocking laughter; then the whistling of the gale among the rigging, a long, sonorous, most discordant wail, as if every rope were a demon's harpstring; maddened screams of terror and despair, as of captives in a flaming prison-house; heart-chilling hisses, as if a thousand furious serpents were twining about the masts. The ship rolled and pitched and lurched as if she would overset; at every surge that struck her

she would quiver from deck to keel as if she had
run upon a rock, while plank and timber groaned
and cracked again, and the senses thrilled as at the
graze of a falling axe or the wind of a ball that cuts
the hair away. At every plunge it was as if the
stroke of a vast and monstrous paw had torn a piece
out of the ship. Thud after thud there came as a
hundred tons of water ruined down upon the deck
like a cataract from on high, and then the rush of a
hundred streams from side to side, like so many
hordes of vengeful pirates. What the ship would
do next I could not tell at all. She was a helpless
creature, cuffed and kicked; she was a ball thrown
one way and struck another by a resistless Titan's
hand. The engine had its pauses, as if stricken with
paralysis; the shaft would bang and struggle; the
screw, hove out of water, would race madly for an
instant, and then plunge down again with a blow
that shook the vessel like an earthquake. And, in
the pauses of the greater uproar, were heard, above,
the rushing of eager feet, the whirr of the electric
bell, weird cries and shouts that sounded strange as
echoes from a snow-filled valley, wails from the
staterooms, retchings choked, strangled, agonized, as
if all within were coming up. Then, suddenly there
came an upward blow so violent that the water jug
flew out of the rack, and was dashed to pieces against
the deck above; whereon began a still more fiendish
orgie of the unchained elements, the ship gave leap

after leap, and I was as if hurled from peak to peak
across a measureless abyss. Every plunge seemed
as if it would be the last. Again and again I said,
"It is all over!" I could not believe but that the
deck was split open above my head, the floor bursting up beneath my feet, the ship's great ribs twisted,
her knees torn from their fastenings, her keel snapped
short across, her bolts and nails drawn shrieking out,
her whole frame dismembered. "What, not yet?
The next time then—she'll never stand another!"
Then came a chaos of ideas, memories of old times
and things of yesterday, a giddy whirl of faces and
of places, all confused and distorted as by a fever of
the brain, and all aglow with livid light; a fierce,
disordered stream of sighs, of weeping and lament, of
prayers without any words, of caresses, and of remorse,—and all this swept back and forth as by the
breath of the dreadful wind outside.

From time to time a stupor, a lull in the thoughts
like that produced by chloroform; a short relief, and
then again, more frightful than before, the grim
reality as if two tremendous hands had shaken me
by the shoulders, and a terrible voice had shouted
in my ear: "It's you! It's you, and no one else!
Here you are, and you must die!" Alas! how vain
the thought that comes in tranquil moments, that it
is all one how we pass away! Oh, to die with a bul-
let in my heart! Oh, to die upon my bed with dear
ones around me, and loving friends to care for me!

Oh, to be laid in my little bit of earth, and have my children come and say above me, " Here he lies " ! At times these thoughts would cease, and it seemed for a moment as if the fury of the tempest were re- laxing, but another surge would come, and a giddy whirl of the screw, as the vessel's stern sprang out of water, swept the flattering unction from my soul. I remember, too, an invincible horror of looking at the sea, a shuddering aversion like that of the victim for his assassin, as if in that dread hour I could per- ceive a live ferocity, a hatred of man in the sweep of the crested billows, and see hideous faces grinning horribly at me through the glass of the air port. I could not look; I turned my eyes away at the first glimpse of those Cyclopean walls, those black, rolling, thundering mountains, as they fell and dashed each other into spray ; and as the volleyed lightning streaked with fire those threatening heaps of murky cloud, it was a light that seemed to be neither night nor day—not a gleam of earth but the glare of a dream landscape where our own sun is not. All sense of time was lost. I could not tell how long the storm had lasted, or guess how many hours it would endure. It seemed as if it must last for- ever, for I could not conceive what there might be that should put an end to so tremendous a convul- sion. Impossible I thought that the gulfs of night below were not stirred up. Impossible to believe that certain fathoms down in the great deep there

was tranquil water; that on the dry land there were
peaceful people and there was quiet business. A
lull; an instant's respite, as I thus reflected, and
then another roller dashed its surge against her side
with a shock as of a cannon-ball; the ship bounded
like a harpooned whale, her timbers groaned, her
planks creaked, her bolts and nails shrieked once
more, and a fresh sense came over me of my hideous
peril, of death standing in the very doorway. This
is the last of earth, I thought; and the anguish of a
year was crowded into a moment. How long, O,
Lord, how long?

It was many hours, seven or eight it may have
been, when my ever-passing, still-recurring idea that
the gale was blowing itself out seemed to stay longer
as it came back; it changed into a hope that the
soul hardly dared cherish, but which the senses
gradually confirmed. The ship still rolled and
dashed with fury, but that hateful, angry howling in
the rigging seemed quieted a little, and the beating
of the sea, if not less fierce, yet certainly less frequent. It was a good sign that I felt how bruised
and tired my body was with those acrobatic feats to
which I had been forced for so many hours. Until
now I had noticed nothing of the kind. And I had
a little curiosity as to what was going on around
me. Through the groaning of the timbers and the
roaring of the sea I heard the wails of the Brazilian
baby, and childlike sobs and cries that must have

come from women. Feeble voices called out here
and there for the stewards. Bells jingled. Trunks
and boxes still went raging up and down the corridors like so many wild beasts broken loose. But,
choosing well my time, so as not to break my head
against the wall, I made a dart and seized the jamb
of the doorway to look out. I saw certain human
forms with wild hair and clothes in disorder dragging
themselves about and staggering like drunken men.

Among these was the Marsigliese with all the
marks in his face of a deadly fright which was passing off but would not leave him altogether. And
in fact a new lurch of the ship from time to time,
and a fresh cracking of her poor strained ribs, drove
me back to hold on with both hands to my berth as
if the fiendish dance were to go on with more fury
than ever. Between one recrudescence and another,
I strained my ears to hear whether in the next stateroom the anguish of a common danger had not slackened somewhat the high-strung cords of hatred. I
was amazed to catch sounds as of a reconciliation,
but soon changed my mind as an evil voice hissed
out distinctly, " Ah ! you hoped it was all over, did
you ? " There was no reply. The first note of real
encouragement was a general laugh from the direction of the Argentines. From the door opposite I
heard the voice of the tenor attempting a shake.
The sound was cut short by a dull thump that
seemed uncommonly like a collision between a hu-

man head and the side of the ship. Then for a
space I heard no more voices. The groaning of the
ship and the roar of the sea were still enough to
stun the senses, and the rolling fit to break four legs,
not to say two. But it was possible to get out.
Swinging myself from one support to another, and
calculating every step, I managed to reach where the
corridors crossed. What a sight ! The doors of the
staterooms were slamming to and fro, and one could
mark an indescribable raffle of trunks and pillows
and clothes and boots ; heads dangling over basins ;
bodies lying as if dead ; garments in disorder ; jugs
and pitchers rolling about the floor. Still the motion was less violent, so I moved on and met the
Genoese, who with bandaged head was bumping
along the wall and using exceedingly bad language.
" What is the matter ? " I asked. He swore, but
proceeded to explain. Perishing with hunger, he
had crawled down to the pantry for a bit of ham, a
biscuit, or something, and a roll of the ship had
flung him against the sideboard, cutting his forehead
open. Then came a clear voice from the stateroom
of the Argentines :

> Hijo audaz de la llanura
> Y guardian de nuestro cielo . . .

The rogues were hymning the *pampero* to which
they owed those eight hours in the jaws of death.

But the gale had blown itself out, though there
was still a high sea running. Haggard faces looked

out of the doorways with inquiring air and quickly drew back. A voice which I took for that of the first officer called from the head of the stairs, " It 's over, good people ! " And answering exclamations from the staterooms : " Thank God ! thank God ! Oh ! can it be true ? *Laudate Dominum!* We 're well out of that ! " But a thrill of life ran through the place as in a cemetery where the buried dead begin to rub their eyes and stretch their limbs. Someone touched me on the shoulder. It was the agent, in a dressing-gown, a bruise upon his chin, but joyous. " Ah ! what a scene ! " he said ; " I heard it all." He was speaking of the bride and bridegroom. In the midst of the peril they had fallen to praying, he said, then they had exchanged farewells, sobbing ; he had begged her to forgive him for having brought her on that voyage ; then a last kiss—a good many last kisses, in fact. " *Ah! Nina mia !* " " *Ah! moe poveo Géumo.*" And more last kisses, you know, but no Spanish grammar. So saying, he disappeared, but straightway returned, devious, and beckoned me to come quickly, for there was something worth see· ing. I followed him as best I might. He stopped before the open door of the advocate's stateroom, and, bursting with laughter, bade me look in. Such a creature was never seen ! I hardly recognized hu· manity in the formless thing that I saw stretched upon the floor, and from which came such wailings as Ernesto Rossi utters when, in his part of Louis

XI., he is struck down by Nemours. It was the advocate, flat on his face. Dressed in some English or American life-preserving garment or other, stuffed with cork, he had a hump on his back and a hump on his breast covered with a cuirass of stout cotton-cloth, and round his chest there was a string of inflated bladders that made him look like some strange mammal which, with much swollen glands, had fallen senseless to the earth. This outrageous load of ridicule awakened an infinite compassion for the poor crushed and unhappy man. The agent bent over him to try and bring him to his senses, and I left him to his pious task.

With difficulty I reached the saloon, where there were already many passengers, the Marsigliese, the Tuscan, the mill-owner, the French commercial traveller, the tall priest, and others. Not one lady. The lightning still flashed from time to time, but the thunder was infrequent and far off. The sea was high and black, and no one could keep his feet. Strange nature of man! It was already plain to be seen from the bearing of these people that the very tempest was a thing agreeable to their self-love, as if their not going to the bottom had somehow been the effect of every man's own conduct, and that they were having even then a foretaste of the pride with which in after years they would tell how they had fearlessly faced that dreadful peril. Amazing to see the coolness with which more than one whom I had

seen as pale as the dying put on the look of courage
before those to whom he had exhibited not long before the most evident signs of abject terror.   Some
would pace back and forth
from table to table, showing off their sea legs as
it were, and laughing
at every remark
with lips
that
were
still
bloodless.
The Mar-
sigliese re-
m a r k e d :
"*Je me suis
enormément am-
usé.*" The mill-owner
pretended to read the cabin
album !   Meanwhile the
stewards brought the news
from on deck.   The sea had
carried away some boats, had damaged the turkey
coops a good deal, had drowned two bullocks, and
stove in a deadeye forward.   A sailor, hurled against
the foremast, had been badly cut in the head.   The
canteen was a good deal shattered.   But the mighty
hull of the *Galileo* had suffered no further harm, and

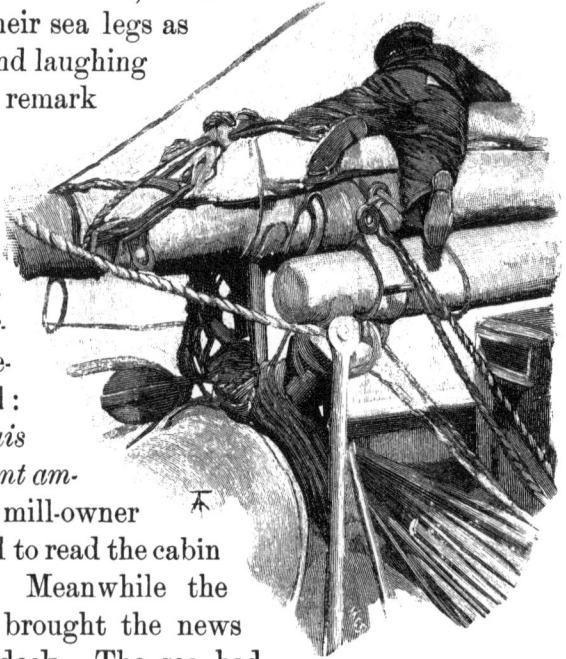

had not stopped moving for an instant. At this last bit of news the flashing eyes of everyone gave token that human pride, but now humiliated, was set up once more, with bold faith in the work which the science and the industry of the race had made; a work against which the full force of the mighty ocean had been vain menace and nothing more, hardly noticed and already forgotten. Yet, all the same, when opened doors gave us permission to go out, not one but heaved a sigh of satisfaction, as if only then assured that it was all over.

Ah! Formidable monster! There you are again, and we are looking one another in the face once more! Ugly and threatening, still, he was. Huge black rollers, crested with foam, rushed on in their dark tumult, shutting in the horizon on every side, and canopied by a gloomy vault of clouds, broken here and there with gray rifts of twilight, while there rolled beneath a mass of vapor in rapid and ill-boding motion, as if the strife were about to begin once more. The ship was soaking wet as if for those eight hours she had been under water. Everywhere were dirty running streams and spreading pools. The deck houses, the masts, the boats were dripping with the sweat of battle. Aft and forward the men were hurrying about in their huge boots, drenched from head to foot, their wet hair plastered on face and neck, their bodies beaten out with fatigue. We met in the covered way the captain, panting, perspiring, red in the face. He passed on without notice. And so, tumbling against both sides of the gangway, wading through the coal-colored slush, and, jostled by the busy sailors, we reached the forecastle.

Here were many persons come out of the cabins and holding on to the life-lines stretched across the deck for the use of the crew. They presented the doleful appearance of a throng that has been fleeing for days before an invading army. The commissary, who had repeatedly gone down into the cabin, described scenes fit to wring the heart and upset the stomach. He had seen down there tangled heaps of human bodies lying across each other; breast to back, feet thrust into faces, clothes in disorder, legs, arms, dishevelled hair; sprawling, rolling on the unclean deck in the tainted air; with sobs and wails and cries of despair, and callings on the saints resounding in every direction. Women on their knees in groups, with heads bent down, telling their beads and beating their breasts. Some in loud voice were making vows to go to a certain sanctuary if ever they saw their native land again; for others nothing would do but they must confess themselves, and weeping they begged the commissary to bring the friar, who was, the while, exercising his office among the men. Several women had passionately prayed for permission to take leave of their husbands before they died; others again to go on deck one instant only, and cast into the sea some saintly image or some crucifix to calm the waves. There were those who adjured him in God's name to turn the ship around and go back. One of the most frightened was that counterfeit lioness of a Bolognese, who sobbed and tore her hair, and called upon the saints like an actress on the stage. And he told one or two cases of the most naïve terror. A poor old woman had called him to her berth, and, placing in his hand seventy francs in silver, had begged him, in a voice choked with sobs, to see that this money reached her brother at Parana, since they all were to go to the bottom; as if it were a law of nature that, whatever happened, the officers and crew would reach their destination. A poor peasant woman falling from her berth had had a miscarriage; others had lost their speech from fright, and could only gesticulate and rave. Even then there were many who would not believe that the peril was over, but still clung convulsively to their berths and refused all comfort.

These women, poor creatures, excited the more compassion because they had no pride to make them conceal their feelings. Those already on deck, all dazed and exhausted, and some with bruised faces and bandaged heads, looked at the sea with that eye which is said to be natural in the Green-landers; petrified, as it were, by gazing all the while upon dismal gloom; and gave a dolorous idea of the condition to which those below had been reduced. The talkative vivacity which usually succeeds an escape from peril had not yet supervened. All were yet so shaken that at every roller larger than the rest, at every deeper lurch, they crowded back from the bulwarks; and, ready once more to fall into the old terror, would look at the bridge as if to get an encouragement from the faces of the officers. They only then began to grow a little calm when they saw the relieved fireman's watch, stripped to the waist, with crimson faces and bathed in sweat, come up from below, proud of their exertions and their victory, and right glad of a little rest; for during the gale they had all been on duty,—those who were shovelling coal held firmly by the rest lest they should be dashed against the boilers or hurled into the burning furnaces.

But as the first stars came out, light-hearted carelessness returned, and there arose a cackle as if all the sixteen hundred passengers were talking at once. Everybody was telling about it; and there were descriptions—excited, interminable, a dozen times repeated—of all sorts of trifling occurrences, exaggerated in each one's imagination until they grew to be events worthy of history or poetry. The half of these people, forgetting or denying their own abject fear, jeered at, pretended to despise, and, perhaps, really did despise the other half for the abject terror they had shown.

After supper the forward part of the ship was vocal with singing and tipsy shouting. And at our table, too, there was mirth and jollity. We all fed like wolves for joy of being alive, and we set the terrors of the sea at nought. The feast wound up with a toast from the Marsigliese to the *intrepidité froide* of the captain, pronounced with the knowing air of one who has been there before. The advocate did not appear. And, to the great sorrow of all, the young lady from Mestre also was not in her place. She had been much shaken by those eight hours of terror and fatigue, and had been attacked with bleeding at the lungs.

CHAPTER XVIII.

HE next morning sea and sky were lovely, and the whole population of the *Galileo* was early in motion; for, if the good weather held, we were to reach America the next evening,—perhaps early enough to land; and it was time to get things ready, to consult with friends and relatives as to what was to be done. The most important matter was registering—having their names put down for going ashore; deciding, that is to say, whether or no they were to go to the commissary and be enrolled as intending to avail themselves of the Argentine Government's offer to pay the expense of landing to such immigrants as should ask it, giving board and lodging for five days and a free journey to those who meant to go up into the interior. This act of inscribing or not inscribing their names was called by the immigrants being or not being "*of*

the immigration." No doubt the advantages were great; but they mistrusted also greatly lest this generosity on the part of the Government, if it was a Government, should conceal a snare; and that to accept it would bind them in some way as to their choice of place to work and condi- tions of contract. Nevertheless the greater part accepted; and there was a continual procession to the commissary's room, which was as if turned into an agency. They went in, and after giving their names, mangled the one defenceless word they had to say in a hundred ways : Write me down for the *a*migration.—I accept the *an*migration.—I go with the *ini*migration.—Or else, bluntly and curtly : So and so, *mi*gration. Many, moreover, went there without having made up their minds—just as one goes to consult a lawyer,—and then said no. The women were the most perplexed. They stopped to bethink themselves once more at the very door, scratching their foreheads as if the destiny of their lives were at stake ; and some, after giving their names and going away, came back to take them off the list again, saying they had heard that the Govern- ment was *treacherous*.

Besides these, there was a crowd of emigrants who came to inquire about the custom-house, whether this article or that had to pay duty, and whether by favor or cleverness they might get out of it. And it was pitiful to hear what small matters they all were; poor little presents they were bringing to their friends and relatives in America; a bottle of *special* wine, a cheese, a sausage, a pound of cakes from Naples or Genoa, a quart or so of oil, a box of dried figs, even an apron full of beans, but from their own place, that corner of the garden which their friends would be sure to remember so well. And they asked whether a fife, or a bagpipe, or a blackbird, or a chest full of old pots and pans would be subject to duty. They all seemed full of terror at the idea of the custom-house at Montevideo and at Buenos Ayres, of which they had heard the most horrible tales; and they spoke of it as of an accursed forest, where were outlaws who would leave them but the bare shirt. The most to be pitied were the invalids and some lonely old people who feared that their sickly look would catch the eye of the American doctor as they went ashore, and they be sent to the lazzaretto. Others again were tormented by the dread lest their brothers or their friends should not, as promised, get on board in time to answer for their subsistence; as the Argentine law allows no useless mouths to land. They all came to the commissary to ask what would happen to them in such or such a case, and then went out, sadly shaking their heads.

And still the commissary wrote and wrote; and saw pass before him, one after another, the pro-

testors of the " Mountain " whom he had repri-
manded, the young girls who had made undesired
love to him, the mothers who had disgusted him
with their jealousies, the quarrellers whom he had
had to separate and punish, the impudent lovers,
the mischievous gossips. Each of these he recognized ; and had a smile, a nod of the head, or a good
word for all of them. As I sat by his side I was
never tired of looking at that little room, full of lists
and registers, and thinking over the endless tales of
wretchedness, the romantic lies of young damsels,
the sobs of women, and the fierce words of disputants he had listened to. More than all, however, the post-bags, tied, sealed, and heaped in a
corner, attracted me. For these were snatches of
the great dialogue between the two worlds. Who
knows how many letters there were here from
women for the third or fourth time beseeching news
of a son or husband who had given no sign for
years ; prayers that these would return or send for
them ; supplications for aid ; announcements of
sickness or death ; pictures of girls which their
fathers would not recognize ; despairing complaints
addressed to faithless lovers; shameless lies from
faithless wives ; latest counsels from the old ;—all
this, mingled with bankers' letters bristling with
figures ; amorous notes from ballerinas ; circulars
from dealers in vermouth ; bundles of newspapers
for Italian colonists eager after news of their coun-

try; perhaps the last poem of Carducci, or Verga's new novel; a confusion of papers of every color, written with weeping, with laughter, and with frenzy, in hovels, in palaces, in workshops. All these sacks were to be sent far and wide in a few days from the mouths of the Plata to the confines of Brazil, to the shores of the Pacific, to the interior of Paraguay and up the slopes of the Andes; awakening joy, fear, grief, remorse, which, in their turn crammed into other sacks, would go back over the same journey; and heaped up in a little room, just as these that were before me, would see other poor creatures pass by returning to the Old World, less poor perhaps, but not more happy than when they had left it with hopes of better fortune.

Meanwhile the procession went on: " So and so, under the Government."—" Tizio, with the migration."—" Caio, landing and shelter." The unexpected appearance of the Bolognese here made an interruption. She came filled with fury at a new and mortal offence from a *canaglia d'erbóff*, who passing by and touching the mysterious pouch had said, in evident allusion to the preposterous surmise : " They pay duty, I suppose." She wanted him on deck, in irons, legs and arms, or she would make declaration before all the consuls in America, that the ship's officers encouraged the most shameless clodhoppers (*boletàri*) in the third class to insult well-conducted girls. As she was near America she did not speak of her relatives in the journalism.   The commissary cut her short (*la rim-becco*) but without losing his temper ; promised as soon as the inscription was over he would see her righted ; and turned short round to a couple of angry peasants who came to have their names taken off the list, for they did not want to fall into the hands of those hangman thieves (*boia de lader*) who offered to land emigrants gratis so as to be the first to plunder them and make up to their women.   They had evidently picked up something fresh and hot in their part of the ship, where agitators were working to excite them.

I went forward, and there, sure enough, was the old fellow in the green jacket haranguing

"The big Bolognese."

22

away to a larger audience than usual; and leaning, from political sympathy, perhaps, on the anchor, which was painted red, and shaking his loose gray locks. The short work which the captain had made of the Forty-

"Haranguing away to a larger audience than usual."

seven Protest had not intimidated him in the least, and he had threatened to *write to the papers*. His nearness to the land of liberty emboldened him all

the more, and not only did he not lower his voice
when one of those suckers of the people's blood
passed by, but rather raised it, rude and harsh as it
was, like the sound of a tin horn, while the veins of
the neck swelled fit to burst the skin.   He spoke as
if he were not making the voyage for the first time ;
said they must look out for the Argentines, the
Italian agents, the consuls, the go-betweens of every
color, who were all in swindling league together to
get fat out of the immigration.   They were to look
after their things as they went ashore, or they would
be robbed outright ; they were to have an eye to
their wives and daughters.   Dreadful things had
been done by the government people in the face of
day before the very eyes of fathers and mothers.
And as for shelter, tumble-down sheds ; the rain
came through the roof on to the beds ; there was
either nothing to eat or else they put something
into the soup which made a man too stupid to put
two and two together, and then the rascals came
and made a contract with him.   " Look out, *figliuoli*,"
he shouted ; " Look to it or you will be skinned
[*assassinati*] worse than in the old country.   He is
a gone man that trusts them ! "

But he was not the only one to hold forth.   Other
groups here and there were hanging on the words of
other orators who had started up that morning.   On
the midship-deck was the professor ex-cook, the
player on the *ocarina*.   He had been everywhere

and done everything, had advice to give to everybody into whatever part of America they were
going, just as if he had lived there many years, and
had plied every trade in every quarter of the globe.
He spoke of the snares laid for emigrants when they
had a little money; lands, far-away lands sold for a
song, fertile, well watered, where they were to become rich in ten years' time; and the poor gulls,
when they reached the spot with empty pockets,
found sandy deserts, fever in the air, the Indians all
around them, lions on the prowl by night, and serpents five yards long crawling through the houses.
And fleeing from starvation they had to go afoot
hundreds of miles before finding a habitable spot,
drenched with rain for weeks at a time, or scourged
with hideous gales, which swept away cows and
dogs like dried leaves. At this many of his hearers
suspected some exaggeration, shrugged their shoulders and went away; while many more swallowed it
all and stood there with their eyes upon the deck.

But in other groups the optimists had the floor. A
new world—no more taxes—no more military service—no more tyranny. The soil teemed as soon as
touched by the plough; meat at fifty centimes the
kilogramme (five cents the pound); tracts with four
thousand inhabitants where the sour face of a *signore*
was never seen. And they told of quick fortunes,
overflowing granaries; of field laborers who had
private tutors for their children. America forever!

Sangue d'un cane! Will you hold your tongues,
you calamity howlers !

In the midst of all this preoccupation it was evident that immortal woman had taken, for the present,
a back seat,—that many attachments would have to
be thrown over.   No more were seen those steady
eyes that watched the fair one hour by hour for the
chance of putting a word in her ear or a black and
blue mark on her arm.   But this very preoccupation left the few faithful ones only the more free.
Amongst these last I marked the poor Modenese
bookkeeper who had gone back to his old contem-
plation, a little farther off than before but more dead
in love than ever; as if the rough handling he had
received, the boxed ears and the disgrace he had
suffered,—poor wretch,—had only enhanced the love-
liness of her for whom he had gone through so much.
I looked at him from the bridge for a long time.
He never moved his head or bent his neck or turned
his eyes for a single instant from the girl.   She was
in her usual place, knitting, with her little brother
at her side, her fair form more upright, sweet, and
fresh than ever.   Her face, clouded for many days,
was placid again ; and I was not long in perceiving
that all this lowly and unwearied adoration from
the poor, lonely, scorned young fellow had awakened
a sisterly feeling of pity and kindness which perhaps
she thought it was due to him to let him perceive ;
for as I was on the point of moving away I saw her

usual quiet, indifferent look as she cast it around her, fixed for an instant, perhaps not for the first time, upon his face with a lovely expression of kindness and sympathy. Ah! Ye Gods! The fellow lighted up like a mirror when the sun falls upon it; he shook all over, he heaved a sigh and passed a hand over his forehead as if astounded that the whole ship should not be aware of the wonder that had come to pass.

But no one took any heed. And this general pre-occupation gave me the chance to move about freely for a while among the crowd and catch, flying, many a bit of talk. The expectation of landing soon had aroused in almost all of them some curiosity about the cities and the regions they were to live in. They asked the officers about them,—or the more educated of their fellow-passengers ; pulling out old creased letters from their kinsfolk and acquaintance, gesticulating over them, re-reading them or handing them about with that extraordinary reverence which your illiterate always shows for a written docu-ment, which he supposes, and naturally enough, capable of various subtle interpretations. I heard mention made of many farm colonies with names dear to my soul,—Esperanza, Pilar, Cavour, Garibaldi, New Turin, Candelaria.

But, gracious Heaven! what it was to see the dense ignorance in which they almost all were plunged ; their utter lack of any ideas about States or bound-

aries, as if South America were an island a hundred
miles or so in circuit, where the provinces were
within gunshot of one another—Buenos Ayres,
Tucuman, Mendoza, Assumption, Montevideo,
Entre Rios, Chili, the United States,—all forming in
the minds of the greater part an inextricable mass
of confusion ; so that the keenest and most patient
man in the world would have been at a loss where to
begin to get order out of the chaos, or throw light on
any part of it.   And to think that many even of the
youngest had been to school and had learned to
read and write ! It was hopeless. Here and there
little family groups were discussing ways and means:
" So, five for the landing, three for the inn; we 'll
say so much for the first day."   Farther on : *Vapu-
rino pe Rusario, quatto pezz' e mèza—nu muorz' e
pane pe' u viaggio ; restano cinche ducate, senza cuntà
e scarpe pe Ciccillo.* " The tender up to Rosario,
four dollars and a half—and a mouthful to eat on
the way ; there 'll be five ducats over without
counting little Dicky's shoes."

I heard among other things that there was bad news
of the young lady from Mestre, upon whom nearly
all of them were depending for advice and patronage.
They seemed to think she had had a fall ; and even
supposed she might be dying, but that it was kept
secret because the captain was somehow (they had
not the slightest idea how) in fault. The Mestre
peasant anxiously inquired about her. All his family

were once more crouched in the old nest between
the turkey pens and the great hogshead, under an
awning of diapers put out to dry, beneath whose
shade young Galileo, red as a boiled lobster, was
having his little dinner like a calf. " *Ah, povareta!* "
cried the peasant, "that such a thing should happen
to an angel like that! She is too good, she cannot
live long!" And the wife added: "Tell her that
we will pray to our saint for her, God bless her!"

The father was going to trust the Government;
had put his name down for the *amigrazion,* he was
not going to believe all the clown's chatter *(panta-
lonae)* which those idiots on the forecastle got off.
Then he asked me if it were really true, what the
ex-cook, the wiseacre of the midship-deck, had told
them, that from the equator on, the water was fit to
drink *(la gera bona da bevar),* because the great
American river drove back the waves of the sea.
But he interrupted himself to exclaim: " Here are
our new *(paroni)* masters!" It was the five Argentines in company with the Neapolitan priest, who
came forward for the first time to have a look at
their guests. The priest must have been discussing some financial matter; for he said loudly,
moving his hand like a fan: " *Si se encontràran los
accionistas para un gran banco agricola-colonizador.*"
And I joined them, urged by a stronger sympathy
in those last days for the children of the land where
so many of my fellow-citizens were to have their lot

in life. And I searched their faces to find what
impression was made; but they looked on and said
nothing. Nevertheless, their eyes and their every
movement betrayed the proud satisfaction they felt
at seeing all those people who were come to seek
hospitality in their country, the greater part for life,
and whose children would grow up citizens of the
republic, would speak its language and not their
own, and would perhaps be, as often happens,
ashamed of their foreign origin.

Perhaps in looking at the emigrants the gentlemen saw in imagination all these clodhoppers
(mangiatori di terra) and Ligurian traffickers at
work, beheld loaded barks glide down the waters
of the Paranà and the Uruguay, and saw the new
railways of the tropics stretch across the forest, the
sugar-cane rise on the plains of Tucuman, the vine
upon the slopes of Mendoza, the tobacco plant upon
the Gran Chaco,—saw houses and palaces rise by
hundreds and by thousands, and leagues upon
leagues of desert glow and blossom under the sweat-
rain of their hard toil. There came surging into my
mind so many things to say to them: "You will receive all these people kindly will you not? They are
hardy volunteers who have come to swell the ranks
of that army with which you are conquering a
world. They are worthy men, believe me; they are
industrious, as you will see; they are sober, they are
patient, they do not emigrate to get rich, but to find

bread for their children, and will easily grow fond of
the country that feeds them. They are poor, but
not because they have not worked; they are un-
taught, but not from any fault of theirs; proud of
their country, but it is because they have a vague
sense of its bygone glory; sometimes they are
quick in quarrel, but you, descendants of the con-
querors of Mexico and Peru, are you not also sometimes quick in quarrel? Let them love and boast of
their far-off country, for if they could have the heart
to be false to its memory they could not become
attached to your soil. Protect them from dishonest
middlemen, do them justice when they require it,
and do not make them feel, poor creatures, that
they are tolerated intruders. Treat them gently
and kindly. We shall all be so thankful to you
for it. They are our blood; we love them. Into
your hands we commend them and with all our
hearts !"

I do not know what stupid—and worse than
stupid, cowardly—reserve it was that held me back
from saying all this. They would have listened
with amazement, no doubt, but they might have
been moved; perhaps not without being a little
softened. The sea was so lovely. It seemed as if
it ought to be reflected in every bosom. Since morning many sailing ships and steamers had been seen
bound for the Plata River, and flights of birds had
come around the *Galileo* to bid her welcome.

As soon as the bustle of inscription was over, everything had quieted down and people were inclined to
be good-natured.   Some emigrants, who had got
leave to come into the after-cabin to get up a raffle
for a silver watch and an engraving of the Madonna,
on behalf of a poor family, were very successful indeed at sixty centimes the ticket.   The drawing, as
the prospectus set forth, was to take place on the
morrow, " with the necessary guarantees," behind
the butcher's shop.   Not a quarrel arose after dinner.
The emigrants were treated to a dish of *braciole*
and potatoes (Irish stew) that softened many a
heart.   Our repast too was such as to make the
single eye of the Genoese gleam with satisfaction,
and had an additional flavor from the idea of that
"something to follow" which Brillat-Savarin says
is necessary to the perfect success of a dinner.   This
"something" was the thought of what the ship
would look like on the morrow when the land hove
in sight.

The talk, under the attraction of America, all ran
upon the countries we were approaching, as if we had
been there before.   In three days we should hear
Polyeucte at the Colon Theatre; and at the Solis,
Crespino e la Comare with Baldelli.   The plan of
the new Square at Buenos Ayres and that of the
new Italian Hospital at Montevideo were discussed.
The presidents of the two republics were dissected
joint by joint, and many heated comments made upon

those newspapers which were opposed to or in favor of Italian immigration. The Garibaldian alone said nothing, and the veil of sadness on his face was deeper than usual. My two next-door neighbors were silent too, but on their faces there was an unusual expression; the look of hate, of course,—but now animated by a new thought, the expectation of something to happen, which each hoped would decide their contest unfavorably to the other. They did not look at one another, but there seemed to be a grim, silent fight between the two, as if they were secretly stabbing one another beneath the table-cloth. They both reached out at once for the salt, but perceiving in time that their hands would touch, drew back and took no salt. The mere thought that I was soon to reach America and have that miserable spectacle before my eyes no longer, was enough to cheer me.

Suddenly I remarked that the lady of the Chartreuse and the mother of the piano-player were missing; and as I could not suppose they were sea-sick at that late day, I asked the agent, who was between me and the advocate, what the matter was. "What! You don't know! You are in America already one would think! A regular scene!" For some days the "tamer" had had hints that the other was speaking ill of her and had shrewd notions what it was about. She had seen it in the faces of some of the passengers, who would look at her and smile, at certain hours, and would peep into her

stateroom as they passed. That morning, however,
her maid, set on to watch had found out all about
it. Our serpent in petticoats had declared she was
getting *delirium tremens*; was giving horrid accounts
of her stateroom, where indeed she had been several
times to taste her Maraschino di Zara, and was
saying that it was a perfect liquor shop, with bottles
under the pillows, sticky glasses all over everywhere,
and a large collection of all sorts of mineral waters
powders, and pastilles, to repair in the morning the
damage done by drinking overnight. But now she
said it was no use trying to repair it; the thing had
gone too far, and the doctor had remarked that the
gentlemen had better not go too near her with their
lighted cigars. The fat lady had heard all this
exactly at the moment when she had been having a
fresh nip, had gone straight to the dear creature's stateroom, and, meeting her in the corridor when two or
three people were by, had said in an uncommonly
distinct voice three words to her—not more than
three,—but spoken with the look and tone of her
profession, and of that kind which good old, mellow
Chartreuse, the true authentic article made by the
well-deserving Friars, and taken in suitable doses, is
alone capable of inspiring. The other, undaunted,
had answered with a single word of three syllables
(one in English), worth her adversary's three together. Then—but then the stewardesses ran up,
and the contestants in a paroxysm of rage had retired,

storming, each to her own stateroom, where half an hour afterwards they fainted.

But as he said this the agent suddenly bethought himself and seemed to be trying to intercept glances between two persons at the table who were at a distance from him. And, sure enough, I heard him the next moment singing to himself Hamlet's long cry in the little Theatre of the Palace *(sic)* : "O-o-o-o-h! my prophetic soul!" Straightway he seized my arm and confided to me his amazing discovery. "Look!" he said, "but don't let them see you doing it." And I did look and was not long in seeing what he meant. Every two or three minutes the fair, blue, vacant eyes of the blonde lady would rest for an instant on the captain; and his hard red countenance would gleam for an instant with a smile half concealed by his bushy eyebrows and bristling mustaches, like a bit of blue that shows through a rift in the clouds, and then is covered; but the blue eyes looked again, and the rift appeared again. Not a doubt about it, the little game went on regularly; there was an understanding between the fair blonde crown and the rough red poll. The siren had sung, the rugged bear had listened; the *Galileo* was brought to. "Ah! now I understand," said the agent, in a rage, "why there was no 'scene'—Ah! *Porcaie a bordo no ne véuggio*, forsooth! U'gh! You old sea Tartuffe! This is too much!" All the same he was not ill pleased at being relieved from the incubus of an unsolved mystery. And as we went on deck he rubbed his hands. "One more—Now what we have to do is to find out whom yonder young lady will next snip with her scissors,—if indeed there be another to snip."

So he and the others laughed with all their might as they nodded and looked at the round back of the professor, who leaned over the rail and discoursed with the Neapolitan priest about the constellation of Orion. It was a charming night and a smiling augury of a good end to the voyage. To the west, among myriads of stars, arose the zodiacal light, in form of a huge whitish pyramid, the apex almost reaching the zenith and the circuit embracing a quarter of the horizon. The track of the Milky Way, between the Scorpion and the Centaur, and the four flaming diamonds of the Southern Cross, stood out clear and vivid. The Magellan Clouds, those vast, solitary nebulæ which-made the heart of Humboldt beat and his pen blaze, formed around the Southern Pole two wondrous white spots, which shaded off into the infinite. Falling stars, seeming larger than with us, from the pure atmosphere, were seen on every side like shooting rockets which streaked the sky with silvery red and blue and golden light. So clear was the sky, that the ship with every black spar and shroud and rope was sharply drawn upon it; and, looking from the piaz-zetta, there were stars among the yards, the lifts, the braces, and stars reflected by the glassy sea; so that we seemed to move along in an airy bark amid the splendors of the firmament. Yet scarcely any one looked at all this. Each of those seventeen hundred living atoms had some hope or fear or regret within him, compared with which these millions of worlds were of no more importance than the dust which his foot strikes out of the earth.

In the forward part of the ship there was indeed a busy hum of conversation, but more steady and intense than on other evenings. No singing, no shouting. It was clear that all were talking of serious matters. At the moment of separation between the men and the women there could be heard many a "Good-night!" full of meaning and "To-morrow, then!" in a hundred ringing tones. "It is the last night! We land to-morrow! Twenty-four hours and we are in America!" And even when they had been below some time there floated up through the hatches a sonorous murmur as of an excited crowd. It was the tide made in a sea of souls by a world as they drew near to it.

CHAPTER XIX.

AMERICA.

WHAT a pleasant awakening! Those words! "To-day we shall be on shore," which expressed the sentiments of everyone, had a fresh sound and renewed power for us all. And one felt, in saying them over, the physical pleasure which is had in throwing the arms around a good solid granite column. Without taking other reasons into account, we were most anxious to get on shore, because in a long voyage a man grows tired, exasperated beyond endurance at that perpetual reeling and staggering, that bending and dodging to which he is forced by the motion of the ship and the narrowness of everything; that continual salt smell, that constant odor of wood and of tar. What pleasure to see the streets, to snuff the country air, to sleep between four walls that stay upright and not feel that the house we are in is thrilling with a special life and one on which after all our own depends. It did so happen that we passed the Canaries and the Cape Verdes at night; and for the same reason we had missed the little Brazilian island of Fernando de Noronha, which everyone had longed to get a glimpse of, so as to break for a moment the interminable monotony of the sea. Not a hand's breadth of land for eighteen days since we passed the Straits of Gibraltar. I should have liked to hold a clod of earth in my fingers for the pleasure of feeling it and smelling it, like forbidden fruit. And at last, at last, we were to have enough of it: a couple of pear shaped pieces, namely, covering together thirty-eight millions of square kilometres, and each equal to about seventy Italies.

As we expected to reach Montevideo by daylight, there began at dawn of day among the emigrants a general scrubbing, hasty and unsparing, for they desired not to compromise the national honor by making their appearance in America as savage and slovenly beggars. Fresh water was served out freely, since it was the last day; and they began to wash furiously, like so many coal miners just come up. There was a plunging of heads into basins and a puffing and a sluicing and a splashing; while the water ran about the decks as if it rained. Many were dragging combs through capillary forests, virgin since Genoa; others, barefooted, were polishing up their shoes with moistened rags. They overhauled their creased and threadbare clothes, they brushed and they beat them. The Venetian barber, imitator of dogs, had set up an open-air shop near the bulwark on the port side, where the to-be-shaved ones, seated in long rows like Turks at Constantinople, awaited each his turn, scraping their cheeks with both hands and chaffing one another. Arms and shoulders of naked babies, and of women in their petticoats gleamed by hundreds everywhere. Some brushed each other's hair and thinned out the too flourishing population of the boys' heads. Others hastily patched and darned their jackets and their stockings, pulling over tattered old bags and valises for fresh clothes and linen. Joyful anticipation had reawakened cordiality; families helped one another with little services and spoke their mutual thanks loudly and heartily. A thrill of young life was awakened everywhere. And above the lively murmur of the throng was heard from time to time the cry "Viva l' America!" or the high shrill falsetto with which the people of North Italy finish the verses of a song. At breakfast, enlivened by the notes of fife and bagpipe *(piffero, zampogna)*, a special ration of biscuit was served out. Everyone filled his pockets, and the canteen man poured out endless glasses of rum, like a regimental sutler on the day of battle. After all which the passengers sat down quietly or leaned over the rail, awaiting the appearance of the New World.

But the hours went by and the land did not heave

in sight. The sky was covered with clouds, but the horizon was clear, and the sharp blue sea line was unbroken by a shade of promise. After eight bells, the passengers began to show symptoms of weariness. They that had so much patience for three weeks had hardly a crumb left for the last few hours. Many complained angrily: "Why did we not see land? Was the reckoning wrong? We should have seen it long ago. Now we shall not get there by daylight. The Lord knows when we shall get there. Italian steamers! There's the whole story. Lucky if we get there in a year." And they glowered and made cutting remarks when an officer passed by. Some, too, feigning to give up all hope of getting there, shrugged their shoulders, turned away from the sea, and pretended to busy themselves with something else. But, all the same, every time the signal officer who had charge of the watch looked through his glass, as he stood on the bridge, they fixed their eyes on him in breathless silence, and not a murmur was heard until the careless air with which he lowered his instrument destroyed hope. But he did not move from his post, which showed that he expected every moment to catch sight of something. The peasant with the abbreviated nose, bent on being the first to announce America, stood halfway up the ladder, ready to catch the first indication from the officer and cry out; and every time the glass was levelled he gave the crowd a majestically comic sign

for silence, like a tribune of the people at a moment
of crisis.

Among us also in the after part of the ship there
was expectation. The ladies were seated facing the
west, the men were
strung about the
poop much excited.
The young lady
from Mestre was in
her usual place, be-
tween the Garibal-
dian and her aunt,
paler in face and
feebler in look than
ever before, but not
more sad ; indeed
her eyes w e r e
brighter than we
had yet seen them,
and in her counte-
nance there was a
wondrous s w e e t-

The Signal Officer.

ness, as if a fresh beauty had come there since her
attack of bleeding. For the first time she was
all in black, and the translucent clearness of her
complexion was set off so strikingly by the dress
she wore that it was like the sight of a living face
under a sable pall. She, with her aunt, appeared
to be delicately folding up little packets of some-

thing upon her lap. There also were the mother of the piano-player, and the plump lady, seated on the opposite side of the deck; the former with an hysterical face showed fine white teeth and looked more venomous than ever; the latter with her great round countenance, seemed steeped in alcoholic beatitude, and thought, as it would seem, of nothing at all. The other ladies, sitting about in their light dresses, made masses of brilliant color, like a row of flags hung out on a holiday. But here too there were signs of impatience. Little feet patted the deck; hands switched fans about with nervous abruptness; heads were tossed; the conversation took a bilious turn, and though they did not utter the cross nonsense that the third-class people did about the officers, it was in the minds and flashed from the eyes of all of them.

But now the young lady rose, leaning on her aunt's arm, and the two, with their little parcels, went towards the third class. On the piazzetta they were joined by the Venetian servant, who was waiting for them with other matters in her hands. As this was to be the lady's last visit to the forward part of the ship I was anxious to see what she did; so I ran through the second-class gangway and gained the bridge.

She had probably chosen that time so as to be less observed, the attention of all the passengers being fixed upon the horizon. From the bridge I could follow all her movements in that crowd of people, and was amazed to see how many she knew and how much good she had done in those few days. She gave the poor peasant, ill of fever, and his wife, the fruit she had got together; gave clothes to another family near the foremast; to another she gave letters and papers. Then she approached the Genoese girl, and though I could not see well for the crowds around, I thought she slipped a ring on the girl's finger. The boys gathered around her from every side; some of the smallest followed her about, and she patted their cheeks with one hand and gave them sweetmeats with the other. She went to speak with the family from Mestre and kissed young Galileo. Several men came up to her, hat in hand, and seemed to ask advice. Here and there she shook hands as if to take leave. Her white face and faded hair would be lost for an instant in the throng and then appear again. She passed within the forecastle, then came out once more at the canteen, went down to the sick bay, and I saw her next by the capstan, in midst of a group of women who thrust out their little babies for her to touch. Wherever she went, grinning faces were composed, loud voices lowered; all moved out of the way and faced round towards her. Her face showed mortal weariness, but wore throughout the same sweet smile, while a faint tremor in her pale lips and filmy eyes, where all her life seemed centred, was like the last gleam of the sun upon a fair white rose already declining to the earth. When she reached the covered way to go aft again, she stopped and panted with a hand upon her breast. The peasant woman from Mestre came up at this moment, fervently kissed the sleeve of her dress, and then ran hastily away. The lady moved on slowly.

And the land did not heave in sight. But I felt no impatience. I was half angry with myself, because the idea of reaching that America so much longed for raised in me no more emotion. It was another moral phenomenon like what I had felt during the first days of the voyage on reaching the Yellow Sea; a kind of syncope, a total abeyance of curiosity and of pleasure. As if not one of the ardent longings with which I had come on board were left with me, the idea of this new land awakened only miserable forebodings of the annoyance there would be on landing,— and then I had a disagreeable taste in my mouth from a bad cigar. Even the excitement of the others disgusted me; fools, to wish to go back to every-day troubles, as if these last three weeks had not been one of the pleasantest periods of their lives. So much so, that to get out of their way I went and sat down in the commissary's room and positively fell to reading over an old number of the *Caffaro*, cursing, between one column and another, books, travellers, tales, lectures, the press, which make us familiar with foreign countries and

preclude all possibility of first impressions. Great
Heaven! it is a fact and I ought to be ashamed to
confess it; but here, a few miles only from the
shores of America, I cudgelled my brains over a
ridiculous charade in a Genoese newspaper, a charade of which I could not guess "my second":

> "My second is always in motion,"

and I pervaded in thought the realms of nature to find
the secret, while the old hunch-backed mariner, as
indifferent to America as I, polished the brass handle
of the door, droning out a Ligurian ballad:

> "Gh' ëa na votta na bælla figgia—
> Once I saw a pretty maid—"

in a cracked and nasal tone which finally sent me
to sleep.

All at once the song ceased as if the old fellow's
attention had been suddenly attracted elsewhere, and
I heard from the bridge a long, long, endless, doleful
cry: "Land ho!"

A thrill ran through me. It was like the announcement of a great unexpected event, the wide, formless
vision of a world, which reawakened at once within
me curiosity, wonder, enthusiasm, joy, and made me
spring to my feet with face suffused.

Another cry, the cry of a thousand voices, answered
the first, and at once the ship rolled heavily to starboard as the crowd all rushed that way.

I ran on deck and searched the horizon. For a

few moments I saw nothing; then looking closely I distinguished a reddish streak which was lost to right and left in two long tongues, like a light cloud that was kissing the face of ocean.

And I stood there for a moment, gazing like the rest, and amazed I knew not why.

Many cries broke out around me : " *Estàmos a casa ! Ghe semmo finalmente! Quatre heures, vingt-cinq minutes* !" exclaimed the Marsigliese, looking at his watch, " *l'heure que j'avais prévue.*" " Ecco la vera tierra del progreso !—There is the true land of progress !" cried the mill-owner. The tenor merely said in a weighty manner: " L' America ! " The plump lady, somewhat elevated, called companionably to one and to another by name to look and be joyful over that strip of land. Perhaps it looked larger to her than to us. The only locked-up face was that of the Garibaldian; and I felt a new sense of repulsion. It was too much, I thought, and a poor-spirited thing, to regard the whole universe as dead because one has lost half a dozen illusions.

I ran forward where a great silence had succeeded to the first tumult. All stood with eyes fixed on that strip of bare earth, all quiet and absorbed as if before the face of the Sphynx from whom they would gladly have extorted the secret of their future life ; or as if beyond that reddish streak they could see already the boundless plains where they were to sweat and toil and leave their bones at last. Few

spoke. The ship drove on and the streak grew
higher and longer. It was the coast of Uruguay.
No sign of vegetation or of habitation. Many who
had been looking forward to a land of wonders cried
out. "Why, it's just like our own country!" A
group was talking of Garibaldi who had fought
upon that shore; and to find after so many days an
unknown land where his name was as great as in
their own country, enhanced his glory most enor-
mously. A young peasant woman with her child
upon her knee began to cry. Her husband nudged
her hard with his elbow and said she was *fabioca*,—
a silly little fool. I asked a woman near by what it
was about. " *Un' idea*," she said. "The sight of
America is enough to give her a pang, because it
makes her think she will never see her own land
again, and so she cannot help crying."

I went on towards the forecastle and there I found
a couple of Turinese workmen seated against the
bulwark. Ah! I never shall forget that! On the
broad ocean, in sight of the New World and within
reach of their new life, they were disputing as to the
precise whereabouts of the Trattoria di Casal Bor-
gone, just as if they had been at the corner of the
Via del Deposito and the Via del Carmine or of the
Via del Carmine and the Via dei Quartieri. One of
them got angry about it. In general the women
were more thoughtful than the men. None were
really merry but the boys who kicked and pinched

each other for very joy. Some of the old people
turned their backs to the sea as if they had nothing
to hope from that strip of earth except to die there,
in peace; and the old, old couple of the forecastle
seated on the bitts as usual, were fast asleep.

But a little later, when the first effects of that
sight had worn off, there broke out, as if by concert, a
boundless jollity, a chorus of singing and whistling, a
shouting of people who crowded around the canteen
holding up pots and glasses ; a sparkling up in every
direction, as if they had in these few moments swallowed large draughts of generous wine. All the
performers performed. The old fellow of the midship deck began to grunt in character, surrounded
by admirers grinning from ear to ear. The noseless
peasant took off the faces of women frightened during the late gale, and drew down a hurricane of ap-
plause. The hairy mountebank came from forward
and with sad face made cartwheels upon the deck
between two rows of delighted women; and the
ex-porter himself, he of the bald head, in a transport
of joy tore out the leaves of his famous album and
gave them to his friends, who straightway formed
each around himself a circle of chuckling sight-seers ;
so that from the kitchen to the butcher's shop it was
nothing but suggestive shrieks of laughter, grinning
faces, shaking shoulders, and a deafening clatter of
music, singing and tipsy cries, above which rose from
time to time the long-drawn howl of the Venetian

barber as he made himself a dog and bayed the moon.

The sun, meanwhile, had gone down, right before us over the land, and we saw a twilight as beautiful as any yet presented to us within the tropics. These sights, so frequent in these regions, are the result of a great mass of vapor which rises from the Plata River and from the huge streams which form it. These vapors collecting on high when the air is calm, are flooded with light, which they refract and shade off into tints and colors which pass all imagination. The horizon was one flaming zone broken into shapes of golden cathedral spires; pyramids of rubies; towers of white-hot iron; lofty arches built of burning coals, which slowly made way for other shapes less lofty but more strange, until nothing was there but the glowing ruins of a demolished city and at last an endless row of fierce Titanic eyes that glared at us. The sky above was dark, the sea below was black. At the sight, silence settled down upon the fore deck once more, as if all were some mysterious manifestation belonging to this region alone. An island or two were seen, Lobos on the left, Gorriti on the right. Then Flores, and then the light on the Archimedes bank. The silence forward was so profound that the throb of the engine was distinctly heard. The ship moved as if upon the waters of a lake.

"What a calm sea!" exclaimed an emigrant.

" We are not at sea," said a sailor near me, " we are in the river."

The emigrant and those about him turned to look for the other shore and, seeing nothing but the clear line of the sea horizon, were somewhat doubtful; but we were indeed in the Plata River, whose right bank was more than a hundred miles away.

When the last rays of the twilight had disappeared, we saw the light-house of Montevideo, a forest of masts, and a confused line of buildings lighted vaguely here and there.

By this time, it was clear that we were not to land that evening. Everybody was fatigued by the emotions of the morning, but all remained on deck to enjoy the sight of coming to anchor.

Accordingly, a little farther on, the ship began to slow down until she hardly moved, and at last that mighty heart of fire and iron, which had been beating so unweariedly for twenty-two days, gave its final throb and the great Colossus stopped—dead. A whistle from the bridge, and two huge anchors fell from the bows, dragged, with thunder sound and lightning speed, the great chains from the hawse-hole eyes, which flashed fire the while; the sea foamed, the ship trembled and then was still. Her two huge talons had fastened upon the bottom of the river.

The emigrants stood a few moments to taste the new sensation of utter quiet, and then, in long procession, descended to their cabin. The first-class passengers, no longer tempted by the cool breeze, for it fanned us no more when the ship came to a stand-still, soon went down also.

And I remained there, almost alone, amazed that, after having so often thought the voyage insupport-ably long, it should at this moment seem to have been so short, so like a vague passing dream, although there was so much that I remembered. Having seen nothing by the way to fix the distance in my mind by any distinct landmarks, so to speak, each day was exactly like the rest; and I seemed to have crossed that mighty stretch of water at a leap. Except, perhaps, the hurricane, no incident of the voyage has remained stamped on my memory like the impressions of these, its last moments. The mighty stream was moveless and still, as if its weary waters were resting after their two-thousand-mile journey from the mountains of Brazil; the sky was dark and tranquil; the city of Montevideo was asleep, not a sound or a movement in the harbor; the ship was quiet; the profoundest silence weighed upon everything ; a silence that seemed to come from far, from great rivers, from boundless plains, from vast forests, from the thousand summits of the Andes ; the mysterious and awful silence of a slumbering continent.

The captain roused me from my reflections as he passed me by, rubbing his hands—a most unusual thing—as if in that rough old sea-dog head of his there was the comfortable expectation of a quiet night. I was tempted to give him his own refrain . *Porcaie a bordo* . . .

But he prevented me by asking me with a serious face:

"What do you think your friends at home are about just now ?"

I looked at my watch, and answered: "At this hour my house is all dark and everyone is asleep."

He began to laugh, and rubbed his hands more than ever: "*Anche voscid scid gh'è cheito!* (Anche lei c' è cascato)—Ah ! my dear sir, have I caught you too ! At this hour it is broad day at home, and your children are wanting their coffee and their milk. "

I had not thought of that.

But the fine old captain, who was in high good-humor, asked me if before leaving I had charged the agent to inform my family as soon as he heard of our arrival ?

I had done so.

" Well, then," he said, " in three hours your family will know that we have reached America—all well."

I had not thought of that any more than of the other, so in high good-humor myself, I went below to sleep for the last time under the deck of the *Galileo*.

CHAPTER XX

TO sleep? *Mentita speme!* False Hope!—

As happens to everyone after a day of agitation, to be followed by one not less agitating, the passengers slept no more than they were forced to do by absolute fatigue. Towards two in the morning all were awake, and what with sighs from the ladies, yawns from the men, and talk in undertones which in the silence of the moveless vessel sounded like the humming of great flies, there was no more quiet. An hour before dawn, hurried steps were heard and the voice of the doctor, sent for in haste to the Signorina from Mestre who had fainted. The effort she had made to go on deck and visit the forecastle once more had been too much for her. Then the little Brazilian began to scream, the negress to croon to him; and after that everyone, springing from his berth, began noisily to get his things in order, chatting and talking without any regard whatever. And when at daylight the stewards and stewardesses, after wrangling for half an hour in the passages, came into our staterooms with the coffee, they found everyone on foot, washed and brushed and with the expected gratuity ready to hand over.

Ruy Blas, as he presented the tray, wished me a long and happy sojourn in America, and his air was as correct as the air of any valet on the boards; but his voice was so languid and his eye so utterly fishy that any child could perceive how broken down he meant to have it understood that he was at the prospect of parting with that mysterious creature who possessed his affections. While I was absorbing the coffee, he was looking at the sky through the airport; biting his underlip as if to repress the utterances of a wounded heart; and then, as he accepted my little offering, he tempered the humility of that act with a bow full of elegance and dignity. Slipping out immediately after him, I saw him enter the stateroom of the priest, whose big voice I straightway heard counting slowly—*Dos, tres, cinco, seis*; francs, as I surmise, which Ruy Blas had to receive with open hand like a beggar, but quivering with shame as he thought of the queen of his soul.

On deck I found the captain and officers on duty. A gallooned official of the port of Montevideo and a doctor had come on board; the former a great big

man with a thread of a voice, the latter a little man
with a voice like a bass drum; and, having inquired
into the sanitary condition of the passengers, the two
went forward to count the crew. All the third-
class passengers, the while, were being assembled on
the main deck in order to pass in review before the
Uruguayan official, that he might number them, and
before the doctor that he might set aside suspected
cases. From amidships they were to pass one by
one over the bridge which spans the piazzetta, and
then, leaving the deck by the starboard ladder, go
forward again. Upon the ample midship deck there
was not one square foot of empty space; a crowd
as dense as a regiment in column covered it from
one end to the other; all silent, save for a slight
murmur. The sky was cloudy; the enormous river
of a yellow mud color. The far-off city of Montevideo appeared like a long whitish streak upon the
brown coast, rising at the western end upon the
solitary *Cerro*, the hill of Garibaldi: a simple and
majestic landscape which silently awaited the coming of the sun. In the distance could be perceived
the smoke of two or three small steamers that were
coming out to us.

I went on deck to see for the last time my sixteen
hundred fellow-travellers. The captain, the officers,
the ship's surgeon, and the Uruguayan official with
the doctor came up a moment afterwards and the
sad procession commenced. Sad, not only in itself,

but because, counting that throng like a herd of animals without care for any name, gave the idea that the poor creatures were told off for sale; that we saw not citizens of a European state, but victims of a raid of kidnappers upon the shores of Africa or Asia. The first passed slowly, but seeing that the port official showed impatience, the captain made a sign and the rest moved on more rapidly, filing by almost on the run. Families passed together; the father first, then the women with their infants in their arms and leading the older children by the hand; the old people came last. Almost all had with them bundles of property too precious to be left in the cabin. Many were neat and clean; dressed in good clothes which they had kept for that occasion. Others were worse off than when they set out; ragged, and soiled with all the uncleanness to be gathered by lying about for three weeks in every corner of a crowded ship. There were unshaven beards and bare necks. There were some with toes out of their shoes; some even hatless; and more than one holding together with both hands a buttonless jacket to conceal the hairy nakedness of his breast. Pretty girls, bowed old men, striplings of twenty years old, workmen in blouses, long-haired priests, Calabrese peasant women with their green corsets, North Lombardy pipers, Brianza women with the radiating crown of long pins stuck in their hair, and women from the mountains of Piedmont with their white caps.

Harbor Steamer and Barge.

All these came on in endless procession, each one
stepping in the other's tracks, as on a scaffold at the
back when the flight of a whole people is to be represented on the stage. Some skipped along as if to
show how light-hearted they were; others passed
with grim faces, looking at no one, as if offended at
this exposure that was made of them. The bourgeois and the middle-class women, who yet had
about them some signs of former prosperity, went by
with heads down, all ashamed. The slow old people
and the encumbered women were shoved aside or
driven brutally on by those who came behind; the
children cried for fear of being trodden on; those
who were jostled cursed and swore. How many
faces that I knew well did I see go by! There is
the man that sent the telegram to his wife, his face
full of jolly wrinkles and looking as if he believed
us yet. There is that old orator in the green frock,
running by with his gray head bare as usual, and
casting a look of hate and defiance at the first-class
passengers on the deck above. There is the tattooed
mountebank; the two slatternly choristers; the family from Mestre, with young Galileo, who takes his
breakfast as he goes along; there is the ex-porter
with his pictures; the fair Genoese, who goes by
with blushing cheek and eyes cast down; the large
Bolognese crossing the bridge with imperial walk,
her inseparable satchel at her side; the Madonna of
Capracotta, the barking barber, the putative homi-

cide of the forecastle, and the poor widow of the
murdered man.

As they filed along, all the sad and comical inci-
dents of that strange life of twenty-two days passed
through my mind ; the varied feelings of disgust
and of sympathy, of kindness and of mistrust, which
those people had raised in me ; all now lost in one
deep sentiment of sorrowful and tender pity. And
still they went by as if their number had been
doubled in the night. Family after family, children and yet more children, city faces, country faces,
from Northern Italy, from Southern Italy; good
honest creatures, brigands, invalids, ascetics, old
soldiers, beggars, rebels, passing ever fast and faster,
as if urged by the dread of not reaching America in
time to get their bit of bread and their strip of earth.

What a procession ! Endless, most pitiful ! And
at the back of all this grievous misery, imagination
held up to me, as in mockery, the patriotic rejoicings
of the idle, the prosperous, and the unthinking, as they
shout with holiday enthusiasm in the banner-dressed
and glittering squares of Italy. I felt a humiliation
which made me shun the regard of foreigners who
were in the ship with me and whose affected exclamations of pity and surprise were only so many
reproaches to my country. And still those ragged
garments, those white hairs, those withered women,
those children without a country, that nakedness,
that shame, that misery kept filing on. The spec-

tacle endured for half an hour, which seemed a whole
eternity. At length the friar with his face of wax,
his hands buried in his sleeves, went slowly by;
then came the little band of Swiss with their red
caps, and at last,—at last there was an end of it.

From the first tender that reached us there came
on board a tribe of people, friends and relatives of
the passengers; who, running through the ship,
sought for the faces and called out the names of
those they were to meet. Then began the greetings,
the embracings, and the kissings. Three gentlemen
approached the one we had called the "thief," and
while we were waiting to see them take him into
custody, uncovered, and profoundly bowing addressed
him as *Monsieur le Ministre.* There! That is what
it is to judge of a man by what one can see. But
we had not time to be properly astonished, for our
attention was straightway drawn to a painful scene.
A young gentleman, well dressed and handsome, but
repellent of look, came rushing towards my two
neighbors of below, who ran to meet him exclaiming
"Attilio!" But at a couple of paces off they stood
still, waiting for him to select one for the first embrace, as if that choice were to be his final judgment
of the past and their sentence for the future. The
youth hesitated for a moment, looking at them both
but wholly without emotion; then flung himself into
the lady's arms. She clasped him to her breast with
what would have seemed deep tenderness had it

not been belied by a Satanic look of triumph which she cast in that very moment at her husband. He turned as pale as death and seemed about to fall to the deck, but he controlled himself with an effort and looked around him with a smile most dreadful and most piteous to see. The young gentleman, leaving the mother, approached him and pressed upon his pale cheek a cold kiss which the father seemed powerless to return. All turned their eyes away with horror, as if from the sight of murder; and I myself hastened forward without daring to cast another look upon the unhappy man.

And here another piteous scene awaited me. A knot of old people, men and women, surrounded the commissary; frightened, anxious, and begging with trembling lips for comfort and advice. These were the solitary sexagenarians who could not land without some relative to answer for their subsistence. But the relatives they expected had not appeared; and naturally enough, for the landing was to be made at Buenos Ayres; but, confounding Uruguay with Argentina, they gave themselves up for lost. What was to become of them! Imagine the despair and agony of these poor creatures, who, having left Europe, found themselves, as they supposed, rejected from America like useless human carcasses, not even good for fertilizing the ground, and frantic already with the idea of returning to a country where they would find no one to love them, no house to live in, no bread to eat. The commissary tried to persuade them that they were in Uruguay and not in Argentina, that their friends were to meet them in Buenos Ayres, on the other side of the river which they saw before them, that they were tormenting themselves about nothing, that they should take courage. But they would hear no reason, they were stunned with fright, and seemed only the more miserable and unhappy in the midst of the joyous and noisy young fellows who jostled them at every moment, crying out: " Courage, old fellows !—Long live the Republic !—Viva l'America !—Viva la Plata ! "

I managed to get the commissary aside for a moment, and in taking leave of him gathered some final news of the poor young bookkeeper. In despair at seeing the last of his fair Genoese, who landed at Montevideo, he was in convulsions and was upsetting the whole cabin. Then I went to shake hands with the other officers, whom I was to see two months later at Buenos Ayres, after their return from Italy once more. And I wished also to see my poor old hunchback. I found him at the door of the kitchen with a saucepan in his hand. " Oh ! at last ! " he exclaimed, with a sigh of satisfaction. " Twelve days without any women ! " " Yes," I said, " and I suppose you will end by taking a wife." *Mi !* he answered, touching his bosom with his finger. *Piggià moggé !*—" I a wife ! " Then, speaking Italian with a queer declamatory accent, " That will never be"; and he whispered joyously in my ear "Twelve days!" But seeing the captain coming, he squeezed my hand and hurriedly saying "*Scignoria, bon viaggio!*" he turned his poor crooked back and was seen no more.

Meanwhile some more tenders had come along-side and one was at the after gangway. I went on deck again to say good-bye to the passengers who were getting into her in a confusion of baggage and a turmoil of hand-shaking and mutual good wishes. Here, too, was another proof of how difficult it is to know much about people on a voyage. Some passengers, with whom I had been all the time on terms of intimacy almost friendly, went off without saying so much as "Go to the deuce!" (*Crepa!*), or at most with a tip of the hat, as if they had forgotten me. Others, with whom I had not exchanged a word, came to take leave with an affectionate sincerity that amazed me. And the same thing happened to other people. The Marsigliese was cordial. He said over and over again that he was fond of Italy, because men like himself were superior to the jealousies of governments, and that he was going to do his best to make Italians and French get on with one another in Argentina. *Tachez d'en faire autant parmi vos compatriotes. Quant' à moi, on me connait dans les deux colonies. On sait,* he concluded with a solemn gesture, *que j'apporte la paix. Adieu!* The agent presented himself to take leave of the young couple who were embarrassed by their just dread of a Parthian shot. " I imagine," he said, that you will not have any more difficulty with the language in America after so much practice— you know."—And they ran down the ladder. Then he set upon the poor advocate, who was just descending with a round roll of something, probably a life preserver, under his arm. " Avvocato," he said, " I suppose you feel now that all your troubles are over." But the other, eying the water askance, growled out: " There's no knowing ; sometimes this beastly river is worse than the Atlantic Ocean "— and down he went, with all possible precaution, taking no notice of anybody. The blonde lady and her husband passed down, then my neighbors with their son, then the " beast tamer," the pianist with her mother, the Frenchmen, the priest, the second-class passengers, and others.

When all were off and seated on the little quarter-deck, the agent gave me a nudge with his elbow, exclaiming " Eureka !" Following his eye, I looked to the right and saw on the deck of the *Galileo*, leaning against the bulwark in the correct attitude of a thoughtful and afflicted lover, Ruy Blas, his regards fixed upon the tender. They pointed directly at the little piano-player, pale and impassive as ever, but with her eyes fastened upon him and giving no uncertain promise on the first occasion of one of those mad letters, those rash outbreaks of

writing, in which she worked off from a distance her
morsels of suppressed passion. "Ah poor little
Maria of Neubourg," said the agent, "Queen of
dead cats!" But the tender was moving off. All
waved their hands. The plump lady blew a kiss to
the *Galileo* with an ardent gesture. I saw once
more my poor neighbor seated at a distance from
his wife and son. A fresh life of misery and torture
was beginning for him. And I caught flying as it
were a queer salute from the Swiss lady, who, not
knowing which to select from the many friends who
were looking at her from above, took in with one
wide glance of sweet gratitude the whole of the
Galileo's quarter-deck. The last one that I marked
was the professor seated next her, his back bent,
smiling with half-shut eyes and his tongue in his
cheek, as if in mockery of his wife, her lovers, the
Atlantic Ocean, the old continent and the new.
Then all these faces melted away and were lost to
my sight forever.

Meanwhile there came alongside another tender,
which was to take off the Argentines, the Brazilian
family, and all the rest. But from delicacy no one
would go down before the young lady from Mestre,
who as was well known would have to be carried
and who had not yet appeared on deck. The captain shook his head when asked about her. All
were waiting in double line at the door of the
saloon. First came out the Garibaldian, who, taking

what was a mark of respect for mere curiosity, cast
round him a glance of scorn. The poor sick lady,
dressed in black and pale as a corpse, rested her
head on the back of the chair and her hands on her
knees as if she could no longer lift them, but in her
eyes so quenched and languid, and on her lips through
which no breathing seemed to pass, there was still
that smile of hers so sad and yet so infinitely sweet.
All uncovered as she passed, and her only answer
was a kind but soundless motion of the lips. The
sailors who were bearing her stopped at the entering port. The captain, hat in hand, saluted her with
the curt speech under which many gruff men conceal real emotion. "Pleasant journey to you, signorina; I hope you will get well." Then turned
sharply to order that the emigrants who were crowding around to see the young lady and were keeping
the air from her, should be made to stand back.
They stood back, murmuring angrily, but ascended to
the deck above to see her carried down and watch
her departure. The Garibaldian was the last to
speak to her at the head of the ladder. She gave
him her hand, which he kissed, and then, raising her
forefinger with a kind reproving air, she said a word
which I did not catch. He bent his head without
reply. The two sailors began to descend with great
care, one lifting the chair in front and one behind
and begging the invalid to hold on well. The aunt
came after them, warning her niece not to look at

"As they sail out of harbor."

the water. When they reached the bottom, a hand on board the tender helped the other two, and quite gently they placed her on the after deck with her face to the steamer. The other passengers then went down and took their places. The Garibaldian alone remained on board, leaning on the bulwark not far from me. And the tender moved off.

Then the emigrants crowding against the rail of the upper deck broke out into gratitude and admiration of that angelic creature, whom they had seen so often amongst their number, touched by their misery, gentle to them as a sister, and from whom so many of them had received consolation and substantial gifts. No cry was heard, but rather a long murmur of greetings in which there seemed to go out to her all the good and all the purity which the bitterness and sorrow of a toilsome existence had left in these poor people. "Buon viaggio,—signorina! —God bless you!—God restore you!—Don't forget us!—Fair befall our friend!—Adieu!—Good-bye!" And they waved their hats and handkerchiefs. But she answered only with a feeble motion of the hand; and then, raising her sweet dim eyes to her friend's stern face, she made with the same hand the same motion, with the forefinger as before, as if to say, "Remember!"

The tender was already at a distance, but the young creature's form came out clear on the quarter-deck, like a dark flower in a nosegay of many

colors. When it showed but as a black dot in the
distance, something white was seen to move in front
of it. The waving of a handkerchief. It was for
him. I looked. Ah! that is too much! Not to be
moved at such a moment! But, as I said this to myself, his brow frowned, his lip trembled, his bosom
swelled, and a sob burst from his very heart—one
only,—short, sharp, deep, irrepressible, as if his whole
soul had surged up like a billow of ocean. He
covered his face with his hands. Had the tears
come at last! Perhaps it was human kindness, love,
patriotism, pity for his fellow-creature's trouble;
perhaps it was all the deep, strong virtues of his
generous nature that had rushed back into that
breast of iron through the little rift made by the
waft of a dying hand. Perhaps it was that the
storm-hardened soldier, as his great mother, Nature,
laid a finger on his shoulder, flung himself upon her
breast, once more entreating her forgiveness and
promising to love and serve her as in the bright
years of his faith and his enthusiasm. The vision
had passed, the bright creature was soon to die, but
her last smile, which was something more than human,
would light his pathway to the end, and that fluttering bit of white would ever dwell upon the horizon
of his life, the sign of his redemption.

He remained leaning with folded arms against the
bulwark, as if riveted in his place by some new and
deep emotion which had fastened upon his soul.

He was still there as, standing among a group of friends on board another tug, I saw the colossal *Galileo* grow short and low before my eyes, but still with the thousand heads of those emigrants swarming at her bulwarks, like a crowd of people on the bastion of a solitary fortress. And passing rapidly in review that twenty-two days' journey, I seemed to have been living in a world apart, a life which, reproducing in miniature the events and passions of the universe, had cleared and quickened my judgment of men and things. Much wickedness there is, much shameful sin, much violence, but far more misery and sorrow. The larger part of humanity is more sinned against than sinning, and suffers more than it inflicts. After hating and despising mankind, with no other result than to embitter life, and aggravate around us that very wickedness that has rendered it odious and detestable, we come back to the only feeling that is wise and good:—to love and pity for mankind; a feeling from which all good arises, and out of which the sure and certain hope springs up that, in spite of dubious signs, the enormous mass of misery in the world is getting less and less, and the soul of man is surely growing better.

As I put foot on shore I turned to look at the *Galileo*, and my heart swelled at bidding her adieu, as if she were a little strip of my own country which had sailed across the sea and brought me to that spot. She was but a black dash upon the horizon of that mighty river, yet I could see her flag as it flowed and floated in the early rays of the American sun. It was as if Italy, with a last salute, commended her wandering children to their new adopted mother.

FINIS.

Lightning Source UK Ltd.
Milton Keynes UK
UKHW010731050521
383174UK00002B/198

9 781410 104557